A Gary Paulsen Collection

Also by Gary Paulsen

Tracker

Dancing Carl

Dogsong

Sentries

Hatchet

Woodsong

Edited by Gary Paulsen

Shelf Life: Stories by the Book

A Gary Paulsen Collection

Three novels by
best-selling author
Gary Paulsen

TRACKER

DOGSONG

HATCHET

ATHENEUM BOOKS FOR YOUNG READERS
New York London Toronto Sydney

Book design by Daniel Roode
Manufactured in the United States of America
Library of Congress Control Number: 2004101690
ISBN 1-4169-0618-5

These titles were originally published individually by
Atheneum Books for Young Readers.

A Gary Paulsen Collection

Also by Gary Paulsen

DANCING CARL

DOGSONG

SENTRIES

HATCHET

WOODSONG

TRACKER

BY GARY PAULSEN

A Richard Jackson Book
Atheneum Books for Young Readers

ATHENEUM BOOKS FOR YOUNG READERS
An imprint of Simon & Schuster Children's Publishing Division
1230 Avenue of the Americas
New York, New York 10020

Manufactured in the United States of America
20 19 18 17 16 15 14 13
The text of this book is set in 11 pt Aster.
Library of Congress Cataloging in Publication Data
Paulsen, Gary.
Tracker.
Summary: Only thirteen, John must track a deer in the Minnesota woods for his family's winter meat, and in doing so finds himself drawn to the doe who leads him and hating his role as hunter.
[Hunting—Fiction. 2. Deer—Fiction] I. Title.
PZ7.P2843Tr 1984 [Fic] 83-22447
ISBN 0-689-84088-8

To Nancy Polette,
who earned it

TRACKER

ONE

John Borne sat at the breakfast table and tried to see the look of death on his grandfather. He could not. If a change were there, he could not see it.

Clay Borne had ruddy cheeks, a head of white hair, clear eyes and steady hands as he buttered a great slab of fresh bread hot from the wood stove, and humor in the corners of his eyes just as he always had.

He is life, John thought—*not death.*

He will never be death. Whenever I turn around and need him, Grandpa will be there.

But that's not what the doctors said. Two weeks ago, at the hospital in Grand Forks, the doctors had asked them to come into a small green room—or had asked his grandparents and John had gone with them because nobody said he couldn't.

"There is nothing more to do," the doctors said. They looked sad. But it was a sadness that would go away. "We can't stop the cancer."

And John had watched his grandmother sag. She made no sound but just sagged. A part of her went out at the words and she started down and John caught her on one side and his grandfather on the other and they put her in a chair.

"It will be all right," Clay told her gently. "It will be all right."

But how could it be?

The doctors had done tests and more tests and worked with chemicals and knives and finally had sent John Borne's grandfather home to die in peace on the small farm at the edge of the woods, the farm where he had been born and lived all his life, the farm where John had lived for nine years, since he was four and his parents were killed in a plane crash in the northern woods.

Home.

"You're not eating, John." His grandmother turned from the stove. "Cold breakfast sits hard, and a hard breakfast won't warm you on a snowy morning."

He nodded and put food in his mouth but tasted nothing, felt only the texture of the eggs and crumbled bacon. His grandmother talked like that, as though she were just about to break into poetry. When John listened to her for a while he caught himself expecting things to rhyme but they never quite did.

She had cried for a time, for days, but she was through with that now just as John had cried but was through with it now. Crying changed nothing.

There was still the fact that the doctors said his grandfather had only a few months to live and so John had tried to see the look of death on him but could not.

He had seen it on many things. They lived close to the land and made all their own meat, and to make meat it was necessary to make death. He had helped his grandfather slaughter cattle and seen death there, and once on a man, the farmer who had lived next door. His tractor had backed over him and John had been the one to find the body when he went to deliver eggs and there had been death on the ground.

But it wasn't here now.

There wasn't the looseness of death or the hot-sweet smell of it or even the tiredness of it. There was no change in his grandfather, no change at all. He kept right on working and carving the little woodcarvings in the kitchen at night and laughing and playing small jokes and eating well and looking to the next day. Always looking to the next day.

His grandfather glanced up from his plate suddenly, his fork halfway to his mouth. "Isn't the food good enough for you?"

John had stopped eating again without knowing it. "Of course . . ." He took another mouthful.

"There's an inch of snow out there." The old man chewed slowly and carefully. "Deer season starts Saturday. The snow will be good for tracking."

They hunted deer every year and normally John would start getting excited two or three days before season. He'd clean and reclean his rifle, look more and more to the woods and start losing sleep. This year was different. Normally they would get up at three in the morning and do chores and the milking so they could be in the woods by first gray light; and they would do that for the entire two weeks of deer season or until they got a deer. But this year that was all changed.

His grandfather wasn't going to hunt this year. "I'll stay home and do the chores," he'd said one morning, sitting in the yellow glow of the kerosene lamp on the kitchen table, his hands folded in front of him on the oilcloth. "It's time you hunted alone."

And John had nodded but it had been wrong, too wrong. They always hunted together, they always did everything together.

John had started hunting deer when he was ten, first without a gun, just going with his grandfather. Then when he was eleven he took a shotgun and got his first deer and he had taken deer every season since, using a rifle after the first year. He was now thirteen.

Three deer he had taken with his grandfather, hunting the cold crisp mornings in November, hunting down the long cold trails in the swamps in the new snow. Three times he had given death to the deer, seen the new blood on the snow, seen the look of death . . .

He stopped thinking, concentrated on eating the pancakes his grandmother had put in front of him. But it was impossible to keep the memories out. *Things don't change,* he thought. *People don't die. They couldn't* . . . It was always somebody else who died, never people you were close to. Even though his parents had gone down in a plane crash and were surely dead, it had happened when he was very young and so he didn't know them. He had not seen the change brought by death—the change that was supposed to come but, for John, never did.

But for his grandfather to stay home from hunting deer—that was too much. Too much of a change. It was like admitting that death was coming.

He got the last of the pancakes down. They tasted like sticky wood. Then he took his plate to the sink and used the hand pump to rinse the syrup down the drain.

"I'll go do chores," he said, turning from the pump, looking at his grandfather at the table but still not looking, saying but not saying. *I'll go do chores and you can't die,* he thought, a scream in his mind. "I'll go start milking."

His grandfather nodded. "I'll be out in a minute, after I finish my coffee."

And that wasn't a change. He always hung back and had coffee with Agatha, John's grandmother. They sat in the morning dark, in the yellow of the lamp, and sipped coffee and talked about what the day might bring and at least that hadn't changed.

John threw his chores jacket with all the holes over his shirt and pulled on the rubber barn boots and went outside into the cold, crunching in the new snow. His breath made small puffs, led the way to the warm smells of the barn.

Once he was out of the house in the dark of the morning he could use his mind to make things all right. It was still a cold clear morning, he was still going to milk the cows and clean the barn and feed and water the stock, still going to smell and feel the heat of the barn.

Those things hadn't changed and so maybe the other thing wouldn't change, maybe the doctors were wrong. They were just people. They could be wrong.

He kicked the ice from the barn door and went in, swinging the door wide and brushing the new snow back. letting his spirits come up.

It was impossible to feel bad when you entered

a barn in the winter where the cows were waiting to be fed; impossible to be sad when there was work to do.

He started chores.

TWO

His grandfather did not come out to help with chores and John did them alone.

He didn't mind. It had happened before many times and in some ways he liked it. During the week, the school bus came before chores were finished and John had to leave the farm then. He always felt as if he were missing something. Now that it was Sunday he did not have to leave and so he could work morning chores all the way to done. That's how his grandfather always talked about work—you didn't just work so many hours or days. You worked a job to done. All the way to done. No matter how long it took.

And chores, morning chores, milking, and cleaning the barn and feeding calves and pigs and chickens was work but more, too. There was something about it that lifted it above work for John.

At school his best friend was a boy named Emil Peterson and Emil thought he was crazy to like chores.

"That's just hard work, that's all it is," he'd told John more than once. Emil hated chores at his own place, or anyplace else for that matter. "You think it's fun to slop around in cow crap all morning? You're crazy."

John had tried to explain but nothing had come out right. Chores was the first thing of the day, it was the new thing of each day and it was work but it touched something else in his mind, touched a place that made him think of good things, of growing and rich things.

More than once in the winter he had come into

the barn only to stop just inside the door and listen and smell and feel the richness of it. The stink of the manure was even rich, and the rumbling of the cows' stomachs in the dark, the fresh warm smell of them just after he came in from the bitter cold, the sound of their teeth as they chewed their cuds, the quiet grunts and chuckles that came from the horses in the stalls at the end . . .

"It's gentle," he'd tried to tell Emil. "Gentle and right, somehow. The feeling of the barn in the morning."

But Emil hadn't agreed and John hadn't brought it up again because when somebody doesn't want to see a thing you can't make him see it.

His grandfather had fought the Japanese in World War II and had been wounded and later had been in the occupying force in Japan, and the hating part of war had gone and he had come to love them. That's how he put it, talking to John one morning during the morning lunch break.

"I came to love them and the beauty they see in things and the way they see the beauty. They look for small beauty, look for the beauty in even ugly things, and they compose songs and poetry to celebrate that beauty. Whole poems have been written about a single petal on a flower. One tear on a child's cheek."

And in a way that was what morning chores were for John—a whole series of small beauties. All the sounds and smells and feelings came as separate little bursts of beauty and he found himself making small poems in his mind while he did even the dirtiest work.

The cows greet
gently.
On a cold morning.

The words went through his head while he was taking the manure fork and sweeping it down the gutter to clean the night's mess and he decided he would tell them to his grandfather when he came out.

The ritual of chores was always the same, at least in the fall and winter when the cows were kept in: clean the gutters, feed hay, feed silage—the warm rich smell of the hot corn from the silo always made his mouth water—and milk. There were seventeen milk cows and four about to come in to milk season and when the milking was done it was time to feed milk to the calves in buckets and separate the rest of the milk and cream in the separator.

John could have done it with his eyes closed by the time he was twelve. At thirteen it was so automatic that he didn't have to use his mind at all and could think of other things.

He brought the milk stool from where it hung and settled in alongside Eunice, the first cow, and nestled his head in her flank and began pulling milk into the bucket with a hissy tingling foamy sound.

Don't watch the milk, he thought. After you'd been milking for a while you learned to not watch the milk, because it came in a small stream and never seemed to fill the bucket if you watched it. But if you looked away for a time and then looked back, the level in the bucket would have come up, and he wondered while he milked how many other things were like that. Wondered if there were many parts of living that only changed when you looked away and looked back.

Like Grandpa.

It came in like a hot worm, the thought—like a needle in a blister. He didn't want to think of his grandfather. Not now, not yet. There would be time for that later, too much time for that later.

But it came. He couldn't stop it. The thought slid in the side and with it a small hope.

If I don't see what is happening to him, the hope said, *then it isn't happening.*

It's the opposite of filling the bucket with milk. If I watch him all the time I won't see the change that death is bringing and so it can't be.

Can't be.

Death couldn't come if you were watching for it.

John went to the next cow, Marge, a big Holstein who was an easy milker because she dropped the milk as soon as you started pulling.

The ritual again. The foamy hiss of the milk, the head cradled in the flank of the cow, the warm-sweet smell of milk coming up and the thinking.

The thinking came again. There was school tomorrow, school all week and then deer season would start. He would think about that: getting through school all week and going deer hunting.

If he worked at that the other thing wouldn't come in. If he kept his mind going on school and going deer hunting . . .

School was a strange time for John. He was pretty much a loner, except for his best friend Emil, and he didn't get the entertainment part of school at all.

He approached school like a job—work to do. Something that had to get done, like chores. Usually he brought none of his home life to school and very little school came home.

But he did talk to Emil about his grandfather. The pressure had been too great—a building, blinding thing—and he had told Emil about it last week by their lockers.

All around was noise, kids moving, hall traffic with teachers watching.

"He's going to die," John had said.

"What?" Emil slammed his locker. It wouldn't catch any other way.

"Grandpa's going to die," John repeated, slightly louder. "Of cancer."

Emil looked directly into his eyes. "That's not fair. He's too good. Too good for dying."

"Just the same," John said, starting to cry. "Just the same—the doctors said."

"That doesn't make it fair."

And Emil was right. It wasn't fair.

He thought suddenly of the deer he had killed.

Three of them. The first one a doe, then a buck and a doe, and he had killed them all.

Jolts of noise and violence—that's what he remembered—the slam of the shotgun as it recoiled into his shoulder, the flat-crack of the bullet leaving the barrel, the second that hung forever in his mind as he saw the bullet hit the deer just in back of the shoulder, the hair and blood that flew with the bullet and the deer staggering sideways with the shock of being hit.

Sideways and down, he remembered, and the eyes looking, always looking for what had happened, looking in confusion and pain and finally clouding as death came; clouding and filming over with death.

The first deer.

And the thought crept in that maybe the deer had been good, just as his grandfather was good, and maybe it wasn't fair for the deer, either.

The second deer had been worse. The bullet had taken it too far back, in the lungs, and death had come slowly and John had to shoot again to kill it and it had seen him and that bothered him.

For a time.

Then that thing happened that happens to all people who hunt, or to everybody he'd talked to about deer hunting. They were sad about it, but the sad part only lasted a short time and wore off and was replaced by a hard feeling, almost an excitement. And after that it wasn't hard to kill deer anymore, wasn't hard to give them death, and sometimes that bothered John, too. More than he admitted to other kids at school or even to his grandfather.

He wasn't sure it was right to feel that hard way about killing, about death, about shooting animals and giving them death.

He realized with a start that he was crying while he milked, the tears dropping off his cheeks into the foam of the milk at the side of the bucket, making round holes down through the foam.

He couldn't remember starting to cry, couldn't think when the great sadness came down on his shoulders, but it was there and he thought of his grandfather and the crying got worse and he buried his face in the cow's flank and ground his teeth together and made the crying stop. There would be nothing from crying, he felt—nothing to help at all from crying.

But still the sobs came, jerking his head as he milked, the tears dripping down in the foam.

THREE

During the next week things almost went back to normal, if a bit quiet, around the house. Now and then John would catch his grandmother crying, just little tears as she worked, and once he saw his grandfather staring out the window when there was nothing to see but darkness, his hands still upon the carving he was working on. But other than that things were almost the same as always.

And in a way the week was the same as the ritual of the chores. There was getting up and working in the barn and then school, and for a change John liked school—it gave him something outside himself to think about, forced him to look away from his own life.

In the mornings at breakfast he forced himself to not stare at his grandfather and by Tuesday it was easier and he could talk without his voice catching.

They talked as if nothing were going to happen. As if things would go on and on.

"Those calves will have to come on hay in a couple of weeks, hay and a little silage, or they won't be ready for grass in the spring when we let them out," his grandfather said Wednesday morning. "We don't want them to bloat when they hit the pastures."

John nodded. "I'll see to it."

"We'll have to check the traces on the stoneboat for hauling manure out to the back forty sometime this week. If we don't I think they might break with the load and we need to get manure on top of the snow this winter so it can soak in or we won't make good corn next spring . . ."

"I'll see to it after school."

"There'll be a lot of work."

"I'll handle it."

And his grandfather had gone back to carving the small figures, the way it had always been. In the evenings they would sit in the kitchen and take heat from the kitchen wood stove and his grandfather would carve little horses and men from the old logging days and talk of all the work that had to be done and John would nod and smile and eat pie and drink cold milk from the well house and finally go to sleep, right at the table if he didn't catch himself.

The work went on. After school there was a small amount of homework and then the work of the farm. John fixed the stoneboat traces, put new boards in the workhorse stalls where the team had cribbed the old ones, drained the tractor for winter, sealed the granary to hold the harvest. The work went on. It fed on itself so that work made more work.

Once the stoneboat traces were fixed it was necessary to use the stoneboat to clean out the large manure pile behind the barn and that meant using the two horses and *that* meant still more work.

"They call them workhorses because it's a lot

of work to use them," his grandfather said almost every time they harnessed the team. "But it's a good work, a full work. And they always start up in the winter, horses do—always. Not like tractors in the cold."

John liked using the team, even with the extra work. The horses were huge and immensely strong and yet full of a kind of gentle courtesy, a slow thoughtfulness that made them better than a tractor.

When he harnessed them they stood to the collar and put their heads in and made it easy for him to reach up and around and to throw the harnesses over their backs. They were named Jim and Lars and they were both brown and had white blazes on their faces, but they had different minds. Jim would stand tight in the harness, leaning forward slightly against the load, while Lars stood easy and relaxed and jerked out when told to get up.

John hauled manure for three nights after chores, late into the night. The work kept him from thinking. When milking was done, his grandfather would help him harness and he would use the fork to load the stoneboat from the manure pile in back of the barn, then stand in front of the load on the planking while the horses took the stoneboat out to the field.

They had been doing it so long that he could leave the reins tied to the rein bracket in front. They knew where to go and what had to be done when they got the load out there, and John stood leaning against the fork in the darkness while the steel runners crunched through the shallow snow.

It was cold, November cold when the body isn't used to it yet, and he wore his heavy chores jacket, so when he got to the field he had to take it off because it would be too warm when he started to fork the manure off. And it was while he was taking his coat off Wednesday night that he saw the deer.

The horses were standing in their own steam and he had jammed the fork down in the manure and pulled one arm out of his jacket sleeve and turned in the moonlight—and there she stood.

It was a doe, a small one—he could tell by her neck and lack of antlers. She wasn't thirty feet away to his right rear.

Deer often came out to check the manure, that wasn't unusual. There were seeds which passed through the cows and horses, and after snow the deer had to work a little harder for food, so the seeds were easy picking.

Many times in the past John had seen deer working through the clumps of manure. But this one was different.

She stood and stared at him for what seemed like hours, stood with little puffs of steam coming out of her nostrils in the moonlight, flaring to smell him, and didn't run.

Usually when deer separated the man from the horse smell they ran—man killed, man was the death smell.

But she stood, stood as if waiting for something, and John hung with one sleeve off and one on and stared at her, saw every part of her, saw her ears flick and her eyes move and then she was gone—gone so fast that she might not ever have been there.

But she left something in John, a picture of beauty that hung in his mind the way a picture will sometimes stay in your eyes when you close them, burned in.

The horses took the stoneboat down the field and he threw the manure off to each side, a fork left and a fork right, and still the picture was in his thoughts, and on the way home, the quarter mile back to the barn, he realized that the only way he could make the picture whole would be to compose a poem about it, the way his grandfather said the Japanese did.

The doe stood
in puffs of steam
waiting.

Later that night in the kitchen after supper he told his grandfather about it, about the way the deer stood and the beauty of it and the poem he had composed.

"A rare moment," Clay said. "But the poem only has partial meaning for me. What was she waiting for?"

John thought, wondering why the word had come into the poem in the first place. "I don't know."

"Sometimes the best beauty comes from that."

"From what?"

"From where you don't know, from instinct." His grandfather smiled. "The best joy and beauty are the kinds that are unplanned, and the same is true of painting or poetry. Don't chew at it too much. It's beautiful, and it makes you remember a beautiful part of your life and that's enough."

John nodded but he couldn't get her out of his mind just the same. Tired as he was, late as it was, he lay in his bed upstairs and remembered the deer and the small poem and tried to think of what she might have been waiting for—why she would have stood looking at him for so long. Especially in fall, in snow, only two days before deer season when all the deer seem to sense danger around them and get jumpy and will actually run from each other, let alone a man.

It was as if she had been waiting for him, waiting for John, standing in the moonlight against the snow, waiting for him.

But to do what?

FOUR

Deer season.

The time for the taking of meat, the time for the giving of death to the deer for the taking of meat to get through the winter.

John did not think of hunting in the normally accepted manner. Once, a man came up from another state to go deer hunting and he talked of why he hunted.

He talked of how it made him more of a man to hunt and kill a deer. He talked of all the skill it took to kill a deer, all the knowledge it took to kill a deer.

John's grandfather would not allow the man to hunt on his land because he made deer hunting more than it should be.

"We take meat," he told John, watching the man drive away. "That's all we do—we take meat with a gun. It doesn't make you a man. It doesn't make you anything to kill. We make meat, that's all."

And that's how John thought of hunting—a way to put meat up for the winter.

After four years, the edge was largely gone from hunting, but there was still a nudge of excitement the night before season, a small thrum in the back of John's mind as he took down the rifle and began to clean it, to make sure the sights were set correctly.

He worked at the kitchen table with a small screwdriver and took the rifle apart completely and used an old toothbrush to clean each part and screw.

His grandfather carved, and drank tea and nodded approval now and then, though it wasn't required.

"If you work that swamp down to the north

early in the morning you should come on some nice bucks. Get a buck first for the tallow. You can take a doe later for good meat."

John nodded. "I thought about the swamp, but it might be a little rough going with the new snow." It was snowing outside as they talked, large flakes with almost no weight. They would make a light powder, ideal for tracking. With new snow in the morning any track John saw would be fresh. "I wish you were coming with me."

"Not this time. I'll take a year off." His grandfather's hands stopped carving for a moment and he looked out the window. "I'll pass this year—I've had plenty of hunting."

John felt his eyes moisten and fought the feeling down. "Well. I'll make meat all right but, you know, it's just more fun with you . . ."

For a time neither of them said anything and his grandmother turned from the stove where she was kneading bread on top of the water reservoir. She said nothing but looked at the table, at them, then looked back and John saw she was crying.

"Dammit. That's enough of that now. There's been enough of that damn caterwauling and carrying on around here . . ."

John was startled. Rarely did his grandfather swear, and never in the house. He put the parts of the rifle down and sat still.

"What's happening to me happens to every single human being on the face of this earth—nobody gets away from it. Nobody. So quit all this misting up and raining and let's get to the business at hand."

He sat still, very still, and stayed looking out the window—as if he might have been talking to the world, though it was dark and nothing showed but flakes now and then as they came into the glow from the table lamp.

John's grandmother looked at his back for a full ten seconds and then fled from the room crying and John waited another half a minute before picking up his rifle and starting to clean it again, though it was clean enough.

His grandfather sighed. "I didn't do that well, I'm afraid. I meant it to come out better, come out nice. But you see what I mean, don't you?"

John nodded. "Sort of. It's just that—well—you know. It's you this time, not somebody else. And when it's somebody close . . ." He let the thought trail off.

"I know. But that doesn't change anything, does

it? It still happens. That's the one fact that holds true about this sort of business, no matter what you do, you can't change it. It's coming."

How strange it is, John thought, *for him to talk about it this way. He's talking about his own death, his own end. The end of him.*

"When I was young I used to think it couldn't be." The old man started carving again, looking down at the wood in his hands. He was making a workhorse that would go on a small sled which he had yet to make. The chips and shavings curled off and dropped on the table and when he had a small pile of them he carefully scraped them together and got up and put them in the wood stove. Then he started carving again, gentle curves coming off the soft clear pine. "But I was wrong."

For a time there was silence, John staring down at the rifle on the table, his grandfather carving. Before they spoke again John's grandmother came back. Her eyes were moist and some hair had loosened from the gray bun at the back of her neck. She stood over the stove but there was nothing to cook and she was just waiting.

"I'm sorry, Aggie," Clay said, still carving. "Sometimes I lose control and . . . I'm sorry."

"Don't be silly."

And John thought that just then, that second, things were back to normal. He was carving and she was at the stove and there was that making-business sound in her voice, as if they had been fooling around and joking the way they sometimes did and she wanted them to stop.

"You bring the liver home when you get a deer, hear?" His grandfather looked up from the wood. "I've been thinking of fresh liver for a long time. You bring it home."

"I will." For the last two years there had been rumors circulating that deer livers were not good because they had some kind of tiny worms, and they had left the livers in the woods when they gutted the deer out. "I promise."

"Good. You take a fresh liver and fry it up with some fresh onions and some good greasy potatoes and you got a meal."

"Grease isn't good for you." Agatha turned from the sink, where she was pumping water to refill the reservoir on the stove. "Too much grease is bad."

The old man smiled. "Well. Yes. I suppose it is—but I'm not too sure it matters anymore. I think if I want to get a little greasy with my food it should be all right."

"Just the same, just the same."

"I'll get the liver," John cut in. "Don't worry. The liver and the heart. If I get a deer."

"You'll get one. You've got the touch of it. Some people hunt and hunt and never get a deer and some go out and get one every year. You'll get one just the way I always get one."

"I wish you were going out with me this year." It came without John calling for it, just slipped loose and was gone and he saw the corners of the old man's eyes tighten and he hated himself then, hated himself for the stupidity of what he had said, hated himself for causing hurt.

"I'll stay back and do the chores," his grandfather said, looking down. "This is your year to go alone. This is your year, not mine."

John clamped his teeth together and went back to cleaning the rifle as, outside, the new flakes came down, roiling in the slight puffs of wind, taking life briefly as they slid past the window and hit the yellow glow from the lamp.

FIVE

John awakened before the alarm went off and sat bolt upright in bed. It was opening morning, deer season, and the old ways had come back, the old excitement. At least for the moment.

He kicked out from under the quilt and put his feet on the floor, the cold floor. John had an upstairs room without heating grates and when the wood stove went down to a smolder in the kitchen, the upstairs cooled fast. He pulled on wool socks, thick ones his grandmother had knitted out of raw wool, and pulled his pants on over them with a scrape of cold cloth.

He could see his breath. *It must have dropped quite a bit during the night and that's good,* he thought. If it got down around zero and there was new snow it would be still and clear and that was good for hunting.

Downstairs he heard his grandmother moving about in the kitchen and he smiled. It was three in the morning—earlier than he normally got up, so he could do chores before he hit the woods—and it still didn't matter. He couldn't get up ahead of her, even if he tried. She always got up first and put coffee on the stove and had the fire going before he made it to the kitchen.

John pulled his shirt on and went downstairs, two steps at a time but quietly because he knew his grandfather would still be asleep. He was sleeping later now, and needing it.

In the kitchen he was assailed by smells. The tang of the pine kindling in the wood stove cut above everything, but it was mixed with the soft smell of bread warming on the warming rack and of raw potatoes frying with canned venison from the year before.

"Good morning." John's mouth was watering already. "Sure smells good in here."

"Morning." His grandmother smiled. "I'll have breakfast for you after chores."

John went to the door and pulled on his jacket. Outside he was met with a wall of cold. It was, he guessed, a little below zero—he could tell because the hair in his nose froze and stuck together—but it felt colder because he'd just come out of a warm room.

The rubber on his shoe pacs stiffened and the snow crunched as he walked to the barn in the dark.

Inside the barn it was warm, as always, and he quickly fed the cows and scraped the gutters and went back to the house for the buckets and separator parts while the cows were eating.

He was surprised to see his grandfather sitting at the kitchen table when he came back in. He was sipping a cup of hot coffee, the steam working up around his cheeks.

"Good morning," John said.

The old man nodded his greeting. "How are things in the barn?"

"Fine. Calves are all right, cows standing to

milk. I fed silage and hay. Grained the horses. I'm going back out to milk."

"You go ahead and milk and separate. I'll take it after that so you can hit the woods."

John hesitated. "Are you sure? There's plenty of time and I can just as easily do it all."

"No. It'll gray up in the east pretty soon and you want to be out by the swamp when it comes into light."

John nodded. That was right: hunt early, eat early is what they said. Hunt late, stand and wait. "All right. If you're sure."

"Absolutely. I'll be fine."

John went back out to the barn with all the buckets and got to milking. It was still pitch dark but some of the chickadees around the granary were starting to make morning sounds and it spurred him a bit.

Milking went well. Nobody kicked over any buckets or was froggy—hopping around—and he got through it without problems. Also, hunting had entered his mind and it kept him from thinking about his grandfather quite so much, took his thoughts away from bad things.

When he finished separating the milk and cream he carried the cream back to the house and left the milk in buckets for the calves. He debated about feeding the calves but his grandfather would have become angry and perhaps would have felt useless, and John didn't want that.

Outside, the morning was coming. John stopped halfway to the house and looked to the east. Not enough light yet to hunt, certainly—he couldn't see the front sight on the rifle—but it was coming.

He walked a little faster. Inside the kitchen, breakfast was on the table and he smiled. It amazed him how his grandmother always knew when he was coming in to eat. He could be out in the fields with the tractor, have a breakdown and walk in for a part and there would be food on the table when he walked in the door. She always knew. *She always knows everything,* he thought—*just quietly always knows everything there is to know.*

John asked her one evening how she knew so much. They were sitting in the kitchen, just the two of them, and John had been asking about his parents.

"I don't know that much about people," she said, flustering. But John could tell she was pleased by the question. "I just try to know as much as I can about something before I talk about it."

She'd gone on to tell John about his parents. Facts about them—how they looked, how they acted under certain conditions. And when she was done, John knew his parents in one way, her way, but he knew that it was honest knowledge.

When he thought of his grandmother that's the word that came to mind—honest. She was honest, and soft, and gentle. An honest, soft gentle person.

He set the cream in the cool-hole by the pump, where it would stay cool, but not freeze, until they went into town later in the week to sell cream, and hung his jacket up.

"I could eat a wolf," he said. "Raw."

His grandfather had been in the privy and he came in. "Set to food. I'll take care of the calves."

John nodded, glad that he had not fed the calves himself. It would have been wrong to take the work away from his grandfather—like saying he couldn't do it, somehow.

Clay went out and John washed at the pump and sat at the table. In the middle was a pile of fresh raw-fried potatoes and strips of venison; he loaded his plate. There was also syrup and he put some on the meat, sprinkled salt and pepper and started eating. He had learned about syrup on meat from Emil; it had looked bad at first, but when he tried it the taste was great. Especially on a cold morning.

"I set some aside for sandwiches for you, so you don't have to save any."

"What about Grandpa?"

"He's already had—just set to. You can't hunt hungry, especially if you hunt long."

She seemed different, somehow. Almost cheerful. Something he couldn't pin down but definitely something new had slipped into her actions.

The depression of the night before had vanished, almost as if a mist had left the house, and he ate heartily. Meat and potatoes with syrup was the best breakfast, better than pancakes any day, and he ate until he started to feel full and then stopped. Normally he would have gone past full and had food for all day, but when you hunt you want to hunt with a little edge on your belly—that's how his grandfather put it. Not hungry, but so the full feeling has worn off when you hit the woods—it makes it easier to see things. To shoot things.

When he'd finished eating John took his plate

to the sink and kissed his grandmother on the cheek and went to the entryway. There he put his coat on and a scarf and a wool hat and wool mittens Agatha had knitted. She brought two sandwiches wrapped in wax paper, which he slipped into his jacket pocket, and she handed him an apple with the other hand, a barrel apple from the basement, which he knew would be tangy and sweet at the same time.

The rifle was in the rack by the door and he took it down, as well as the box of shells from the shelf on the gun rack. John knew he wouldn't need the whole box so he just took out five cartridges, brassy and shiny with copper bullets tipped in silver, and dumped them in the top pocket of his jacket. He decided he would load in the woods.

He waited.

". . . It's going to be all right."

He thought about that and knew that she was wrong. It wasn't going to be all right. A part of him knew that his grandfather was going to end, end and be gone. But there was that small edge of hope in her voice, hope which she held the way a drowning person holds a stick. And John would not damage that hope, so he nodded and smiled. "I know, I know. I'll see you when I get back."

Outside, the cold hit him again, harder because he'd been in and his body had gotten used to the warm kitchen and the warm food. He felt it come in around his cuffs past the mittens, around the back of his neck.

By the barn he could see the glow from the lantern and he thought of going to say goodbye to his grandfather, but he would be busy and it would bother him.

Instead John wheeled left off the porch and walked straight north from the house across the pasture until he came to the trees that marked the edge of the woods.

Just inside the tree line he stopped and loaded the rifle, sliding the cartridges into the side-loading gate slowly, carefully. When all five were in the tube magazine he worked the lever once and brought a shell up into the chamber. Then he let the hammer down to the safety half cock and cradled the gun in the crook of his arm and paused, getting a feel for the morning and the woods.

It had stopped snowing and there was a gray light from false dawn coming off the snow. It still wasn't light enough for hunting, but close, very close, and he knew that by the time he reached the edges of the great swamp there would be enough light to see the sights of the rifle.

The woods were still. The new snow took down sound the way a blanket would, holding sound low and muffled, and with the freshness for tracking and the quiet it was nearly a perfect morning for hunting deer.

He turned his back on the farm and headed into the woods.

SIX

John knew there were many ways to hunt deer. Some hunters drove them into other men who were posted with guns. Others walked around until they saw a deer and tried to shoot it. Still others picked a spot near a deer trail and stood and waited for a deer to come along.

And now and then a hunter would use the

stalking method—move quietly on fresh tracks and try to catch a deer off guard. This final method was very difficult to do successfully and demanded total concentration and complete knowledge of deer.

John used a combination of methods—he did some stalking and some standing. He would move through the woods as quietly as possible for a distance—perhaps a quarter of a mile—and then he would stop and stand for a time, usually half an hour or so.

He had learned it from his grandfather.

"You have to think deer," Clay had told him. "You have to think deer, you have to *be* deer inside your head. Be quiet, move quiet, and be deer."

The country he was hunting was very good deer country but hard to hunt. His grandfather's farm lay on the edge of a huge peat swamp-bog that covered all of northern central Minnesota. The bog extended over two counties, and in the spring and summer it was a mucky quagmire that had defied people forever. Ducks and geese nested there by the thousands; moose and timber wolves and deer lived on spruce "islands" that stuck above the level of the swamp.

It was not a place, in the summer, where life was easy. Even the deer and moose and small game had trouble. Deer were discovered wandering blind from the ravaging flies that chewed at their eyes, and moose had been found dead from loss of blood because of ticks.

But in the fall life comes to the swamp; relatively easy life. The bugs are down for the winter, the peat is frozen solid and the land becomes passable.

John's great grandfather had made his farm along the edge of this swamp. Far enough away to avoid the worst clouds of mosquitoes, close enough to get good soil. And while Clay had trouble now and then with wolves, the farm had easy access to good deer hunting.

The swamp was perfect cover for the raising of deer, for hiding fawns from wolves, and that was important. The wolves hunted deer, coursed through them, in the winter, like sharks hitting schools of fish.

When he was small and came across his first wolf kill, it had bothered John. When wolves killed it was usually in brutal fashion, at least by some human standards—a slow and tearing death. A pulling down and closing off of life.

But later John realized that there wasn't a

right or wrong way about wolves hunting and killing the deer. There was just the wolves' way. That was the way they were and had nothing to do with what man thought was right or wrong. John still didn't like it, but at least he thought he understood it and that helped him when he discovered the fawns the wolves had taken and torn to pieces.

But because the wolves were so active in the fall, the deer moved away from them and that meant they moved out of the swamp, which in turn meant that deer hunting became very good around the edges of the swamp. John now worked on the western edge. Or perhaps it might be best to say that he was at the edge of the edge, working in.

Around the outside there were huge hardwood forests that had once been logged off but were now coming back and they were mixed with stands of poplar and willows. The deer browsed in the willows when the snow got too deep for them to get at low plants, and John moved quietly through the willows, stooping and weaving, taking deliberate steps, stopping often to listen.

Deer are not silent. When they run through the willows in the fall and the willows are dry and hard it sounds like somebody tipping over a lumber cart.

But there was no sound this gray dawn and John decided the deer hadn't yet moved this far out of the swamp. Then, too, there were no new tracks in the fresh snow.

He worked slowly further into the edge of the swamp, hitting the deep grass and the open areas of the bog.

It was full light now, with the top edge of the sun slipping up over the tree line to the east. Tight cold had come down and he felt it working into his shoulders. He had just rezipped his jacket when he heard the noise.

It was a releasing sound, as if a branch or tree which had been held had been turned loose—a kind of *swoosh*—in back of him, back to his right, and he froze, waiting for another sound to guide him.

None came.

He turned and took two steps, then two more, and so covered a distance of perhaps thirty yards through the willows until he came to a deer bed.

It was about a yard across, where snow had melted down to bare swamp grass in a cupped little warm place under a stand of willows.

Very cozy, he thought. It almost looked inviting. He knelt next to the bed and felt the grass and it was still warm. That had been the sound. A deer had been here in its storm bed—John knew they holed up sometimes when it snowed—and he had walked past it and it had jumped up, apparently hitting the willow on the way.

It must have surprised the deer, his coming, because the first tracks were more than ten feet from the bed. The deer had bounded up and away. The next tracks were twenty feet from the first ones, out into a clearing and across, craters in the new snow where the deer had run.

Well, he thought. *I was close to one, anyway, even if I didn't know it.* He decided to follow the tracks, or work in the same direction as the deer.

Better, he thought, *to go after one you know is fresh than to hunt blind and hope.* It wasn't likely he'd see the deer soon, but it could happen and if it did he might get a shot and make meat early so he could get back and take care of work around the farm so his grandfather wouldn't have to.

It came to him suddenly that he hadn't thought about his grandfather for nearly an hour and he didn't know if that was good or if that was bad.

He brought his mind back around to the tracks.

There was a saying among the old-timers that you could either hunt deer or you could do something else. You could not do two things when it came to hunting deer—hunting required too much concentration.

John went back to hunting.

SEVEN

In the clearings the snow hung on top of the matted swamp grass and it made hard going. His foot came down through the snow and then on past another eight inches to the peat beneath the grass. It was slow, stumbling work.

And in the willows he had to weave back and forth, so while it was easier walking—the grass was not so deep in the willows—it was still slow.

By midmorning he had only gone two miles, moving with the tracks. He had not seen the deer again but knew several things about it just the same. It was either a doe or a small buck—he could tell that by the size of the tracks, but he was not yet good enough to tell its sex. Older hunters could, but he wasn't sure of it; it had something to do with the way the foot came down.

He knew the deer wasn't unduly frightened. After he had jumped it out of the bed it had bounded for two hundred yards but then it had settled down to an even pace, just walking-running ahead of him easily. It wasn't panicking or running hard, the way deer did when the wolves got close.

He knew this deer was healthy. The steps were even, the weight came down evenly—it didn't limp or weave.

And he knew the deer wasn't a yearling, or a first-year fawn, which he wouldn't have shot even if he'd gotten a chance. His grandfather didn't kill first-year animals and he didn't either. If it had been a yearling it would have been all over the place, wandering as it fed, and probably running in spurts if it felt that it was being followed.

It wasn't until he reached one of the pine and spruce islands in the swamp that he came close to the deer again.

The island was about a hundred yards long, shaped in a large oval, and John worked across another clearing to get to it, wading through the snow-grass, stopping often to listen and watch.

It was easy to follow the tracks. The snow was all new and there didn't seem to be any other tracks in the area, except for rabbits. They had moved during the snow storm and left a patchwork of trails.

As he entered the pines on the island he stopped once more and listened, letting his eyes work ahead through the underbrush. It was like a make-believe land, what his grandmother would have called a fairy place; a place shot with silver and beauty.

The sun was as high as it was going to get now, an orb in the midsouth sky, and the light came down through the pines to make diamonds of the snow. Light sparkled all around, caught in the ice crystals as he stepped, showering his way with gold. He'd never seen anything like it and he looked down to see the snow move away from his legs in fire and when he looked up he saw her. A doe.

She had been in back of a spruce, all covered with snow and looking like a picture on a Christmas card and when he looked up she stepped out and saw him and was gone, that fast, but she left an image in his mind the way the snow had. When she jumped out from in back of the spruce the snow showered out and around and caught the fire from the sun and took the light to make her something other than what she was.

He held his breath. It had only lasted part of two seconds and yet he held his breath for half a minute, thinking of it. The rifle had come up of its own accord, settled against his shoulder, then gone down. There was no real time for a shot.

Then he breathed. It was over, over and gone and his breath came in a burst. He'd never seen anything like it. A shower of gold around a golden doe; beauty splashed through the woods.

After another minute he shook his head and continued. There was much beauty in the woods. His grandfather had told him the woods were *all* beauty. But that didn't change the basic fact: he had to make meat. They needed the food. And a doe was the best meat.

But something nagged at him, something he didn't understand. There was a mixing of things in his mind, or the start of a mixing that he couldn't quite pin down. As he walked the doe's tracks he started thinking of other things again; of his grandfather, of the way they lived, of what was coming for his grandfather. And the lines between the thoughts got blurred; the doe mixed with his grandfather and they both mixed with him.

He had to fight to concentrate on hunting.

He moved on.

As she left the spruce island, the doe had taken great bounds—twenty and thirty feet from print to print, the initial getaway jumps that all deer take when in danger, whether from man or wolf. But inside half a mile the tracks eased down and by the time John had followed another mile, through two more clearings and across two more spruce islands, she had calmed again.

It was when she'd settled into another bed that he finally got a chance to kill her.

EIGHT

John had read several books about deer and deer hunting. One writer would say all deer do this, another would say all deer do that. But in truth the deer didn't read the books and they did just as they wanted.

Some deer slept at night and fed in the day, some bedded down during the day and fed at night. Still others slept and fed intermittently all day and all night. There was not a normal way for deer, John knew—only the deers' way.

The deer that John was following bedded often during the day. In a normal twenty-four hours she might make four or five beds—some in darkness, others during the warm part of the day where the sun could get her.

After her second near brush with John she went farther. She was not yet really alarmed, that much John could see from her tracks. They were still full of purpose, though for half a mile she stretched them out and covered distance with some speed.

By the time John was well into the first half mile of tracks the doe was two miles away. And this distance gave her time to get out of the escape mentality—he could see the tracks settle down, get steady.

In nature, John knew, danger came with great suddenness. A mouse could be feeding peacefully on a stem of grass one second and be in a fox's belly the next instant. Two grouse could be performing the mating ritual and within a heartbeat come under an owl's silent slashing attack.

But if danger comes suddenly it also leaves

quickly. If the fox misses the mouse, it seldom persists; the owl looks for another meal. It takes too much precious energy to chase food that is forewarned; it's much easier to find prey that can be taken without so much effort, off guard.

By the time she'd gone those two miles the doe had forgotten about John. Her tracks settled down and John followed them slowly, carefully.

He knew he could get her, knew by her tracks. She would move ahead of him and stay there for a time but she would forget and all he had to do was stay on the tracks and he would get a shot. And if he got a shot he would get her.

He visualized it. She would move and then stop and he would put the bullet through her shoulder and she would stagger sideways and down with the impact. The life would go out of her, out and out, leaving the gray film on her eyes and he would cut her throat and the red would flow out on the snow, warm and rich and steaming . . .

He shook his head. It was wrong to project when hunting. Nothing came the way it was supposed to come and planning didn't work. You might stand and watch a clearing for hours, waiting for the deer to come out, and it would pass ten feet in back of you and you wouldn't know it.

He washed his mind clear, took a mouthful of snow to wet his tongue and replace some of the moisture he was losing by perspiring. He was not warm, but he knew he was sweating into his clothes because that's what always happened when he worked in the winter.

It was noon now. The sun was peaking and he turned his face toward it as he walked, let the heat warm his cheeks. It would get cold tonight, very cold. Maybe fifteen or twenty below. He would have to be sure to get the doe early so he could start back. If he was out much after dark he would either have to keep moving or stop and build a fire and ride the cold out. He had matches and the sandwiches and his grandparents wouldn't worry. He knew how to handle himself in the woods—he'd had a good teacher in his grandfather. Still, he didn't relish the discomfort of standing over a fire all night.

He would get the doe early, he decided. Work a little harder and catch up, get a shot. He grunted a bit as he stepped over a windfall—a lare poplar the wind had torn out of the swamp, with a disk of roots sticking in the air. His leg came down and went through the deep snow and grass and threw him over at an angle, put him in an awkward position and he looked up and there she stood.

She had made a bed on the far side of the windfall where the sun could warm her, protected by the roots from any wind. John's eyes took it all in. The small cupped bed in the grass, still warm and steaming, the sudden flurry of movement, a blur of red-brown as she got up and the freeze, the freeze as she stood.

John was leaning to his left and while it threw him slightly off balance to stand that way, it did not keep him from being able to use the rifle.

She stood frozen, eyes wide open, staring at him. He'd caught her somehow, off guard. He was on top of her and she panicked and froze and stood now, stood waiting for death.

The rifle came up, floated up to his shoulder in a fluid movement, a movement he'd known many times. It happened with great speed but he visualized it always in slow motion; the rifle coming up, his thumb pulling the hammer back, the bead of the front sight nestling into the sloping buckhorn of the back, the bead coming perfectly to rest on the doe's shoulders where, in back of the hair and muscle, he knew the heart pulsed, pumping, beating.

His finger tightened on the trigger and that, too, was automatic, all part of the same motion, all natural and flowing. The gun up and the hammer back and the sights on target, on her heart, on her death and his finger squeezing and squeezing the trigger to give her that death, to blow her over and down and make her into meat.

But he didn't shoot.

The moment hung for hours, burned into him, became part of him. The doe standing side-on to him, so close he could see her hairs, eyes wide and clear, little puffs of steam from her nose, a twitch in her back leg from a ready muscle held in check. All of it seen over the blue black of the rifle barrel. Two seconds that lasted hours.

Just pull the trigger, he thought. *Pull it and let the sear drop and that will let the hammer fall and set off the primer which will ignite the powder and send the bullet out to take her life.*

His finger was tight on the trigger, knuckle tense and white under the mitten.

But he didn't shoot.

Why am I not shooting? We need the meat and there it is and I've hunted this deer to give her death and make her meat and it's all here for me, for us, and still I don't pull the trigger. Why?

The doe moved.

Her back foot lifted and stepped forward a couple of inches and settled into the snow again but her head was still.

It's the same doe, he thought suddenly, finger still tight on the trigger. *It's the doe from the other night.*

And with that thought came another one: *She knows me.*

She remembers me from the stoneboat and spreading manure and the horses that night. She knows who I am and that's why she isn't running, isn't trying to leave. And he knew that had she moved at first he would have fired and killed her, and he knew that it was getting harder and harder to kill her.

Knowing her made it hard to finish the trigger squeeze and having her know him made it still harder, and still the moment hung, suspended—time in the cold—frozen time.

He had not breathed for twenty seconds now and more, holding only half a breath, and he let it out in a burst that made an explosive sound.

"*Whewwwgh*!"

She jumped. With no gathering of muscle she exploded up and away and came down thirty feet to the side in a great burst of snow and then two more bounds and she was out of sight and gone.

And still he did not shoot.

The snow was still hanging in the air, drifting down like traces of white flour when he lowered the rifle, staring after her, seeing the image of her still, etched in his eyes: the doe standing and the rifle sights on her—and he not shooting.

It made no sense.

He was still leaning over the windfall in a bad position. It took him a few seconds to get his leg loose and drag it over the log, then another two or three to brush the snow off his leg and clean out the top of his boot and when he looked back down the trail he thought he saw the outline of her standing in the willows. He couldn't be sure but he saw the markings of a deer in the vertical gray, caught in the sun, and then it was gone.

He shook his head. Part of all this didn't make sense. Why should he not shoot, and why should she stand to him, stand for death that way?

John looked around, as if trying to see the answer, then up at the blue sky and down at the rifle in his hands and then he started to walk.

He followed her trail in the new snow, followed the part of her that was left behind.

He did not know why.

He knew that he hadn't shot her, and he knew he had wanted to shoot her and that made no sense, no sense at all. He did not understand himself, did not know what made him hold the death back. But there was something later for him, something later on down that he wanted to see, to hear, to feel.

It all meant more than just the deer and the gun and him. It meant something bigger that he couldn't understand just yet.

That's what he thought, anyway. But another part of John told him that he was following her because he really had no choice. He could not hunt another deer having failed on this one, and he could not turn and go home because it was not a finished thing.

He followed the doe's tracks because at that time that was all there was for him—the tracks leading off into the snowy woods.

The tracks called him and he followed.

NINE

He could see the fear in her now.

He was following her and the fear drove her and she ran hard; long and deep in the first burst the way she would have run to get away from wolves—she ran for her life.

John followed the tracks easily, not hurrying. He still wasn't quite sure why he was staying with her, tracking her, but he kept going for another hour and a half to cover the same distance she had covered in eight and a half minutes.

Speed was everything to her, to all deer. When mortal danger threatened the only recourse was speed, burning speed, speed that tore energy from the center of the deer and used her up.

She ran that way now. Ran from the danger of John and while she had paused long, too long, in the freeze position, she made up for it by now getting as much distance as possible in the shortest possible time between her body and the man with the gun.

But running long and hard burned her out. It showed in her tracks, a slight wobble now and then from running past her short-range endurance. She would have to rest soon, he knew, would have to bed down.

John knew this from hunting and from talking with his grandfather and other old hunters. There were stories of men who had taken time and walked deer down and John had always figured they were just that, stories. But he knew that deer had a short burn, nonetheless, and that was in his mind now as he followed her tracks.

The tracks.

The tracks were her and they were more, too. They were small stories in the snow. At first, when she ran scared from him she had torn the snow and left diamonds scattered in the sun across the white. But when she settled down again and began looking for a place to rest, the tracks were more controlled, her feet almost inserted in the snow, with no splashing.

He knew her from the tracks. Knew more about her all the time and kept going at first for that, he thought: to learn more about her, to try and find what it was that made her stick in his mind. She was there already, as if she'd been there before he came hunting.

The second time he got her up she didn't freeze but made off to the left, the north, in a smooth, low run. He could easily have hit her. She started forty yards away and he had a good sixty- or seventy-yard run to get the sights on her but he didn't even raise the rifle.

He cut the corner and again picked up her tracks and started following once more. Again there was panic in the tracks, the long burst, but he knew he wouldn't lose her, because it was all new snow and there were no other deer and it was clear and there wouldn't be any more snow to cover her tracks.

I'll follow for a while, he thought, having used up all the reasons and excuses. *Maybe I can still kill her and take liver for Grandpa. Maybe I can make her into meat,* he thought, knowing that something about that was wrong. *Maybe I'll just stay with her. I'll follow for a while and see what happens.*

The sun was moving toward evening now. It was still well above the southwestern horizon, but it would drop fast and when it did it would get dark. John frowned, trying to remember the moon. Finally he remembered that it would be nearly full so there would be good night light. Sometimes when there was new snow and the moon was full he could almost read at night.

He took a sandwich from his pocket and tore the paper off while walking. His first bite tasted so good that it made his jaws ache but on the second one he remembered that it was a venison sandwich and the meat seemed to take on a taint, not so much a bad taste as a bad feeling.

He did not take a third bite but put the sandwich back in his pocket and instead ate the apple. When he was finished he threw the core away and kept walking, always walking.

He was tiring now, but not exhausted. The calves of his legs ached slightly now and then and his stomach hurt a bit from stepping over the swamp grass, but it was nothing to him yet and he walked easily.

I'll bet, he thought, *I could track her all night. I'll bet I could just keep going in the moonlight and stay on her tracks and then . . .*

He did not know what came next. Just *and then . . .*

He was halfway through a stand of jack pine on a small sand island in the sea of swamp grass when dark caught him.

John knew that starting in November for four months dark hammers down fast in the north. In literally minutes it goes from day to dark night, so fast it catches things. Dark can catch a rabbit in a clearing, letting a fox find him. It catches mice in the open and lets owls have them.

And it caught John.

He stopped then, studied the sky and the terrain. There were times when he was young when he would have worried—being caught in the dark miles from home in a strange woods. But not now. He could see the stars, see the polestar, and though it was cold, the wind had also died so the cold didn't blow in.

And there was the moon. The moon would be south, go to bed in the southwest. "You're never lost when you can see the sun and the stars and the moon," his grandfather had told him. The moon was a pale-blue light that took life from the snow and changed the dark to just a different kind of day, not night at all, so John wasn't lost.

The tracks shone in the moonlight, called to him from the inside, and he started walking again, following.

At first, while he worked the tracks and went deeper and deeper into the swamp he saw other things, saw beauty.

He moved to within fourteen inches of a snowshoe rabbit, frozen in the moonlight like a white ghost, caught by surprise while playing fox-and-geese. John could not tell where the snow ended and the rabbit began; the rabbit was a part of the whiteness.

A timber wolf followed him for a short time, until John turned in a clearing and saw him. The wolf had been looking for mice and for a time John thought he might be after the doe and it angered him and he made a sound in his throat.

It was an animal sound—a sound that wasn't a sound. It came from inside some way, from a pit that he didn't understand. It was a sound for the wolf, a warning for the wolf—a thing that went out from John, out to the wolf.

He did not want to kill the doe. He didn't want

the wolf to do it either and he was glad when the wolf turned away, not in fear, but just naturally.

She is not mine, he thought, stopping suddenly, *but she is of me now, somehow; I will follow her for a while and we shall see.*

I will follow her for a while and I will touch her.

The thought came like a fast wind, working around the sides of his brain into the middle.

I will follow her and I will touch her and she will be mine then, mine without me having to kill and give her death and make her meat.

But why? He had never thought like this before. He was tired now—had been tracking for twelve hours, moving steadily, getting the deer up and pushing her ahead, often without seeing her. But he wasn't odd-tired yet, just tired—and yet he wanted to touch the doe.

He *would* touch her.

He would stay on the trail until she couldn't get away from him anymore, stay and stay and when he caught her he would touch her.

And if I do that, he thought, *if I can follow her and touch her without giving her death then death will be cheated.*

If I touch the deer.

He looked to the moon again and saw that it

was indeed full and there would be good light all night and he started walking.

There was purpose now, an aim. He thought suddenly that it would be better to dump the rifle, to leave it hanging in the branches of a tree. He would pick it up on the way back, if he came this way. If not he'd come out on his tracks and get it later. It was of steel and heavy and meant death and he didn't want to carry it any further. It did not fit with the doe any longer, or with him, and when he put it in the tree he felt a weight lifting from him that was out of proportion to the four pounds the rifle weighed. It was a weight from his thoughts. An extra part was gone, a part that didn't matter. Now there was just John and the doe and the night and the tracks, and he fought the tiredness away and kept going. He picked up the stride and worked to increase the pace.

He did not come to see how the deer was his grandfather, or the spirit of his grandfather's life, until later in the night, almost daylight the next morning.

And by then nothing was the same as it had started out to be. The deer wasn't a deer anymore and he wasn't John Borne anymore, either. Everything was changed.

TEN

Through the night he moved, weaving amongst the willows, flowing across the clearings, following her tracks, watching the doe change from a deer to something more and something less.

She went mad in the night. She ran too hard and went down and fell and he saw the splotch in the snow where it had happened and at first he smiled, some part of him felt good that he had caused her to run, but then it changed to sadness and he hoped that she would not do that again, would not panic and fall and perhaps hurt herself. But she ran in jerks through the night, great tearing runs that took her energy.

She ran across clearings and amongst the willows and pine, away, away—always away from the sound of the steps that kept coming.

And John in some ways became less than he was before—less the hunter, less the man tracking her—and in some ways he became more than he was before. He took strength from the snow and the winter and the beauty of the night, took power from the moon and the white light and kept going.

More than once he fell asleep while he was walking. From three in the morning on to daylight he had a terrible time staying awake. His legs and body kept on but his mind and spirit went out and he dropped, face down in the snow, and it was hard to get up.

Once he simply lay and felt the sleep come and knew that if he didn't get up the sleep might let him freeze, but he still couldn't move and wouldn't have moved except that he heard the deer.

The deer.

He heard her move in the red willows in the white light and he looked and saw her and she was afraid but she was somehow beckoning, too. The sound pulled him and he got up and stood on his feet and started walking again.

In the night he changed.

In the night he changed from following the deer to becoming the deer. A part of him went out to the deer and a part of the deer went out of her into him, across the white light and he wasn't the same. He would never be the same again. He was of the deer and the snow and the night and he kept himself but he lost his spirit and gained a new one.

I am not
but I am.
I am the deer.

It became a chant, a song that he did not sing aloud but which still went out before him down the line of tracks to the deer and he hoped she knew the song, knew the beauty of the song and knew that he meant her no harm.

But she could not know.

She could know only that this man kept following, stayed on her trail the way no wolf would have done, spent energy the way no predator would have done, stayed and stayed and stayed until the fear was alive in her.

Big-eyed terror. She was tiring in the night, her muscles quivering. She ran in bursts ahead of John, ran until she was out of sight and then went down in the grass to rest, but always the steps kept coming.

In panic, in a clearing, she voided all her fluids and solid waste in a small pile that lay steaming in the snow, sinking, and she ran on.

John came upon the pile and it was still hot, still giving off airs and he knelt to smell it. He could taste the smell, acid on the sides of his tongue, and he looked up and he knew her from the smell and the taste, knew that no other deer would have that smell or taste and even if he lost the trail now he could go by smell and that wasn't the same. That made him different. He couldn't smell that way before and that made him part of the doe. He would stay on her, keep after her until he owned her. No, more than that, more than owning.

He would touch her and touch himself and

touch his grandfather's spirit and touch death and he would win.

It was all with the doe, all of it—and he loved her.

He would touch her, and he loved her. Loved her deeply—what she was and the way she looked and what she meant. She had brought him out, danced before him in the winter, danced and pulled him into the swamp. Part of him said that it couldn't be, but another part of him knew that the doe had come for him at the barn—come for him and danced him away.

In the night he was crazy, a little, and some of it came from being tired and some of it from thinking about his grandfather. The craziness came in short flashes and mixed with being not crazy so he couldn't tell the difference. And he didn't care.

The gray of false dawn showed him closer to the doe. He could see her now, see her often. Her bursts of running, open mouthed and hard, stretched only two hundred yards and he saw her moving ahead in the willows and across the clearings, looking back in fright, spit dripping from her tongue out the side of her mouth.

The deer.

And when full light came he hated himself as much as he loved the deer. She was running until her front legs collapsed, running until she caved in, and she plowed down into the snow and then up, staggering, to run again and he hated himself for driving her that way but he couldn't stop, couldn't make himself stop now.

He must touch her.

He must own her.

He must own-love-touch the doe and when that happened his grandfather would not die.

ELEVEN

He had tracked her all that first day and all of that night, following in the moonlight and the new clean snow and through the next morning, and when the sun was highest his brain did not work right anymore.

He was tired beyond bearing, tired beyond the doe, weaving and staggering and falling and still not stopping. By midday there was nothing for him but the doe and the touching of the doe and it was no longer possible to distinguish between what was real and what was not.

Once in the morning light he watched the doe ahead of him and saw her turn and swore there was a light around her head. The light moved with her neck movements, was not a halo so much as a glow that came from within the doe and it was still there even when he wiped his eyes. The light stayed for five or six minutes and did not disappear until the doe staggered into some willows and was lost from sight.

Again, later, he was looking at the doe and it seemed that everything he saw in front of him was a mirror. Seemed that the doe was actually in back of him and that everything that was going to happen had already happened in back of him. It made his mind whirl and then his vision fogged and he fell down and would have stayed down again but for the doe.

She moved and he followed.

By noon she could not run but seemed to fall forward, fall away from him and just keep falling, with her legs catching up only to fall again for miles and miles.

And he came the same way. John was falling and making his legs catch up—he did not feel tired anymore, didn't feel anything.

At one in the afternoon he began seeing the doe all the time. She was blown out completely and could not even make the pretense of running. Instead she worked just to stay ahead of him, just ahead, always in sight—never more than a hundred yards, often less then fifty.

He saw her.

At one point she vomited from stress and there was some blood in it, blood mixed with bits of bark fiber from the last time she'd eaten, over a day before, and when he came on it he was sickened and felt the bile rise and he, too, vomited.

The air was warm and he hung his jacket over a bush, stuck his cap in his back pocket and poured sweat still. The sun was full on his back now as he worked north and he made sounds that weren't human, yet weren't animal—sounds from his throat as he watched her stagger and fall away from him, first to the left and then to the right.

At last when she went down she didn't get up as fast and then each time she fell she was slower to get up and he kept coming.

Coming—until there came a time when he was nearly on her before she got up, only to fall again, and then she didn't get up.

She was blown. Her ribs heaved for air as his did, her eyes showed edges of red, her mouth was open and her tongue stuck out to the side and he thought he'd never seen anything so awful and ugly and beautiful at the same time.

The doe was his and he didn't have to kill her, give her death, and he moved forward to her, on his hands and knees now, crawling, lunging, and she jerked to get away once and fell and he saw it as a picture, the doe on her side, heaving air, the yellow in the snow where she urinated in fear, the fear and the madness around her, the wild eyes, and he reached out and he touched her.

He was there and his hand went out and he touched her and then he fell, down and down in the snow and when he opened his eyes in a minute, an hour, a lifetime, she was gone.

He got up and stood, weaving, looking back on his trail. The sun was afternoon hot and he had touched her and she was gone, gone, but he had done it.

He knew because the yellow was still on the

snow and there were flecks of blood from her nostrils and the imprint of her muzzle in the white.

He had touched her.

And now he had to get home and tell his grandfather that he had done it, he had won and there would be life now—life taken from death. Life taken back.

TWELVE

It was dark again when John reached the farm, dark and cold. He stopped in the woods on a small rise and looked at the house.

He couldn't tell his grandfather what had happened—at least not all of it. He had been chewing on it since he'd left the doe, walking all day in a thought haze. She had run in great loops and circles of fear but not a terrible distance from the farm. When he'd regained some of his thoughts he knew where he was and took a straight line back to the rifle and from there home—a seven-hour walk.

Seven hours of wondering what he would say to his grandfather and now the time had come. He would have to say something but he couldn't tell him of cheating death—that wouldn't work either.

The doe had taught him much, not about death but about life. And yet it was not something he could share with anybody—it was not something he was sure he really understood himself. It was just a thing that *was*—a way for something to be. She made him see a new way, but he could not make others do the same. They had to have their own deer.

His legs were on fire and the pain seemed worse now that he was close to home. He staggered down to the porch and leaned the rifle in the corner and stomped clear of snow and went in.

They were sitting at the kitchen table, just as they always sat. Relief flooded his grandfather's face, a clearing away of wrinkles, but he said nothing.

His grandmother coughed and cleared her throat, and he could see mist in the corners of her eyes, small tears.

"We were worried," she said, controlling her voice. "It came on to being long—longer than you've ever been at hunting."

John shook his coat off and hung it up and sat at the table, still silent.

"For all that you didn't make meat?" His grandfather lit his pipe, making clouds of smoke. He only smoked when he wanted to think before talking, he'd once told John. "Two days and some and no meat?"

John studied him. "It's not like it was before . . ." He trailed off, said nothing more for a long minute.

"What isn't? What's changed?"

And that's it, John thought, the idea searing across the front of his mind—*what has changed?* Had touching the deer altered anything? Was there not still death—still death coming to his grandfather?

"I . . . I found a doe and I followed her," he started, but it wasn't coming out right.

"For two days you followed a doe? And you didn't get a shot?"

John looked out the window yet could see nothing but the reflected room. The tablecloth with the pattern, the glow of the lamp—it was like another world facing the world he was in. A world that was the same and yet the opposite and he wished he were in the mirror world.

"A thing changed," John said. "A thing changed in hunting, in everything, and I walked after her but didn't shoot her."

His grandparents said nothing, waited.

"And I walked for two days and then I touched her. Actually two days, and a night. And when I touched her everything changed—everything about the way we are and what's happening."

He finished lamely, letting it simply end. His grandmother took a plate of meat and potatoes from the oven and put it in front of him. She had known somehow that he was coming because it wasn't stale food, still fresh. Or maybe she'd just kept a different plate warm each night. *No,* he thought, *she'd known somehow—just as she always knows.*

His grandfather put his pipe down. He never smoked when anybody was eating. He looked at John, then out the window. "You touched her? You really touched a live deer?"

John nodded. "I walked and walked and touched her. She couldn't get up."

Another long pause.

"Ain't that something, Aggie?" his grandfather

said. "He walked one down. Ain't that something?"

And there was a thing in his voice that John had never heard before. A touch of pride, perhaps; a building of something.

"I'll take that with me," his grandfather went on. "That's something I'll just take with me."

John had a forkful of meat halfway to his mouth and he stopped, put the fork down. He was surprised to see that his grandfather was crying, crying as he looked at his reflection in the window—or just looked out the window—and two thoughts cut through the tiredness in his mind, burned into his brain.

The first was that his grandfather was going to die. He would die and there was nothing John could do about it—nothing touching the doe could do about it. Death would come.

And the second thing was that death was a part of it all, a part of living. It was awful, a taking of life, but it happened to all things, as his grandfather said, would happen to John someday. Dying was just as much a part of Clay Borne as living.

"Tomorrow, I do the chores," John said. "You take it easy."

After that there was just the food and keeping his eyes open until he went up the stairs to bed where he dreamt of the doe and his grandfather and awakened in sweat when the dream became too real.

But he made no sound and went back to sleep evenly, even thoughts of the doe washed from his mind.

DOGSONG

Also by Gary Paulsen

DANCING CARL

TRACKER

DOGSONG

•

Gary Paulsen

A Richard Jackson Book
Atheneum Books for Young Readers

ATHENEUM BOOKS FOR YOUNG READERS
An imprint of Simon & Schuster Children's Publishing Division
1230 Avenue of the Americas
New York, New York 10020

Printed in the United States of America
15 14
The text of this book is set in 12pt. Janson.
Library of Congress Cataloguing in Publication Data:
Paulsen, Gary Dogsong.
Summary: A fourteen-year-old Eskimo boy who feels assailed by the modernity of his life takes a 1400-mile journey by dog sled across ice, tundra, and mountains seeking his own "song" of himself.
1. Eskimos—Juvenile fiction. 2. Children's stories, American. [1. Eskimos—Fiction] I. Title.
PZ7.P2843Do 1985 [Fic] 84-20443
ISBN 0-689-83960-X

This book is dedicated to
KAY-GWA-DAUSH
to honor her song

C O N T E N T S

PART ONE

THE TRANCE

I

I came wet into the world.
On both sides there were cliffs,
white cliffs that were my mother's thighs.
And I didn't cry though it was cold
by the white cliffs and I was afraid.
I came wet into the world.

—an old Eskimo man relating
the memory of his birth in a
snowhouse on the sea ice.

RUSSEL SUSSKIT rolled out of the bunk and put his feet on the floor and listened in the darkness to the sounds of morning.

They were the same sounds he had always heard, sounds he used to listen for. Now in the small government house—sixteen by twenty—they grated like the ends of a broken bone.

He heard his father get up and hack and cough and spit into the stove. His father smoked cigarettes all day, rolled them with Prince Albert tobacco, and had one hanging on his lip late into the night. In the mornings he had to cough the cigarettes up. The sound tore at Russel more than at his father. It meant something that did not belong on the coast of the sea in a small Eskimo village. The coughing came from Outside, came from the tobacco which came from Outside and Russel hated it.

After the coughing and spitting there was the sound of the fire being lit, a sound he used to look forward to as he woke. The rustle of paper and kindling and diesel fuel, which was used to start the wood, the scratch of a match, the flame taking and the stink of the diesel oil filling the one room. Russel did not like the smell of the diesel oil but he did not hate it the way he hated his father's coughing in the morning.

Russell heard the wind outside and that was good except that it carried the sounds of the village waking, which meant the sound of snowmachine engines starting up.

The snowmachines were loud and scared the seals. To fourteen-year-old Russel the whine of them above the wind hurt as much as the sound of coughing. He was coming to hate them, too.

It was still dark in the house because the village

generator hadn't been turned on for the day. The darkness was cut by the light of the oil lamp on the table as his father touched a match to the wick.

Flat light filled the room and Russel looked around as he always did. It was a standard government house—a winter house. They would move to summer fish-camps later. But in the winter they came into the village and stayed in the government houses. Boxes is what they are, really, he thought: boxes to put people in.

In one corner there was a small table with an oilcloth table cover. The cloth was patterned with roses and Russel did not know why his father had ordered it. There were no women there. Russel's mother had been gone for years, gone with a white trapper. But his father had liked the roses on the tablecloth and had sent for it. Russel had never seen a rose except on the tablecloth and on television over at the central meeting house where there was a set for watching. He did not think roses were as pretty as the small flowers that came in the tundra in the summer while they were taking salmon from the rivers. But his father liked the roses and Russel liked his father so he tried liking the roses.

All around the walls were pictures of Jesus.

His father loved Jesus more than he loved the

roses. When he was young his father had told him about Jesus and Russel had listened but he didn't understand. He supposed the idea was something that came when you got old, the understanding of Jesus, and in the meantime he looked at all the pictures and wondered what they meant.

There was one in which Jesus had thorns on his head and they were cutting into him and making him bleed. Russel had asked his father why Jesus would want to do such a thing.

"Because he is the Son of God and is meant to suffer for your sins," his father said, which made no sense at all to Russel: the story of Jesus happened so long ago, back in the Before Time, and Russel couldn't remember doing anything wrong enough to make a man shove thorns in his head. But he said nothing against it. Jesus kept his father from drinking, in some way which he also did not understand, and that was good. When his father used to drink, things were all bad and if Jesus kept that out of his life, even if He did it mysteriously, that was all right.

But he got bored with the pictures around the walls showing Jesus with light in back of him and bleeding and carrying a cross. Even in the tiny bathroom where there was the bucket there was also a picture of Jesus, and another hung over the stove. All the pictures were cut out of religious magazines which people Outside had sent his father.

Two snowmachines went by the house. They were moving fast, too fast to stop in the dark if something jumped out in front of them. Russel winced at the noise.

Russel owned a snowmachine. Owned a motor sled. And he used it. But he didn't like snowmachines and used one only because he needed a means to get around and he didn't have any dogs. There were almost no dogs in the village. Just one team, owned by old Oogruk. And Oogruk didn't use them but simply kept them for memories.

Russel pulled on his felt-duffel slippers and slipped them inside the rubber shoepacs that made up the outer boot. He had slept in his pants and it took only a moment to pull the undershirt on and a sweater.

He stepped out to the food cache in the dark. It was an elevated wooden hut filled with caribou and seal and fish meat. Earlier in the winter the men and boys of the village had gone back into the hills on snowmachines and found a herd of caribou and they had worked around them with rifles, killing into the center. Russel and his father had taken twelve of them, some others had killed twenty or more, and they brought the meat back on sledges pulled by the snowmachines.

Russel used a hatchet to chop off some slivers of caribou and a tiny bit of seal meat. He took them back in the house.

On the wood stove was a pan and he pulled it over onto the heat and threw in the seal and caribou meat. The frozen seal meat started to melt and give off oil immediately and the caribou began to cook in the oil and soon the smell of the meat filled the room and he liked that.

He stood looking down at the pan and when the meat was warm—still nearly raw—he took out a piece of caribou and put it in his mouth and used an *ulu*—a short curved knife—to cut the meat just on the edge of his lips.

He chewed and swallowed, then took another bite. Cutting it cleanly, chewing, staring at the stove, the pan, at nothing.

"You should cook the meat longer," his father said, coming from the bathroom. "We do not eat it raw anymore."

Russel said nothing, nodded, but took more meat.

"There are small things in the meat to make you sick. Small worms and bugs. When you cook the meat more it kills them."

"I was hungry."

"Well. Next time, eh?"

Russel nodded. "Next time."

His father watched the meat cook. "We used to eat everything raw but now we have learned to cook it. That's one of the good things we learned."

Russel smiled. "Raw meat tastes better. You get the blood then."

"That's true. But you also get the small things to make you sick. It's better to cook it."

"Yes, Father." He wanted to go on and say, *Father, I am not happy with myself*, but he did not. It was not the sort of thing you talked about, this feeling he had, unless you could find out what was causing it. He did not know enough of the feeling to talk.

"There were some of the old things that were not bad," his father said. "I am too young to remember many of them, but I was told a lot of them by my father. You did not meet him because before you were born he died in a bad storm on the sea. His *umiak* was torn by ice when they were walrus hunting and all the men in the boat died but one who rode to the ice on a sealskin float. It was an awful thing, an awful thing. The women cut themselves deep and bled in grief when they learned. I was just a small boy, but I remember the grief."

His father scratched himself and took some meat,

still nearly raw. "I like the blood taste, too." He bit, cut and chewed and put the *ulu* back on the stove top.

"Father, something is bothering me."

He replied around the meat. "I know. I have seen it."

"But I don't know what it is."

"I know that, too. It is part that you are fourteen and have thirteen winters and there are things that happen then which are hard to understand. But the other part that is bothering you I cannot say because I lack knowledge. You must get help from some other place."

Russel nodded, then thought. "But where?"

His father looked at the ceiling, back down, thinking. "When I have trouble that I do not understand I sometimes get help from Jesus Christ."

Russel hesitated. He did not want to sound discourteous but he was sure Jesus wouldn't help.

"But you do not have Jesus so that may not work for you. If you do not have Jesus I think you should go and talk to Oogruk. He is old and sometimes wise and he also tells good stories."

"Oogruk? For help?"

His father laughed. "I know. You think he is old and just babbles. But there are two things there, there are Oogruk's words and there is Oogruk's song. Songs and words are not always the same. They do not always say the same thing. Sometimes words lie—but the song is always true. If you listen to Oogruk's words, sometimes they don't make sense. But if you listen to his song, there is much to learn from Oogruk."

"All right. I will go. But will Oogruk give a song to me?"

Russel had heard about the songs his father spoke of. They were private and belonged only to the person who owned them. Now almost no one had a song.

"That is for him to know. Now go and get more meat. You did not bring in enough." His father thought a moment. "And bring in two of the heads so they will begin to thaw."

"You want the heads?"

"Not for me. For Oogruk. Take the heads when you go, as a gift. He loves the eyes."

Russel nodded and went out into the dark again.

2

There was a time when I was young. It was a bad time when there was not meat anywhere you looked and we had eaten of all the dogs.

We asked our old mother if we could kill her and eat of her until the deer came back and we would have done that thing. We would have done that thing. But that morning a deer came and my uncle took it with an arrow in the right manner and we did not have to do that thing. More deer came and we did not have to eat our old mother.

—an old Eskimo telling of his youth.

RUSSEL HAD been in Oogruk's house many times but he always stopped before he went in. The dogs always drew him, drew his eyes over and he stopped. They were tied near the elevated food cache—a rough log hut up on stilts—and they watched him with interested eyes, slanted, deep eyes, watched him as he threw the caribou heads on the ledge surrounding the food cache.

The dogs.

There were five of them. Great red beasts with blue eyes, a cross between wolf and Mackenzie River huskies with some Coppermine River village blood mixed in. They were shy, aloof dogs who did not want people to touch them except to harness them or feed them. Russel knew little of dogs, but a man who knew dogs said they were good.

They were the only team in the village and never worked, so they were fat. But the fat hid muscle that could go forever.

Russel turned away from them and went to the door of Oogruk's house. Again he stopped, hesitating. It wasn't that he was afraid to go in. Everybody was welcome at Oogruk's. The old man loved company. It was more that Oogruk lived differently and inside the house—which outside looked like any government box—you had to change. The mind had to change, and the nose—Russel thought, grimacing—because Oogruk lived the old way. He would not allow electricity, used a seal-oil lamp and had skins on the floor. Some of the skins, all from caribou, were green tanned and they smelled when they grew warm. It was not a bad smell but it was strong and took some getting used to.

As did Oogruk. The way of Oogruk, the way he looked and was; it took a different thinking.

Russel opened the door without knocking, as

was the custom, and went in and closed the door. Outside there had been bright-light and sea-wind off the frozen sea ice, salt-wind. Inside it was almost pitch-dark. The windows were covered with smoke grime, and the room was full of smoke from the lamp on a box in the corner, a seal-oil lamp with a moss wick that threw a tiny yellow glow around the room.

Leaning against the wall were harpoons and lances, hanging on nails were arrow-bags and bows and small ivory carvings. On other nails were skin clothes, squirrel-skin undergarments and caribou-skin parkas, some old and some not so old, all hanging loosely and thick with the smoke.

Against the far wall sat Oogruk. At first it was hard to know where the smoke ended and Oogruk began. Except for a small breechclout he was nude, and his skin was the same color as the smoke, a tan-brown, rich and oily. His hair had gone white, or would have been white, but it had taken the smoke, too, seemed to have flown into the smoke and become part of the smoke from the lamp.

"Hello. Hello. You sit down and we'll talk for a while." The voice was strong—it always amazed Russel to hear Oogruk's voice. He was so old but the voice moved like strong music. "I will talk for you."

Russel nodded and sat near the right wall, glad

that nobody else was there. Often children would come in to listen—with respect, but out of curiosity more than anything—and Russel was glad that they were not there now. "I brought some deer heads for you," he said when he'd settled on the hides. "With the eyes. They are out on the platform."

Oogruk swiveled his head to face Russel. The eyes were opaque, a milk blindness over them, but Russel never thought of him as blind.

"I eat of the eyes when I can but people don't save them anymore," Oogruk said.

"Should I bring them in?"

"Later. Later. Did you see my dogs when you came in?"

Russel nodded, then remembered the blindness and said aloud, "Yes. They are well. They are fat."

"Good. I don't drive them anymore but they are good dogs and I worry that they don't get fed enough."

"They are being taken care of by everybody—they are all right."

Oogruk said nothing for a time. The eyes moved back to the flame from the lamp so the thick-white caught the yellow of the light and glowed for a second.

"Dogs are like white people," Oogruk said,

looking at the flame. "They do not know how to get a settled mind. They are always turning, looking for a better way to lie down. And if things go wrong they have anger and frustration. They are not like us. It is said that dogs and white people come from the same place." He snorted—a nasal sound, a kind of *chaa* sound through his nose that could have meant anything from scorn to anger to humor. "I do not know how true that is because white people are clearly not dogs. But they have many of the same ways and so one wonders."

Russel nodded but said nothing. One time he had seen a bushpilot who had crashed his plane near the village. The plane was broken in the middle and the pilot had stood screaming at it and kicking it for failing him and falling from the sky. He treated the plane like a living animal until he got tired, then he walked away as a dog would walk away from a stick he'd been tearing at.

Oogruk sighed. "I will tell you about something. We used to have songs for everything, and nobody knows the songs anymore. There were songs for dogs, for good dogs or bad dogs, and songs to make them work or track bear. There were songs for all of everything. I used to know a song that would make the deer come to me so that I could kill it. And I knew a man who could sing a song for whales and make them come to his harpoon."

The flame guttered in the lamp and Russel saw Oogruk use a small ivory tool to brush the burned moss away to clean the flame. A new-yellow filled the room, cut through the smoke, then paled down as the twisted moss burned on the end.

Russel shifted and stuck his legs out straight in front of him—Eskimo fashion—and relaxed. He leaned back against the wall. There were things he wanted to ask but he did not know what they were. Part of his mind was turning over, but another part was full of a strange patience and so he waited. Sometimes it was better to wait.

"Mebbe you could bring in those eyes and put some snow in the pot and we'll warm them up. Cold eyes are bad to eat."

Russel got up and went outside. The wind was stronger now, bringing cold off the ice, but he didn't wear a coat and liked the tightness the cold caused when it worked inside his light shirt. He used his belt knife to pop the caribou eyes out of the two skulls—they levered out with surprising difficulty—and stopped by the door to take down the pan hanging on the wall and fill it with snow.

He put the eyes on top and took the pan and

snow inside and handed them to Oogruk, who held the pan over the lamp.

"One misses women," the old man said. "I had some good wives but they are gone. Two died back before the white men came, died bearing children, and the last one just left. She went up to the mining town to a party and didn't come back. One misses women."

Russel said nothing. He was seated again, leaning against the wall, and as with dogs he knew nothing of women. The girls smiled at him with round faces and merry eyes but he was not ready for women yet and so knew nothing of them.

"They cooked and sewed for me. Eyes and meat taste better when cooked by women. That's the truth."

Russel had never eaten eyes. He knew the fluid in them would be too salty. He smiled. "Were there songs for the women, too?" He wanted Oogruk to talk of the songs again.

Oogruk grinned, the teeth worn down to the gums, the hair hanging down past his cheeks. As the memory grew so did the grin until finally, after a couple of minutes, he laughed openly. "They always shined in the snow houses, shined with fat and oil. It was a thing to be young then—it was everything to be young then. It wasn't that there were songs for women," he said, coming back to the subject, "it's that the women *were* the songs."

Russel reached over. The pot was tipping in Oogruk's hand and the melted snow was about to spill into the lamp and douse the flame.

Oogruk stuck a finger in the water and found it to be warm. He reached into the pan and took out an eye and popped it in his mouth, using his gums to crush it and swallow the juice noisily.

"Have one." He held the pan out. "They are good."

"I brought them for you. Besides, I ate before I left our house. I had meat."

Oogruk nodded and slowly, one by one, ate the other three eyes, smacking his lips with the joy of it. When he was done he slapped his stomach. "They are good. Later, when you are gone for the long time, you will wish you had eaten of them."

Russel almost missed it. Then it hit him. "What do you mean, 'gone for the long time'?"

But Oogruk was again in his memories. "I saw a thing once that was hard to understand. We were talking of songs and this man lived when I was young and he was very old and he had a song for the small birds. They would fly in flocks that moved this way and that and would flick the light of the sun off their breasts. Snowbirds. So this man was named Ulgavik and he had a song to make the birds dance. When he sang it one way they would fly that way and when he wanted them to change he would sing it another way and they would take the light and go the new way.

"It was a thing of beauty."

But Russel was fixed on the earlier comment.

"What did you mean about being gone for the long time?"

"This man Ulgavik knew dogs. He knew birds, but he knew dogs, too, so that when he got old and his eyes went to milk it did not matter. He could run his team blind and knew the dogs so well that what the dogs saw came back up through the sled and he saw that, too. The dogs were his eyes. Maybe if Ulgavik were alive he would tell you how to know dogs and birds."

Russel closed his eyes and thought of Ulgavik running blind out across the sea ice, blind into the white—but such a thing couldn't be.

"What we need is some *muktuk*," Oogruk said. "I haven't had any for a long time. Do you know where there is some *muktuk*?"

"No. Everybody is out of it." Russel thought of the delicate little squares of whale blubber that had been fermented all summer in rancid seal oil. They had a nutty, sweet-stink taste. But the village had not taken a whale that year, which was considered very bad luck. Russel thought it was because of the snowmachines, because they scared the seals and whales away by sending their ugly noise down through the ice. But he didn't say what he thought. "There will be no whales until the ice is gone and then I don't think they will come."

Oogruk was quiet for a time. Then he sighed. "Because of the machines."

Russel started. "Is that what you think?"

"No. That is what you think. I think they will not come because we are wrong now and don't deserve them and they know that. We don't have the songs anymore and they don't hear us singing and so they know we don't deserve *muktuk*. Of course I could be wrong and it could be the machines."

"How did you know I felt that way about the snowmachines?"

Again the flame sputtered and again Oogruk trimmed it to bring the light up and Russel only then realized with a start that if Oogruk was blind, truly blind, he could not see the flame sputter.

"It is the way one thinks," Oogruk said. "I know the way you think and so I know what you feel about the machines and the whales."

"How can you tell when the lamp goes down if you can't see?" Russel blurted.

"Questions. Questions. Did you come here to

ask questions or did you come here to find the way it was?"

And Russel knew he was right. In truth he had not known why he came to Oogruk's house, just that he had to come, that something had been bothering him. Just as his father had known that something had been bothering him, and that Jesus probably wouldn't be able to help him, even though he helped Russel's father quit drinking.

But Oogruk was right. That's why he had come. There was something wrong with the way things were now, something wrong with him. He wanted to be more, somehow, but when he looked ahead he didn't see more, he saw only less.

Oogruk wiped his face with his hands and smoothed the shine of the oil and sweat. He turned to face Russel and his voice grew serious. "Some of my memory is like my eyes, dead and gone. That is the way of age. And so some of the things I should tell you I can't, because they are gone. Just gone. Like melted ice in the spring. I held them as long as I could but many of them are gone now."

"That is all right. Tell me what you can and that will be enough."

"I don't know. I don't know if it will be enough for what you have to do. But it is all I have. Still, one is hungry."

Russel thought of the food cache outside. "Is there meat in your cache? I could bring some in."

Oogruk nodded. "There is much meat. Deer and a seal that some young men brought by. Why don't you bring in a piece of the deer and we'll put it in the pot and get it warm? Maybe the warm meat will help my memory."

Russel went outside and opened the cache. There was no seal but there were some parts of caribou, two back legs and eight or nine front shoulders. Oogruk obviously couldn't hunt for himself and so people brought him spare meat. That explained all the front shoulders—it was not the best part of the animal. The tenderloin down the back was gone—the best part—so Russel took one of the back legs out. He used an ax leaning on the shelf to cut off large slivers, long chunks, of the marbled meat, happy to see the fat streaks and thick layer of fat on the legs.

Fat was everything. And while deer fat wasn't as good as whale or seal or even pig lard from the trading post, it was good enough when it was hot. It turned to tallow on the lips when it cooled, but at first it was all right.

Some of the chips from the ax flew into the nearest dog's circle and he got up slowly and walked out on his chain to pick them up.

"Lazy dog," Russel said aloud and was answered by a low growl. Not one of anger but of shyness and suspicion—a low rumble that came from the dog's chest.

Russel didn't know the dog's name, didn't know any of the dogs. Always they were just Oogruk's dogs; it was Oogruk's dogs making noise howling, or Oogruk's dogs who had bitten somebody, or Oogruk's dogs who had gotten into a fight. He didn't know their names.

With the meat under one arm like large red pages from a thick book he went back into the house. It was still light, hazy light, but the light only held for three hours a day. He knew it would be dark soon. Across the ice would come the late afternoon wind and light, both hitting the village, the light dying as it always did in the winter, dropping fast, and the wind making huge drifts off the beach. Sometimes, in the late middle of the winter, the drifts became so large they covered the houses.

Inside he put a couple of slivers of meat in the pot and Oogruk held it over the lamp to warm it up.

Another question was bothering Russel, one inspired by the dogs and he decided to ask it. "You have dogs but there is no sled. Don't you have a sled?"

Oogruk nodded. "In the lean-to next to the house. It is old but made of hardwood that came from the sea and so has strength."

When the deer meat was heating on the lamp—Oogruk holding it over the flame with a corded arm, a wire arm—the old man let breath out of his nose.

"I have not been counting the summers and winters of my age," he said. "But I am old. I am old enough that I hunted before we had guns, old enough to remember what it was like before."

Russel was once again seated, legs sticking out straight, leaning back against the wall. The smell of the heating deer meat mixed with the smell of the smoke from the lamp and made him hungry. The smoke smelled like burned meat, the salty smell of burned meat. "It must have been something back then."

Oogruk made the *chaa* sound. "It was more than that. We lived so differently, so far back and different that it almost cannot be understood now. Now they use guns and make noise, back then we were quiet and the animals felt different about dying. But that's just one thing, one little thing that was different."

A third time Russel got up. He went to the wall where the weapons hung and took down a small bow, made of wood laminated with slivers of horn, wrapped with rawhide. It had a string made of sinew and after much grunting and heaving he got the bow strung. When he tried to pull it back his shoulders knotted but the string only came back four or five inches.

All this while Oogruk sat quietly, waiting, an air of study on his face.

Russel unstrung the bow and put it back on the wall. There was a skin pouch of arrows that he took down and he pulled several arrows out of it. They had bone and antler points, some with jagged barbs, others with smooth edges.

"There is a museum in the mining town," Russel said. "I was there once when I was sick and went up to the doctor. In the museum are many things like this bow and those lances. Some of them from back a long time."

Oogruk nodded. "I have not been up to the town, though I have had many chances. But I have heard of the museum and the old tools. There is a difference. I have used these weapons to take meat. They do not belong in a museum," he snorted, "any more than I belong in a museum. These tools are for using, not looking at."

Russel took down a lance. The shaft was of wood that had been scraped and straightened to take the ivory cup and point on the end. The point itself was a small toggle, razor sharp, that would tip once it entered the animal and be impossible to pull out. The toggle point was attached to a piece of supple leather, a long lashing, that had been kept soft and greased. Just as the bow and arrows had been kept in good shape.

"All these years," Russel said. "All this time you have taken care of these things."

"When I was a young man I came down this coast in a *umiak* with four other men. We had some trouble back in a village up north and we came down to make this village. After we found meat we went to get wives and we made this place where we are now."

"You made this village?"

"At first just us. Then others came because there were good fish here and much game. And so it was a good place and we had good food and good songs. Everybody had a song then and that song was just for that person. That's how it was."

"What happened to the songs? Why don't we have them anymore?"

Oogruk set the pot down and rested his arm. The meat was still too cold to eat. He picked the pot up and held it over the flame again, using the small tool to clean the moss wick first. "We had those songs until the first missionary came. He said they were wrong for some reason or another, like dancing was wrong. At first nobody believed him and we laughed at him. But he kept talking about it being wrong to have the songs and the dances and said how we would go to hell if we did not give them up. Of course we laughed again because we did not understand what this hell was . . ."

He took a breath. Russel knew about hell from his father, the same way he knew about Jesus.

"It was not that we were stupid," Oogruk continued. "Just that we didn't know about hell. So he told us. About fire and pain and these demons—as he called them—who would tear the strips of meat off us. So, many of the people quit singing and dancing because they feared hell. And even when the missionary became crazy with the winter and we had to drive him out the damage was done. People were afraid to sing and dance and we lost our songs."

Russel frowned. "Can we get them back? Could I get a song?"

Oogruk thought for a time. "It is not like that. You don't get songs, you *are* a song. When we gave up our songs because we feared hell we gave up our insides as well. If we lived the way we used to live, mebbe the songs would come back. Mebbe if we lived the right way again." His voice took on a sadness and became soft. "But nobody is doing that."

"I will."

It came without Russel knowing it was coming. A simple statement. Two words. And when he said them he knew he meant them. He needed to go back and become a song.

"I will," he repeated, leaning once more against the wall. "I will try to get a song. No. I *will* get a song, I will be a song. But I don't know what to do. I don't know how to do it."

Oogruk nodded. "That is true. There has been nobody to teach you. All the fathers have moved from the old ways and so have the mothers and so the long time required to pass on the right information is not there." Oogruk fell into silence.

"If you wanted to," Russel prompted,"you could tell me the way."

At length Oogruk nodded again. "That is why you are here, of course. You are here to learn. And I will try. I will try. But I do not know it all and there will be things I miss. Still, we will do what we can."

All this time he had been holding the meat pot over the fire and now he set it aside. The meat was steaming and he took a piece out and produced an *ulu* and bit down and cut and chewed with worn gums, swallowing when the meat was softened. Russel took some meat and tore with his teeth—he had no knife with him—and chewed and swallowed and they made no talk while they ate.

There was some fat on the meat and the grease ran down their chins and hardened and Russel used his arm to wipe it away.

They ate until the meat was gone. And when they were done with the meat Oogruk picked up the pot and drank deeply and handed it to Russel, who did the same. The water-blood soup was still warm and went down easily.

The silence grew when they'd finished eating but it was not wrong. Russel felt like sleeping yet when he closed his eyes it wasn't sleep that came. It was more a trance, a gentle lowering of his thoughts until he was relaxed, his belly full of warm meat and juice, his mouth full of the taste of the deer meat.

And while he was so, his mind warm and down, the wind tearing through the darkness around the house, bringing snow off the ice to make the big drifts, covering the dogs and the garbage of the village; while he was down, down and back, Oogruk started to talk.

3

I was round and had great beauty. For that reason I had no trouble getting husbands and that was good because they all died. I had three husbands and they all died before I had twenty summers. The sea took two of them when their kayaks were ripped and a great bear took the third. All I found was his head on the ice. It was hard then but not bad although I missed my husbands for a time. But I got a new one and he lasted.

—Eskimo woman relating her youth.

NORTH AND EAST of the village the land rose away from the sea in rolling hills that led to mountains. Even in the middle of the winter the land fought to hold the snow. The short tundra grass gave no foothold and so often the surface was blown free of snow and the grass was out all winter.

Arctic hares fed in the bare areas, as did ptarmigan, the small white grouselike birds sometimes flocking two and three hundred birds in a single place. Now and then, even in the dark-cold of winter, it was possible to see a frozen blue or purple flower—winter flowers.

Russel sat on the edge of the sled and looked down at one such flower by his foot. It had four petals, and he did not understand how it could have gotten through the fall and into the middle of winter. But it had. And it had grown in beauty for it, the color rich against the cold brown of the grass.

Much had changed.

Oogruk had talked until he was done and when he was done he had fallen silent. It might have taken days and nights, it felt like years, and when he was finished Russel had fallen asleep, a real sleep this time. He slept without moving, leaning against the wall and when he awakened the room was cool—still not cold—and he got up stiffly and stretched.

Oogruk was silent, with his eyes closed, the lamp burned out. For a moment Russel thought he was dead, but he was still breathing and Russel took a deerskin and wrapped it around the old man's shoulders.

He knew what to do. From the walls he took the lances and bow and arrows. He also took a pair of bearskin pants and the squirrel underparka and the deerskin outerparka with the hair on the inside. Some of the hair was brittle on the deerskin but it was still thick and warm.

He did not think of the objects as belonging to him, just thought of them as being what he needed. Oogruk had told him to use what he needed, including the dogs and sled and Russel followed those thoughts as if they had been his own, as in some way they were.

He was wearing store pants and a coat and he took them off and hung them on the pegs. For a moment he stood naked in the cooling room, felt his skin tighten. Then he pulled on the bearskin pants, with the hair out, the skin soft and supple. Oogruk had worked oil into the leather to maintain them as he had taken care of everything. At the top there was a drawcord and he pulled it tight. The pants were just slightly large, but the right length.

On the wall were sealskin mukluks. He took them down and felt inside. The grass bottoms were still good and he pulled them on, tied them up around his calves over the bearskin.

Then came the squirrelskin innerparka with the hair out, soft and fine, like leather silk. Last he pulled over the outerparka, thick deerhide, with the hair in, and when that was on and shrugged in place he took down a pair of deer-hide mittens with a shoulder thong and pulled them on.

As soon as he was dressed he went outside before he could heat up. He had to get the sled out of the lean-to on the side of the house and see how much work it needed. The harnesses were also there and the gangline.

It was cold, standing cold. So cold you could spit and it would bounce. When the wind hit him he pulled up the hood and tightened the drawstring through the wolverine ruff. The long fur came in around his face and stopped the wind. Then he pulled up the mitten cuffs and felt the air movement through the parka stop. His body brought the temperature up almost immediately.

Around the sea side of the house Oogruk or somebody had made a lean-to. The door had leather hinges and a wooden pin through the latch. Russel pulled the pin and worked the door open against the snow.

Inside stood a dogsled and there were harnesses on a peg on the wall. He reached in and pulled the sled out to examine it more closely. The sky was light now, a gray all-around haze off the sea and out of the clouds at the same time, and he thought he'd never seen anything so beautiful as the sled in the gray light.

It was the old kind of sled, the kind they called basket sleds. When the modern, white mushers ran the races, they used toboggans made with plastic and bolted together. Ugly little tough sleds.

But in the old days the people used sleds of delicate hardwood lashed with rawhide, all flexible and curved gracefully. Oogruk's was like a carving of a sled, with birch rails down the side and elegant curved stanchions. Around the front was a warped-wood brushbow—something he'd never need unless he ran where there were trees—and it had one-eighth-inch brass runner shoes that looked almost new.

There was a steel snowhook tied to the bridle and a rope gangline with tugs and neck-lines already in place.

He spread it out on the snow and studied everything carefully. The lashing on the sled looked old, but had been oiled and was in good shape. The rope on the gangline was a corded nylon and looked also to be in top condition.

He pulled the harnesses down and spread them out and went over them carefully as well. They were clean, had been patched a few times but were good for all of that.

All he needed was a dog team.

The harnesses all seemed the same size so he put them on the tugs, using the small ivory toggles to tie them in. Then he set the snowhook and pulled the gangline out in front of the sled and stopped to see what he had.

He had never run a team himself. But he'd seen mushers go by in races—one long-distance race went by the village—and he knew how things should look.

He took the lead dog off the chain. It growled at him and raised its hair but he tightened his grip and paid no attention to the snarl. The dog held back and Russel had to drag him to the gangline. The dogs had run for Oogruk but that was more that two years earlier. They had not run since for anybody. And this stranger had to earn their respect, earn the run. The leader turned his shoulder in the curve that meant threat, the curve that meant attack, and lifted his lip to Russel. It was an open challenge and Russel cuffed him across the head with a stiff hand. Still the dog growled and now took a cut at Russel's leg and Russel hit the dog harder.

Then a thing happened, a thing from the trance with Oogruk, and he leaned down so his head was over the top of the leader's head and he growled down at the dog. He did not know why he did this, did not know for certain what the growl meant but when it was finished he curved his head over the dog's head and, still without knowing for sure why, he bit down, hard, across the bridge of the dog's nose.

The leader growled and flashed teeth but quickly backed down and that was the end of it. He stood to in harness, pulling the gangline out tight while Russel turned to bring the rest of the team.

The other four dogs came nicely and settled into harness as if they'd been working all along. Russel smiled. It almost looked like a dog team.

He had in mind this first time to just take the dogs out on the ice and see what happened. He took no weapons or other gear because he wasn't sure if he could control the team and didn't want to lose anything if the sled flipped.

The first run was rough. The dogs ran as a gaggle, wide open, in a tangled bunch and not lined out as they should have been. Russel ran into them with the sled more than once when they stopped—before he could get the brake on—and when they hit the so-called pressure ridges a mile offshore, where the ice from the sea ground against the shore ice and piled up, he almost lost the sled.

They tipped him and dragged him on his face

for a quarter of a mile before he could get the snowhook set in a crack.

When he had stopped them he put the sled upright and sat on it for a moment to think. It was close to dark, the quick three-hour day all but gone, and he would have to head back to the village, yet he did not want to leave the run.

The wind cut at his cheeks and he turned his hood away from the force, took the cold.

"You will have to know me," he said quietly to the dogs after a time. "Just as I will have to know you."

Two of them looked back at him. It was perhaps not an invitation. It was perhaps not a look that meant anything at all except that they looked back and their eyes caught his eyes and he knew they would run. He *knew* they would run. He knew when he put his feet to the sled and took the handlebar in his hands that they would run and he did not know how he knew this but only that it was so.

When he was on the runners he reached down and disengaged the snowhook and used the small lip-squeak sound that Oogruk had told him to use to get the dogs running.

They were off so fast he was almost jerked backward off the sled. It wasn't a gaggle now, but a pulling force with all the dogs coordinating to line the sled out across the ice, a silent curve of power out ahead of him.

The feeling, he thought, the feeling is that the sled is alive; that I am alive and the sled is alive and the snow is alive and the ice is alive and we are all part of the same life.

He did not try to steer them that first time and they ran up the coast on the ice for three or four miles before their fat caught up with them and they slowed. When they were down to a trot, tongues slavering off the heat from their run, Russel stopped them again.

Oogruk said the leader had been gee-haw trained the same as the white freighters did—to go right on gee, left on haw.

"Gee!" Russel made it a loud command but he needn't have. The lead dog turned off to the right and started out again, back in toward shore. When they got along the beach edge, where the ice was mixed with sand, Russel turned right again and headed back for the village.

The dogs automatically headed for Oogruk's house and their chains, and Russel let them go. When they pulled in he took them out of harness and put them back on the chains and went into the house.

Oogruk was awake and sitting by the lamp. He had moved, Russel could tell by his position, but he was back and he smiled when Russel came in.

"Did they run for you?" the old man asked. "Did they run for you?"

Russel shrugged out of the parkas, down to bare skin. He laughed. "They ran, Grandfather. They ran for me like the wind."

"Ahh. That is fine, that is fine."

"It was a feeling, a feeling like being alive. The sled flew across the ice and I was alive with the sled."

"Yes. Yes. That is so—this is how it should be. You are correct."

"Is there meat left? We should eat meat."

The old man laughed. "You are a true person. Eat when you are happy. No. We ate it all last time. Get more from the cache. But first feed the dogs. Give them meat three times bigger than your fist. Always take care of the dogs first."

The words were not meant as a rebuke but they made Russel stop and think that perhaps he had been inconsiderate. He pulled on the light inner-parka and went outside. It took him a few minutes to chop meat for the dogs and to get some for themselves and when he got back in the cabin Oogruk had the pot on the flame waiting. He had already put snow in the pot to melt and Russel was mystified as to how the old blind man could have gotten out and found snow and gotten back in to sit without Russel seeing him.

Russel put the deer pieces in the pot and took his position on the floor. He had, essentially, moved in with the old man. Not that it was strange. In the normal Eskimo culture people moved around on a whim, especially young people. It was as natural as calling old people grandparents whether they were actually related or not.

"This is good meat," Oogruk said as the deer cooked. "But we need fresh. Fresh meat. You will have to hunt for us."

Russel nodded. "I was thinking the same thing. But what should I hunt?"

Oogruk snorted. "Whatever there is. But maybe you should start small. Go out after we eat and sleep and try to get some hare or ptarmigan."

And they had eaten, and slept, and Russel had the team out in the hills to hunt fresh meat for the old man: for himself and the old man.

He was hunting with the bow and had had many shots at both hares and ptarmigan but hadn't hit any yet. The arrows wouldn't fly true, wouldn't go where he wanted them to go. Always they were just under or over or left or right—just enough to miss. On one ptarmigan he shot six times with the round-headed bird arrows and the bird just sat as the arrows *shusshed* past. Finally he flew.

Russel looked at the dogs. They were all down, but not out of tiredness as much as boredom. The country has nothing for them to see, he thought; it is my mind that is wrong. Not the bow. It is my mind.

"What should I do?" he asked. "What is it that I am doing wrong?"

He closed his eyes and when they were shut the answer came to him. Oogruk had told him during his trance, had told him how to use the lances and the bow.

"Look to the center of the center of where the point will go. Look *inside* the center," the old man had said.

And so he pulled the hook and squeaked the team up and ran a few miles over the rolling hills until the team scared up another flock of ptarmigan. This time the dogs saw them and heard them and he had a good ride until he could get them stopped as they chased the birds. When he finally got them down he set the hook and took the bow off the sled.

The quiver he put over one shoulder but he kept out two of the bird arrows and put one of them in the bow.

The birds had flown over a small ridge and he followed, walking slowly, keeping his head down as he approached the top of the ridge.

Most of them had gone across. But eight or ten had landed just past the high point and two of them were hunkered under a small piece of willow, nearly hidden white-against-white.

Russel drew the bow, but Oogruk's advice stopped him. He looked at the nearest bird more closely. Rather than just see the bird he tried to find the exact spot he wanted the arrow to hit. Then he tried to see in the center of that tiny spot and he drew and released the bowstring and the arrow moved across the space, floated across and took the bird in a shower of feathers, and the commotion frightened the other birds away in a cloud of flying white streaks.

Russel ran over to the bird and picked it up. He had killed many ptarmigan with the small rifle that spit—the .22—but never one in the old way, with the bow.

"When you kill the old way," Oogruk had said, "it is because the animal wishes to be taken then. You must thank the animal by leaving the head with food in the mouth—if it's a land animal. With sea animals, you put fresh water in their mouths."

He pulled off the head and found some dried berries on a branch and put them in the bird's beak and put the head under the bush. "Thank you for this good meat," he said. "It will be enjoyed."

A part of him felt silly for that. He was far enough away from the old way still to almost not believe in it. Yet another part of him felt right, more right than he'd been in a long time.

It was coming dark as he trudged back to the sled. The dogs were sitting up as he came toward them and they wagged their tails when they saw the bird.

"Some meat," he said to them. "Not much but a start. A start."

He put the bird in the sled bag and tied the bow and quiver back on the sled, pulled the hook and called the dogs up.

He did not want to go back to the village yet. Even if it was too dark to hunt more he could run out along the tundra and see the country. There was no trail and he let the dogs have their heads, or let the leader run. The rest followed wherever he went.

Russel stood easily on the runners and held the

handlebar loosely. When he'd first run the dogs he was tight and rigid—afraid of losing them—but he was quickly coming to realize the sled had a life of its own. It was very flexible, giving and taking the bumps with a flowing motion, and it made gentle sounds. The rawhide lashing points creaked softly and the runners hummed, a kind of high-pitched *ssssss* sound that was very pleasant to the ear. Riding was more a matter of fitting in to the sled than trying to control it. With his knees relaxed and his hips loose he could shift his weight only slightly and the sled turned with him. It became almost an extension of his body, just as he was becoming almost an extension of the dogs.

They started down a long slope, across at an angle, perhaps a mile of downhill running, and the snow was packed so they didn't sink in. In seconds they were running wide open, their tongues flying, their ears laid flat, tails down.

Russel kept one foot on the claw brake to keep the sled from running up on them and a great joy grew within him.

The silence was broken by his laugh but the dogs didn't look back. They drove on down the hill, the sled flying from hummock to hummock, Russel laughing and playing the sled back and forth to miss the larger mounds. Twice it flipped on its side but he stayed with it and it bounced back onto its runners, all the time careening down the hill.

When they finally reached the bottom he stopped the team and set the hook.

It was then he saw the caribou. She was standing, side to him, part of the gathering darkness, part of all he could see. She had a ghost quality, the light fur of her belly blending with the snow color. He held his breath.

Hold for me, he thought, hold for me, deer. He moved slowly and took the bow from the case. It was still strung from when he was hunting the ptarmigan and he took out one of the wide-ivory-tipped big-headed arrows and fitted it to the bow.

Inside the center of the center of the caribou, he thought—that's where the arrow must fly.

Still she stood. Waiting, looking at him and the dogs, and he pulled the bow and released it and did not see it fly in the dusk but he knew, he *knew* that it flew as his mind would have it fly.

The caribou hunched slightly at the shoulder and took four steps and folded down, the front legs bending slowly, almost as if she were going to sleep. The dogs had held silently but when they saw her hit and going down it triggered the prey response from the wolf memory and they went mad. They slammed against the harnesses, again and again until the hook jerked out of the snow and the sled came loose and the team was on the deer in a tangled mass, some tearing at her throat, some at her back legs, some at her belly.

Russel ran after them. Using the bow as a club, yelling and hitting and throwing them back, he finally got them under control and off the dying caribou. It took five more minutes to get them lined out in the opposite direction from the animal and when he turned back the deer was dead.

He stopped and looked down at her. The feathers of the arrow protruded from just in back of the shoulder. The arrow had gone through the heart. She had died with her head to the east, which was good, and Russel found some of the sweet tundra grass the caribou liked and put it in her mouth. When the ritual was done he stood away from her and looked above the deer's head and said: "Thank you for this meat, deer. It will be enjoyed."

From the sled back he took the short knife he'd gotten from Oogruk and made the gut cut, from the ribs back, and dropped the large stomach. He reached in for the liver and heart and cut them out and set them aside for Oogruk. The old man could get the eyes later. Reaching up and in he jerked the lungs out and cut them in five pieces and gave them to the dogs, only just keeping his hands safe from their lunging, again using the bow as a club to stop their fighting. The blood smell was strong for them and they wanted to fight.

"Ha!" He snorted. "We are tough now, are we? When we smell the hot guts we are all tough."

The deer was heavy and he had to work hard to get her carcass loaded on the sled. When he had her on and tied in he put the liver and heart back in the open cavity, washed his hands in the snow and put mittens back on. As long as he'd been working on the deer her body heat had kept him warm, but he now realized that it was getting very cold and his hands had lost function in moments. They hurt as the mitts warmed them and he smiled with the cold-pain. He thought of cold not as an enemy but as many different kinds of friend, or a complicated ally.

Cold brought the first ice to the sea, the first strong ice so they could get out and hunt seals. Cold brought the fattening up of game so it was good to eat. It brought snow and made everything clean, it made storing meat and fish easy.

Cold could kill as well. But if treated fairly, if treated as a friend and if caution was taken, cold was good.

Russel's fingers took pain for a time from his friend the cold and he smiled with it, smiled with the deer on the sled and the cold and the dogs: the dogs out in front, coming around in a large curve, heading back for the village with the deer and the ptarmigan, the dogs moving in the dark silently with the hot lungs in their bellies and the joy on them from the kill, the dogs with their shoulders curving over and down with the weight of the deer and Russel pulling back against them as they fought up the hill, fought up with lunges and heaves to pull the sled over, over at last onto the crown of the ridge.

In the distance he could see the lights of the village from the ridge height. It was about ten miles away, but the night was clear and cold now, and almost still. The wind was dying off with the cold and darkness.

Knowing they would spend another night in their kennel the dogs picked up the speed, even with the weight of the deer, until they were moving in a steady easy lope that would cover the distance to the village in thirty minutes.

Russel was full of the night and the dogs as they ran and he felt himself go out to the dogs, out ahead. At first he didn't understand it, couldn't define it enough to give it form. But in moments the feeling grew and in his mind he gave it words, moving words, dog words.

Out before me they go
taking me home.
Out before me they go
I am the dogs.

He realized that it was part of a song, moving through the dark toward the village lights.

He wondered if it was part of his song and decided that it might be. He would make it grow.

Tonight in the village he would let it be known that he was a new person, not the old Russel, and he would tell the story to Oogruk and anybody who would listen, the story of how he took the deer with the arrow that flew across the dark.

And the telling would become part of the song.

4

Those white men came a long time ago. The white men who talked with rocks in their mouths. They came and took and took it all. They used our men as beasts and they took our women for their own and left us with no meat. Left us starving. They took all the fur and then they left. That is what I was told when I was young and in those villages they still don't like the white men who talk with rocks in their mouth.

—Eskimo speaking about the early Russian fur hunters who came for pelts.

SEA ICE IS not the same as fresh-water ice. The salt-water ice is stronger, more elastic, isn't as slippery. Also the sea ice moves all the time, even when it is thick. Sometimes whole cakes of the ice will go out to sea, miles across, sliding out to sea and taking anybody on the cake with it.

On the fourth day after taking the deer with the arrow Russel took the team out on the ice to find seals. Oogruk wanted oil for the lamp and he wanted some seal meat and fat to eat and he said these things in such a way that Russel felt it would be good to find a seal to take with the harpoon. It wasn't that he actually asked, or told Russel to go for seal, but he talked about how it was to hunt in the old days.

"Out on the edge of the ice, where it meets the sea but well back from the edge, sometimes there are seal holes. The seals come up through them and sit on the ice and if you are there when they come you can get the small harpoon point in them. That is the way it was done. Men would leave their dogs well back and pile a mound of snow in front of them and wait for the seal. Wait and wait." Oogruk had scratched with his nails on the wall of the house. "When the seal starts to come there is a scratching sound and the hunter must be ready to put the point in then."

"How long must one wait?" Russel asked.

"There is not a time. Waiting for seals is not something you measure. You get a seal, that is all. Some men go a whole winter and get none, some will get one right away. Hunting seals with the small point and the killing lance is part of the way to live."

So Russel went out on the ice. He took the team away in the daylight and was twenty miles out, working heavily through pressure ridges, when the storm came off the sea.

He had seen many storms. In his years with the village, every winter brought violent storms off the sea, white walls of wind and driven snow. Twice he had been caught out on a snowmachine and had to run for the village ahead of the wall coming across the ice.

But with a dog team you did not run ahead of the wall. As he was crossing a pressure ridge, pushing the dogs up and over the broken, jagged edges, he heaved up on the sled and looked out across the ice, out to sea, and a great boiling wall of white was rising to the sky. In seconds it was impossible to tell where the sky ended and the sea ice began and Russel knew he would have to hide before it hit. He fought the sled down the pressure ridge and brought the dogs around into a small hole under an overlapping ice ledge. There was barely room to pull his legs in.

He tipped the sled over to make a rough door across the opening to block the wind and pulled the dogs in on top of him. Working as fast as he could he tried to pack snow into the slats of the sled bottom but before he could make any headway the wind roared into the pressure ridge.

Russel drew the hood tight on his parka and huddled into the dogs, closing the small opening in the front of his hood by burying his face in dog fur.

The dogs whined for a few moments, then squirmed into better positions, with their noses under their tails, and settled in to ride the storm out the same way dogs and wolves have ridden storms out forever—by sleeping and waiting.

Russel felt a couple of small wind-leaks around the edge of his parka and he stopped them by pulling the drawstrings tighter at the parka's bottom hem. When he had all air movement stopped he could feel the temperature coming up in his clothing and he listened to the wind as it tore at his shelter.

In what seemed like moments but might have been an hour, the wind had piled a drift over his hole and he used a free arm to pack the snow away and clear the space around his body. The dogs remained still and quiet, their heat tight around Russel.

After a time he dozed, and when he awakened it seemed that the wind had diminished to some degree. He used a mittened hand to clear away a hole and he saw that it was getting darker—the short day almost gone again—and that indeed the wind was dying.

He stood, broke through the drift and shrugged the snow off. It was still cloudy but everything seemed to be lifting. The dogs were curled in small balls covered with snow, each of them completely covered except for a small blowhole where a breath had kept the snow melted. Each hole had a tiny bit of steam puffing up as the dogs exhaled and Russel was reluctant to make them stir. They looked so comfortable in their small houses.

Still he had to get home.

"Ha! Hay! Everybody up!" He grabbed the gangline and shook it. The leader stood up and shook his fur clean of snow and that brought the rest of them up. Slowly they stretched and three of them evacuated, showing they understood work. A good dog will always leave waste before going to work, to not carry extra on the run.

In a minute he had them lined out, aimed for home—or where he thought the village was—and when he called them to run they went about thirty yards and stopped. It wasn't abrupt. They were running and they slowed to a trot and then a walk and finally they just stopped.

"What is it?" Russel snorted. "Are we still asleep in our houses? Hai! Get it up and go."

Again they started and went forty or so yards and stopped.

Russel swore. "Get up! Run now or I will find a whip."

And after a time, hesitating still, they finally

got moving. Slowly. At a trot first, then a fast walk, then back up to a trot, they headed across the ice fields.

Russel nodded in satisfaction. He had not run dogs enough to know for certain what it meant when they didn't want to run, but he supposed that it was because they had anticipated staying down for a longer time.

But the man had to run the dogs. That's what Oogruk had said to him. "You must be part of the dogs, but you must run them. If you do not tell them what to do and where to go they will go where they want. And where a dog wants to go is not always the same as where the man wants to go."

The wind had stopped almost as suddenly as it came, in the way of arctic storms, but before it died it seemed to have changed a bit. When it first came it was out of the west, straight in from the sea, but before it stopped Russel noted that it had moved around to the north, was coming down from the blue-black north, the cold places.

Twice more the dogs tried to come to the right, but he made them go back and run his way. At last they lined out and went to work and Russel looked for the lights of the village. He had come out a way, but as the wind died he knew they should show, especially the light up on the hill near the fuel tanks.

He saw nothing. The clouds were still thick and low so he couldn't see the stars. He had nothing to help him tell his true direction.

He ran for several hours, letting the dogs seek their own speed, and once he was sure he should have run into the village he called them down and set the snowhook.

He was going the wrong way.

What has happened, he thought, is that during the storm the ice has caked and turned. A whole, huge plate of ice with Russel and the dogs had rotated and changed all his directions. That's why the dogs had hesitated, held back. They knew the way home and had wanted to head back to the house.

He could have let them run and they would have taken him home. But now—now what would they do?

More now, he thought. More is coming now. It was getting cold, colder than he'd ever seen it. He could feel the cold working into his clothing, see the white steam of the dog's breath coming back over their backs. His feet were starting to hurt. He was lost and the cold was working in and he did not know where to go.

There were just the dogs—the dogs and the sled and him. And the ice, and the snow and the northern night. Nobody would come to look for him because they expected him to be out late—or didn't expect anything at all. He had told nobody other than Oogruk that he was going out for seals and since he was staying at Oogruk's house nobody else could know that he was gone. And Oogruk would not expect him back because Russel was hunting the old way.

He was alone.

And a part of him grew afraid. He had seen bad weather many times. But he'd always had the chance to get out of it. On a snowmachine, unless it broke down, you could ride to safety. But he would have to face the cold now.

He debated what to do for three or four minutes. If he went down without a fire the cold would get bad later—maybe too bad. He had nothing to burn and there was no wood or fuel on the ice.

And what had Oogruk said about that? He fought to remember the trance but nothing came. He knew about problems growing in the cold, or during a storm, from other people. But Oogruk had said nothing about being lost on the ice.

Lost on the ice.

People died when they were lost on the ice. He

had heard stories of people dying, of whole families lost. The ice moved out and away from land and the people had starved to death or drowned when the ice broke up beneath them, stories that came down in the long nights, sad stories.

And now Russel. Now Russel lost on the ice with a dog team and sled.

In the sled bag he had a small piece of meat left over from when he and Oogruk had cooked the deer. He could eat. That would help him stay warm. And then what?

He could wait until the clouds cleared off and he could see stars and they would guide him home. But it might be many days. Sometimes the clouds stayed for weeks.

"So." He talked aloud to the dogs, saw a couple of tails wag in the darkness with his voice. "So there is some trouble. What should we do?"

The leader looked around at him, although it was too dark for Russel to see his face. Still, there was something there, a desire to understand or to help. Russel smiled, a quick sign back in the fur of his hood.

The dogs.

They were the answer. He could not trust himself, couldn't see anything to help him, but he could trust the dogs. Or he thought he could. He would let them run and decide where to go.

"Hai! Enough rest. It is time to take me home. Take me back to the village."

He squeaked with his lips and they got up and started off. At first they traveled in the direction Russel had forced them to go. But as they settled into their trot the leader moved them gently to the right, more and more to the right until he had them going where he had first started them off before Russel had corrected him.

Russel nodded, let them run. They had a purpose in their backs, a pulling sense that he could believe in. He was learning about dogs, just in the few runs he'd taken. He was learning.

And one thing he had to know was that in some ways they were smarter than men. Oorgruk had said that to him.

"Men and dogs are not alike, although some men try to make them so. White men." Oogruk had laughed. "Because they try to make people out of dogs and in this way they make the dogs dumb. But to say that a dog is not smart because it is not as smart as a man is to say that snow is not smart. Dogs are not men. And as dogs, if they are allowed to be dogs, they are often smarter than men."

The problem, Russel knew, was learning when to recognize that dogs were smart. The dogs knew how to run in the dark and see with their heads, with their feet, with their hair and noses. They saw with everything.

At last Russel *knew* that they were heading back for the village in the cold and dark, knew it because he felt it inside.

But they were not home yet.

Running in the dark, even in the tight dark of the north when there is no moon, it is possible to see out ahead a great distance. The snow-ice is white-blue in the dark and if there is no wind to blow the snow around, everything shows up against the white.

Now, suddenly, there was a dark line ahead of the lead dog. A dark line followed by a black space on the snow, an opening of the ice. A lead of open water, so wide Russel could not see across.

Open water. Steam rising into the cold. The ice was moving and he was moving with it.

The team stopped. The lead dog whined and moved back and forth across the edge of the ice. The dogs hated open water, hated to get wet, but they knew that the way home was across the lead.

For a few moments the leader continued to whine and pull back and forth. "Haw! We go left along the ice and see."

The leader slammed to the left gratefully, happy to be relieved of the responsibility.

But the open lead was long. They ran mile after mile along the broken edge of the ice, in and out of the steam wraiths that came from the sea water. New ice was forming rapidly in the deep cold but it was not safe and would not be safe for several days, if then. Besides, it kept breaking away with the shifting of the cake that Russel was running on.

Yet the fear was gone. The fear had come from the unknown, from not acting, and now that he had made a decision to act the fear had gone. He might not make it, he might die on the ice, but he would not die with fear. He would die working to not die.

That was something he could tell Oogruk when he got back. If he got back. The thing with dying was to try to not die and make death take you with surprise.

And with the end of the fear came a feeling of strength. The cold was less strong along the lead because the warmth from the sea water came up as steam. The steam froze on everything, on the gangline and the sled and the dogs. Soon everything glistened with ice, even the dogs looked like jewels running ahead of him in the dark with the ice frozen on their backs.

It was a beauty he could not measure. As so much of running the dogs proved to be—so much of it had a beauty he saw and took into himself but could not explain.

And while he was looking at the beauty he saw that the lead had narrowed. There was still open water, but there were large chunks floating in it and the idea came to him of bridging the open water with one of the chunks.

He stopped the team.

The leader whined. It is perhaps possible that Oogruk has done this, Russel thought, and the dog is scared because he's done it before.

Or it was possible that the dog was reading Russel's mind and knew what they were going to do. Or it might be that the dog had figured out what had to be done on his own.

Whatever the reason, the dog knew and he didn't like it. Russel set the hook and took the harpoon with the line on it out of the sled. He walked to the edge of the lead, holding back to make sure he wouldn't break off the edge and fall in. Death would come instantly with the water. With the weight of the parka and pants wet, he would go down like a stone.

There were several chunks floating in the lead, which had now narrowed to thirty or so feet. Most of them were smaller than he could use, but one was about twenty feet long and four feet wide. It lay sideways, halfway across the opening.

He lay the harpoon line on the ice, in a small loop, and held one end with his left hand. With his right he hefted the harpoon and with an easy toss threw it across the large chunk of ice.

Then he tried to ease it back so that the butt end of the harpoon would hang up on an edge. It was harder than it looked and took him ten or twelve tries before the harpoon shaft caught in a small hole. When it drew tight the point jammed and he took up the strain until he had the weight of the chunk moving. Slowly he pulled the ice through the dark water, slowly and gently heaving on the great weight.

He gradually brought the chunk across the lead until the end butted against the edge he stood on, then, using the harpoon as a prod he jammed and pushed until the ice lay the long way across the lead.

When it was in position he went back to the sled and pulled out the hook. "Up! Up and across the ice."

The leader knew what he wanted, but he held back, whining louder now. The ice didn't look that steady, didn't look safe. He didn't move to the side, but he wouldn't go, either.

Twice more Russel urged him from the sled but

the dog wouldn't go and Russel threw the sled over on its side and walked to the front. The leader shook and crouched down but didn't move away. Russel took his mittens off and hung them by their cords behind his back. Then he grabbed a handful of hair on the dog's neck and another at the root of his tail and heaved the dog out onto the chunk.

The leader fought for balance, found it on the teetering ice, then drove with all his might for the other side of the lead, clawing and scrabbling.

So powerful was his tearing struggle that he pulled the next two dogs after him, and those three then pulled the rest of the team and the sled in a great leap onto the floating ice bridge.

Russel grabbed the handle as it went by and barely got his feet on the runners. A kick left, another to the right and the sled flew across the gap of water at the far end, splashed once as Russel threw his feet up to stay out of the water—and he was across.

Across onto the land ice. Off the floating pack ice. Safe.

Safe with the dogs. Safe and heading for the village. Safe and moving to where he could now see the light of the fuel tank on the hill. Safe out of the steam of the water and back on the solid ice.

5

Shamans had great power in the old times before the church came. They could make stones talk, and the snow, and I knew one once that had two heads that talked to each other. They fought all the time, those two heads, and finally it was said that one of the heads told the body to kill the other. This it did and of course that made the whole body die. Shamans had great power but they weren't always smart.

—an old woman's memory.

RUSSEL HAD moved away from life in the village but he was not rebelling. He was working toward something in his mind, not away from something he didn't like. He had moved in with Oogruk, but his father knew it and approved.

There was school, of course. He was not going to school but he was learning and everybody knew that; it would have been hard to stop him trying to learn what he wanted and needed to know and so nobody tried. It would not have been polite to try it and many considered Russel old enough to know what he was doing.

Life in the village went on as it had before. Men took snowmachines out on the ice to find seals, when they could get through the leads. Other hunters took other snowmachines back into the hills and found caribou, sometimes killing six or seven to bring back for other people who could not hunt.

In the long darkness house life took on a meaning that couldn't exist in the summer. Families sometimes moved in with each other for a time, played games, fought the boredom that could come with the semi-arctic night. The village had a game room with television and it was usually crowded with both adults and children, watching the outside world.

All but Russel.

And Oogruk.

Russel hunted caribou twice more but didn't get any meat either time. He saw them at a distance, but couldn't get the sled close enough to make a stalk and a kill. On the second attempt he set the hook, left the dogs, and with the bow worked up some small creek beds but the deer saw him before he could get close enough for a shot. He took rabbits and ptarmigan home each time, using a small net Oogruk had fashioned and showed him how to use. With the net, laying it on the ground and using a long line, he lured the birds with a handful of berries. When they were on the net he flicked it closed with a jerk of his wrist and caught five and six birds at a time.

So he made meat. Light meat. That's what Oogruk called it. And it was good meat, as far as it went. The small birds tasted sweet and were tender and soft, which suited Oogruk's poor teeth.

But the dogs needed heavy meat, heavy red meat and fat or they could not work, could not run long and hard.

And heavy meat meant deer. Caribou.

Or seal.

So it came on a cold clear morning that Russel decided to go out for seal again. It was still dark when he awakened and sat up on the floor but before he could get his pants on Oogruk was sitting up and had lighted the lamp.

"It is time for me to go out for seals again. For food for the dogs. I will go out on the ice."

Oogruk nodded. "Yes. Yes. I know that. But this time I will go with you."

Russel stopped, his bearskin pants halfway up. He looked at the old man. "To hunt seals?"

"That. And other things. There are certain things that must be done at this time and it is for an old man to do them when the time is right."

Russel waited but Oogruk said nothing further. Instead he stood, slightly stiff, and feeling with his hands found clothes on the side wall. He dressed in pants and mukluks and another squirrelskin underparka. Then he took down an older outer-parka, of deerskin, one with holes and worn places, and shrugged it on over his head.

"I have the good parka," Russel said. "Let me give it to you."

Oogruk shook his head. "Not this time. You keep it. You will need it and I won't. Go now and harness the dogs."

Russel finished dressing and went out for the team. They knew him now, knew him well, and greeted him with tails and barks when they saw him take the harness off the pegs. He laid the gangline out onto the snow and harnessed the team quickly, wondering why the old man wanted to go.

When the dogs were harnessed he took the weapons—two harpoons and one killing lance with a plain sharpened point—and tied them into the sled. When he turned back to the house Oogruk had come out of the door and was looking across the ice.

His milk-white eyes stared across the ice. But he was seeing nothing. Or, Russel thought, maybe he was seeing everything.

"I smell the sea out there," Oogruk said. "It is not too far today. The ice lets the smell come across."

"The dogs are harnessed."

"I know."

"Would you drive them?"

"No. I will ride. Put me in the sled and you drive."

Russel took his hand and put him in the sled, settling him back against the crosspieces at the back. When Oogruk was settled Russel pulled the hook and called the dogs up.

They tore away from the buildings and out across the ice. When he was away on the ice and the fire was burned out of them a bit he dragged the brake down and slowed them and looked back at the village.

Small gray buildings and caches on the dirty snow of the beach, with people here and there. Someone he did not recognize waved at him and he waved back. Dirty smoke came from chimneys and slid off with the wind and he watched as they moved away, picked up speed on the clean ice-snow, until he rounded the point heading north and the buildings were gone.

He waited for some kind of sadness to come but it did not, did not, and he turned back to the sled and the dogs lined out in front and he moved them over to the right a little, using a soft "Gee," to let them know it was a gentle turn. The sea was a blue line on the horizon when they crossed the high points and could see ahead.

Oogruk said nothing, but when they got within a couple of miles of the sea and the spray smell was heavy in the cold air he held up his mittened hand to signal a halt.

"There will be seals. Watch for seals." His voice was excited, hushed but alive. "They will be on the edge of the ice. Watch for them."

Russel looked out on the edge of the ice but saw no seals. The light was half gone now and he knew that he would have to leave the sled to hunt.

"I will leave you with the dogs and go out on foot."

But now Oogruk shook his head. "No. No. It is time to talk one more time and I must leave you. But I wanted to come out here for it because I missed the smell of the sea. I wanted to smell the sea one more time."

Russel looked down in the sled at the old man. "You're leaving me?"

"Yes. But first I must tell you what to do . . ."

"Where are you going?"

"It is time to leave," Oogruk said simply. "It is my time. But there is a thing you must do now to become a man. You must not go home."

"Not go home? I do not understand."

"You must leave with the dogs. Run long and find yourself. When you leave me you must head north and take meat and see the country. When you do that you will become a man. Run as long as you can. That's what used to be. Once I ran for a year to find good birds' eggs. Run with the dogs and become what the dogs will help you become. Do you understand?"

Russel remembered now when Oogruk had said he would take a long journey. He spoke quietly. "I think so. But you, what are you to do?"

"You will leave me here on the ice, out here by the edge of the sea."

"With respect, Grandfather, I can't do that. There is a doctor. Things can be done if something is bothering you."

Oogruk shook his head. "An old man knows when death is coming and he should be left to his own on it. You will leave me here on the ice."

"But . . ."

"You will leave me here on the ice."

Russel said nothing. He didn't help Oogruk,

but the old man got out of the sled himself. When he was standing on the ice he motioned Russel away. "Go now."

Russel couldn't. He held back, held the sled. "I will stay with you."

"You will go." The milk-eyes looked through him to the sea, to the snow, to the line of blue that was the sky. "You will go now."

And there was such strength in his voice that Russel knew he must go. He took the handlebar in one hand and pulled the hook, and the dogs surged away and Russel let them run without looking back. He went mile after mile, and finally he could stand it no more and he called the team around and headed back, his eyes scanning the ice in sweeps as they ran.

When they were still half a mile from where Oogruk had gotten off, Russel could see his small figure sitting on the ice and he smiled.

He would talk the old man into riding back to the village, that's all there was to it. The old man would come back and tell him more about living the old way, would sit at night and tell the stories that made the winter nights short.

But when he drew close he saw that Oogruk was sitting still. Very still. His hands were folded in his lap and his legs were stretched out in front of him and the eyes were open and not blinking with life.

Russel stopped the team before the dogs were close to Oogruk and walked ahead on foot.

Oogruk did not turn his head but stared out to sea, out past the edge of ice where his spirit had flown, out and out. His face was already freezing and there was some blown snow in the corner of his eyes that didn't melt. Russel brushed the snow away with his mitten, a small gesture he made unknowingly, and a place in him wanted to smile and another place wanted to cry. "You left too soon, Grandfather. I was coming back for you."

He stood for a time looking down at the dead old man. Then he thought of something and he went back to the sled and took the small harpoon with the ivory toggle point from the weapons lashing. He put the harpoon across Oogruk's lap so that it balanced on his knees.

"You will want to hunt seals. Use it well and make much sweet meat."

Then he went to the sled. The dogs were nervous. They smelled the death and didn't like it. The leader whined and fidgeted and was glad when Russel called them around and headed north.

Before he let them run he turned back to Oogruk one more time. "I will remember you," he said, then let the dogs go.

He would run north for a time, then cut across the ice and head northeast into the land. He had weapons and dogs and a good sled. The rest would come from the land.

Everything would come from the land.

PART TWO

THE DREAMRUN

6

The Run

OUT.

Into the sweeps, into the great places where the land runs to the sky and into the sky until there is no land and there is no sky.

Out.

Into the distance where all lines end and all lines begin. Into the white line of the ice-blink where the mother of wind lives to send down the white death of the northern storms.

Out.

Into the mother of wind and the father of blue ice.

Russel went out where there is nothing, into the wide center of everything there is.

Into the north.

His village lay on the northern edge of the tree line. Here and there in small valleys nearby there were scrub spruce, ugly dwarfed things torn and ripped by the fierce wind. But as the run went north even these trees vanished to be replaced by small brush and gnarled grass. Snow was scarce, blown, and the landscape looked like something from another planet.

Still there is beauty, Russel thought.

It was hard to believe the beauty of that torn and forlorn place. The small mountains—large hills, really—were sculpted by the wind in shapes of rounded softness, and the light . . .

The light was a soft blue-purple during the day, a gentle color that goes into the eyes and becomes part of the mind and goes still deeper and deeper to enter the soul. Soul color is the daylight.

At night, Russel knew, often the wind would die and go back to its mother and the cold would come down from the father of ice and the northern lights would come to dance.

They went from red to green and back again, moving across the sky in great pulses of joy, rippling the heavens, pushing the stars back, and were so grand to see that many people believed that they were the souls of dead-born children dancing in heaven and playing with balls of grass and leather.

Even in the wind there was beauty to Russel. The wind came from the north in a steady push that made the dogs work evenly, and the wind made the snow move, change into shapes that blended into the light of day and the soft glow from the sky at night.

Out.

When he'd gone far enough north along the coast to miss the village, Russel headed back into shore and moved up onto the land in a small gully, headed mostly north but slightly east.

He moved into the dark. He ran the dogs out and down. Ran them steadily for a full day, eighteen hours, letting them find the way. He stood on the sled's runners and moved to get away from what he knew, ran to get away from death sitting on the ice in Oogruk's form.

When the first dog started to weave with exhaustion, still pulling, but slipping back and forth as it pulled, he sensed their tiredness in the black night and stopped the team. He had a piece of meat in the sled, deer meat from a leg and he cut it in six pieces. When he'd pulled them under an overhanging ledge out of the wind and tipped the sled on its side, he fed them. But they were too tired to eat and slept with the meat between their legs.

He didn't know that they could become that tired and the knowledge frightened him. He was north, in the open, and the dogs wouldn't eat and they were over a hundred and fifty miles to anything. Without the dogs he would die.

Without the dogs he was nothing.

He'd never felt so alone and for a time fear roared in him. The darkness became an enemy, the cold a killer, the night a ghost from the underworld that would take him down where demons would tear strips off him.

He tried a bite of the meat but he wasn't hungry. Not from tiredness. At least he didn't think so.

But he knew he wasn't thinking too well, and so he lay down between the two wheel-dogs and pulled them close on either side and took a kind of sleep.

Brain-rest more than sleep. He closed his eyes and something inside him rested. The darkness came harder and the northern lights danced and he rested. He was not sure how long it might have been, but it was still dark when one of the dogs got up and moved in a circle to find a better resting position.

The dog awakened the remainder of the team and they all ate their meat with quiet growls of satisfaction that came from their stomachs up through their throats. Small rumbles that could be felt more than heard.

When they'd eaten they lay down again, not even pausing to relieve themselves. And Russel let them stay down for all of that long night. He dozed now with his eyes open, still between the two wheel-dogs, until the light came briefly.

Then he stood and stretched, feeling the stiffness. The dogs didn't get up and he had to go up the line and lift them. They shook hard to loosen their muscles and drop the tightness of sleeping long.

"Up now! Up and out."

Out.

They started north again, into a land that Russel did not know. At first the dogs ran poorly, raggedly, hating it. But inside half a mile they had settled into their stride and were a working team once more.

But they had lost weight.

In the long run they had lost much weight and it was necessary for Russel to make meat. He didn't know how long they could go without meat but he didn't think it could be long.

He had to hunt.

If he did not get meat the dogs would go down—and he was nothing without the dogs. He had to get food for them.

The light ended the dark-fears but did not bring much warmth. Only the top edge of the sun slipped into view above the horizon, so there was no heat from it.

To get his body warm again after the long night of being still he held onto the sled and ran between the runners. He would run until his breath grew short, then jump on and catch his wind, then run again. It took a few miles of that to get him warm and as soon as he was, the great hole of hunger opened in his stomach and he nearly fell off the sled.

The hunger lasted until he remembered the small piece of meat he hadn't eaten the night before. He found it in the inside pouch of his parka and ate it. His body heat had thawed the meat and made it soft enough to chew. It was bad meat, tough meat, but it tasted so good that it made his jaws ache.

And with the meat came energy. It rippled through him, up from his stomach like something alive, something hot.

The meat brought strength into his legs and arms and made his eyes sharp. He scanned the hills ahead, the low round hills with grassy sides and small gullies between. That would be where he'd find game. The birds would be on the hillside where there was no snow to eat, but close to the snow so they could fly to the white for protection. The rabbits would be high so they could see when the wolves came. There would be mice in the grass if nothing else. All food.

He headed for the hills and reached into the sled for the bow. When he had it out he stopped the dogs and strung it, marveling again at its beauty, the laminated strips of horn and bone and wood shining in the light.

He took the quiver up and strapped it over his shoulder, letting the dogs run again as he worked. He would hunt with the team, rather than stalk, and hope to get close enough to something for a shot.

And now there was luck.

In many of the hills there were smaller animals. Rabbits and ptarmigan, some small fox—which had a sweet-rich meat and were easy to kill—and the ever-present mice, or lemmings. But sometimes herds of caribou numbering several hundred head moved across the land, taking the grass where they could find it.

Such a herd lay in the gully in front of Russel and the dogs. The only way out for the caribou was to run over the team, or around it. The gully had steep sides with large drifts and the deer had foolishly cornered themselves. A pack of wolves could get into them and take many of them down before they could escape. Or a man could take them. But the deer would think only of running, not where they could run, just that they could run, in blind lines.

The dogs smelled them before Russel saw them. They had seen him take the bow out and they knew he was ready to kill and when they smelled the deer they turned off and headed for the gully where the herd grazed.

There were about a hundred and fifty deer within the confines of the drifts and when the animals at the outside edge saw the dogs coming they wheeled and tried to beat Russel to the opening.

But the dogs were strong and thin and fast and they caught the deer easily. When they ran toward him into the narrowest part, Russel jumped off the sled and got ready. The dogs kept going, crazy now for the smell of deer and the wild running of the herd as it came at them.

The caribou parted around the sled and the dogs wheeled to catch them, missing most, hitting a few with the ancient hamstring tear that ripped and crippled the deer's back leg, and four of these, staggering with bloodied back legs, came by Russel.

Falling, running, they tried to keep up to the other deer but they were doomed now, as doomed as if they had been hit by wolves, and the dogs were working to catch them and pull them down.

Russel took them with arrows, putting a shaft in each one, just in back of the shoulders. He watched the arrows streak into the light and enter the deer cleanly. First one, then the other, then the next two, and they ran-fell for another fifty yards before they went down, blood spraying from their mouths onto the grass and snow.

"My arrows are true," he said aloud. And then, in a poem-song:

They brought the deer down,
They helped the dogs to bring us meat.
My arrows are true.

The dogs were on the deer now, stopping with the first one. Russel ran over to it to hasten the death by cutting its throat but he didn't have to. The eyes were already glazing with the end and he put grass in the deer's mouth, doing the same for the second, third and fourth ones, which were already dead.

Then he pulled the dogs off and tied them away from the four carcasses. There would be food for them, but all in good time.

He would set up camp and he would skin the deer out and cut the meat for easy carrying. Then he would eat and eat, he thought, and after he ate he would sleep, and then eat more. He'd never been so hungry and he could see that the dogs were the same. They were on the edge of eating each other, fresh with the blood smell and tough with the running.

He set up camp and skinned the deer. By now it was getting dark and he cut front shoulder meat for the dogs—a great piece for each—and took a fatty tenderloin from one deer for himself. He used some grass and dried sticks and a match from his sled bag to start a fire and he warmed the meat over the flames until it was pleasant—not hot, just heated. Then he took a chunk in his mouth and bit down and cut it off by his lips with the *ulu*, wolfed it down, then another, and another, until his stomach hurt with the meat.

He mourned not having a pot, but ate snow for water and this, with the blood in the warm meat, was enough moisture to help in digestion.

With his stomach full he put one deerskin on the ground, hair side down, and the other three on top with the raw sides touching. In between the layers he had a fur sleeping bag as warm as the warmest down and he crawled in as the short-lived sun bobbed back down for the long night.

Full-bellied dogs curled into balls in their harness, sleeping next to him. Russel pulled his head under the skins, took his parka and pants off and put them outside, inside out. The moisture from his perspiration would freeze during the sleep and he would scrape the ice off in the morning. With only his squirrel parka on he pulled back into the skins, took his mukluks off and left them inside the sleeping bag to warm up and dry out.

It was a home.

The sled, the dogs, the food, and more food to eat when he awakened.

It was a home.

It was as much of a home as his people had had for thousands of years and he was content. He closed his eyes and heard the wind gently sighing outside past the hides that kept him warm and snug.

It was a home and he let his mind circle and go down, the same way a dog will circle before taking the right bed.

What a thing, he thought—what a thing it is to

have meat and be warm and have a full belly. What a thing of joy.

And he slept.

And while he slept he had a dream.

7

The Dream

THERE WERE swirls of fog like steam off the water in the ice leads; thick fog, heavy fog, that would start to clear and close again, then clear a little more until finally he could see, could see, could see . . .

A skin shelter, a tent, on the side of the ocean. Inside there was an oil lamp, much like the one Oogruk had, burning a smoky yellow that lighted the faces of the people in the tent.

Two children were there. Small and round and wonderfully fat. They were eating of some fat red meat that Russel could not understand, didn't know, but knew as being important. He wanted to know what kind of meat they were eating because it was so red and had coarse texture and rich yellow fat. All over the children's faces and in their hair the grease shone and they were happy with it.

On the other side of the lamp sat a woman, young, round and shining beautiful. She was fat and had eaten of the meat but was done now and worked at tending the lamp. There was much honor in tending the lamp and she took pride in it. The flame was even, if smoky, and in the stone lamp-bowl there was the same yellow fat that was so important for him to name.

One other person was in the skin tent and he couldn't see who it was; it was a man, but he kept back in the shadows and would not come forward.

They were saying nothing, but the children laughed until the laughter was like a kind of music in the background and the woman looked at the man and smiled often. It was the kind of smile all men look for in women, the kind that reaches inside, and Russel felt warm to see it.

But he could not see the man and he did not know the meat, and they were important to him.

The fog came again, and this time when it cleared

the man was standing near the doorway in a parka. The parka was deerskin and he held a long spear with some form of black stone point, chipped black stone that was deep and shining dark. He was going out hunting and Russel knew, sensed, that he was going to hunt whatever had made the coarse meat and yellow fat and Russel wanted to go with him.

The woman kept smiling and the children kept laughing but the woman was worried and said something in a language that Russel could not understand. It was words, and they were similar to what he knew, but enough different so they didn't quite make sense to him.

As the man turned to leave the hut the woman said something to him and he stopped and looked at her.

Her eyes glowed at him and there was much fear in them, so much that Russel was afraid, and he knew that there was some fear in the man, too, but hidden.

Russel would not have known that except that he felt close to the man. More than close somehow.

The man left the tent and went out to harness dogs and they were already in harness, waiting for him, and they were dogs but they were more than dogs, too.

Great gray sides twitching, they stood like

shadows, with wide heads and heavy triangular jaws. Russel had never seen anything like the dogs in the dream. They were higher than the man's waist and had silent yellow eyes that watched everything the man did while he put his gear in the sled and got ready to leave, and the way they watched it was clear that they could either run or turn and eat him. It was up to the man.

He stood to the sled and Russel saw then that it was not of wood but all of bone and ivory, with large rib bones for the runners, and lashed with yellow rawhide. It shone yellow-white and rich in the night light, the color deep and alive, and when the man stepped on the runners the dogs lunged silently but with great speed and power and the fog closed again, swirled in thick and deep.

When it lifted the man was alone out on the sweeps. The stretch of land looked familiar, but there was something different in the dream and after a time Russel could see that it was the grass. Where the snow had been blown away the grass was taller and thinner, with pointed ends. It was bent over in wind, but not twisted like the tundra grass.

There was deeper darkness now and Russel watched as the man worked the dogs without making a sound. They were clearly hunting something, that much was sure, but what they were hunting Russel couldn't tell. He was amazed to see the man handle the dogs with no audible commands.

They ran to his mind, clean and simple. They went out into the sweeps and Russel watched as if from somewhere above, watched as they hunted in and out of the fog until finally, in a clearing, they found the fresh tracks of whatever they were hunting.

The gray dogs put their hair up and ran to the tracks nervously. They wanted to catch the smell but they didn't want to as well. They were still running to the man's mind and he made them follow the tracks but there was fear now.

Great fear.

The tracks were blurred, but huge, and Russel couldn't see what might have made them. He had never seen tracks like them, nor felt the fear that was in the man.

Then there was a shape before him and Russel fought to see it.

Some great thing it was, some great shape in the fog and then the mist was whirled away in a rush of wind and Russel saw two things clearly.

The animal was a woolly mammoth. Immense, it stood with shaggy hair, its giant domed head swaying, it's great tusks curved toward the dogs. The small trunk whipped back and forth in anger and the red eyes tore through the fog like a demon's from the Below World.

The man was to kill the beast if he could, or the beast was to kill the man and the dogs, drive them into the snow and kill them.

That much Russel saw clearly and one more thing.

As the man grabbed the long killing-lance and jumped from the ivory and bone sled, the wind blew off his parka hood and Russel saw the man's face and knew it.

The man was him: Russel, with more hair, longer hair, and a small beard and mustache, but he was Russel and Russel knew fear, deep fear, because with the knowledge that he was the man in the dream he knew that he would have to fight the mammoth. He would have to fight it and kill it.

And the mammoth charged.

The head and tusks thrashed in angry arcs and the huge feet trampled the earth, tearing up clods of dirty snow, as the mighty animal bore down on the man and the dogs and sled.

There was no time for escape, no time for dodging. The man had to face the beast.

The dogs ran to the side, but turned back in as the mammoth rushed by them, heading for the man. But their action caused the animal to swing its head slightly to the side and that revealed the center of the chest.

Crouching and turned away, the man set the shaft of the long lance in the earth and snow in back of him, settled it in as hard as he could and rose to face the oncoming mammoth. With its head sideways to lash at the dogs it roared down on the man as with small arm movements he guided the point of the lance into the center of the chest and let the weight of the animal carry it down the shaft to death.

The lance entered like light, like a beam of light shot into the mammoth and when there should have been death the animal instead wheeled and heaved in a great circle, caught the dogs and threw two of them in the air.

All in silence.

And then the beast stopped. It stood with its head hanging, swaying back and forth, and accepted the death from the broken lance shaft in its chest and went down on its front knees and then its back and in an almost gentle roll slipped to its side and died.

And the man as he saw the animal falter began to sing. Again Russel did not know the words but they sounded familiar to him.

The man sang in exultation.

Sang the death of the great beast, and the mountain of meat lying before him.

Sang the luck of his hunt.

Sang of the fat that would be his for his family and the dogs that now tore at the belly of the mammoth.

Sang the wind that brought his dogs to the tracks and sang the gratitude for the great animal who died and left him much meat.

And Russel felt all those songs inside his soul, felt them even as the man in the dream sang and the fog came again to hide him and the dogs and the mammoth.

Russel knew it all because he knew them all. He was the man and he was the dream.

He was the fog.

8

The Run

THE LIGHT filtered into the skins and he awakened. Some of the dream was still with him and he had a great hunger for the coarse red meat and yellow fat but when he looked out from the skins he saw only the four deer carcasses. The team was chewing on one.

He stuck an arm out and scraped his parka and turned it right side out and put it on. The cold of the skin penetrated his squirrelskin undergarment and brought him totally, instantly wide awake.

Next he put his mukluks on—they were warm from being in the skins all night—and then he threw back the skins and stood.

The dogs had fought while he dreamed and the gangline was bitten in two or three places. He swore and pulled them back from the deer and to the sled and tied them in place, liberally slamming their noses with his mittened hand.

In a few moments they had settled and he went back to the deer. Their bodies had frozen but were small enough to fit roughly on the sled. Legs stuck out but he wanted to keep going and the legs didn't bother him. There were no trees to catch at them.

The skins were more of a problem. Though he had slept in them the raw sides had frozen solid. The hollow hairs had kept his body heat from penetrating the skins and they would not fold. He finally jumped on them in the middle to fold them over and jam-fit them next to the deer carcasses on the sled.

He pulled his hood on, tightened it against the coming wind and called the dogs up. In minutes he was out of sight of the camp area, heading still north. Out. Into the sweeps.

Today was different—as Russel knew all days are different in the north. It was so cold his spit bounced—white men would call it forty below zero—and the air caught in his throat as he warmed it.

The color was new as well. Yesterday had been blue. Today was almost a deep purple with stringers of clouds shooting across the dimly lighted sky, fingers aimed away from an advancing storm.

Russel knew weather as all Eskimos know weather. The storm would come in two days, maybe a little less, but it would not be too bad. Some wind and cold, nothing more. He could ride it out easily.

But there was a strange unease driving him and at first he thought it was the dream. It had been so real-seeming. He could still smell the inside of the dreamigloo-tent, the stink of the mammoth voiding itself in death, the heat of its blood down the shaft of the lance.

He had killed the beast and yet something was pushing him, making him drive the team. They were new now, a new team. It wasn't that the dogs had changed; and yet they were not the same dogs that he'd first seen at Oogruk's. They changed with him, or at least so it seemed, changed with his mind.

It was as if they had gone out of themselves and become more than dogs, more than animal.

They ran to his mind, out and out before him.

With bellies full of deer meat, rich guts and stomach linings, the dogs were strong and driving, had great power, and wanted to run.

He let them run and they seemed to want to head the same way he wanted to go and that, too, became part of his thinking.

Did they know him?

Did they know his mind and run to it the way the wolf-dogs had run to the man's mind in the dream?

And if that were so, which he believed since he seemed to see his thoughts going out ahead, with the lead dog—if that were so, did the dogs know where they were going? Did they know when he didn't know?

And more, did they know *why* they were heading north?

"Why do we run?" he asked aloud and the sudden words broke the silence and startled the dogs. They kept running but broke stride for a few steps before regaining rhythm.

They did not answer.

Twice he looked back but saw nothing and after that he didn't look to the rear again. Out ahead was everything, out ahead was where they were going and he let the dogs decide because that was the same as his deciding.

The snow was right for speed, didn't have the cold-weather scrubbing sound it sometimes did which pulled at the runners, and they ran the daylight out without losing pace.

For five, maybe six, hours he let them run and as the gray dusk was gathering before dark he saw off to the right a small valley between two hills where there was some brush which might make a fire.

He said nothing to the team but they knew and they curved off to the right to head for the valley. There was still light as they came to it. He stopped them near some dried brush, dead in the wind and snow, but the dogs kept pulling forward and he let them go again. Further up there was an overhanging ledge of stone, a shelf, with a place under it to make a shelter. The dogs stopped when they reached the overhang.

He used one skin to shield the opening and scraped enough snow to secure it to the ledge. Then he cut a set of front shoulders up and threw the pieces to the dogs and pulled a second carcass into the lean-to. With the other skins he fashioned a bed and went out and collected bits of brushwood until he had enough to last the night and a little extra.

It was a perfect camp.

He brought the wood into the shelter and pulled the flap down. Using a bit of moss he started a small fire and in moments it was warm inside the shelter. He took his parka off and turned it inside out and put it back outside to freeze.

He heard the dogs growl, but they settled the problem immediately and he turned to warming meat to eat. Using the point of his knife he pried a tenderloin off the middle back of the carcass and held it over the small flame. The smoke was bad at first but he opened a hole at the top of the lean-to and the smoke was quickly sucked out by the wind.

The meat thawed in the flame and was soon warm enough to eat and he put the piece in his mouth and cut it off by his lips.

He was thirsty and he ate more snow with the meat, alternately chewing meat and eating snow until his stomach started to bulge.

He could eat no more yet he was hungry still. He thought of the red coarse meat of the dream, of the rich yellow fat and he closed his eyes.

But there was not sleep at first. Instead he thought of the day's run, then thought of Oogruk asking if they ran for him. It was a pleasant thought and Russel lay back on the hide to rest—but there was a lump beneath his shoulder. He was about to ignore it, to leave it there, but it was such a perfect camp that he wanted the bed to be perfect as well and he folded the skin back to see what the lump was. There was a stone there, a curved piece of stone, and when he pulled at it, it wiggled a bit.

He took his knife and dug around the edge, pulled at it, loosened it more, then dug again. Finally it came free and when it was in his hand he saw that it was more than a stone. It was a stone that had been worked by hand.

It was round, a disc about ten inches in diameter, and smoothly polished. On one side it was completely flat, but on the other it had been hollowed out to form a six inch dish, one edge of which had a small groove in it.

It was an old stone lamp. Older, much older than Oogruk's. Older than the lamps in the museums he had seen that were dug by the college people from the old village up north. Somebody had camped here many years before and either left the lamp or had come upon a disaster which ended what they had been. Only the lamp was left, and Russel held it and wondered at the shiny smoothness of it, the polished beauty.

"See what a man has been given," he said. "By the dogs who brought me. By the night. See what a man has been given." He had dropped into the third person usage without thinking, though it was no longer used very much. He had heard the old people talk that way sometimes out of politeness.

He used the back of his knife to scrape the last of the dirt off the lamp and set it aside. He needed some fat to light it and he went outside once more to the caribou carcass to get stomach fat.

"The best fat to eat is the best fat to burn," Oogruk had said. "Save the best for the flame and you will never be cold. It is a good lesson for a man. Save the best for the flame."

Russel took the stomach fat, pried it off with his knife—it was still frozen—and cut it in chips for the lamp bowl. When he had a small mound of chips he found some moss near the ledge and fashioned a wick. Then he took a burning stick from the fire and tried to light the lamp.

It was necessary to melt the fat into a puddle in the lamp so that as a liquid it could be wicked-up into the moss for burning.

After a good hour of moving the chips around and becoming frustrated he was ready to give up. But he tried once more and was rewarded when the chips of white fat suddenly became fluid and soaked into the moss. Smiling, he lit the wick and set the lamp on a small dirt ledge to the side of the shelter.

The fire died to embers but the lamp glow remained and the sweet yellow of the burning fat kept the night away, kept him warm. The fat was poor, he knew, compared to walrus fat or seal oil. And it burned with some smoke, though much less than the wood fire. But he did not need wood now, as long as he had deer for the fat. And there were many deer.

He could get everything from the deer.

He was sleepy now, again full and round with heat and food. But he didn't know how long the fat would last, or the wick, so he went outside and spent some time getting more fat from the same carcass. When he had a fair small pile of it, cut in chips, he found some more moss and twisted it into wick for later.

He added some chips to the liquid in the bowl and they melted and he saw that it was easy now to keep the level of the liquid up to the edge. Small crackles of rendered fat floated there and with quick fingers he dipped them out and ate them as they cooled.

He took a thin piece of wood and made a scrape-tool to keep the wick even. Then he lay back on the skins as the storm came up and he looked to all he had done and knew Oogruk would have liked it. Where there had been nothing he now had shelter and food and heat and comfort. Where there had been nothing he had become something.

The dogs were fed and down for rest, fed on meat and fat, fed on running and cold, fed and down.

He could sleep now. He would awaken in the night at intervals to add chips of fat to the lamp or to trim the wick, or perhaps to warm and eat a piece of meat or open a leg bone to get at the marrow, which tasted like the butter at the village store, or swallow a bit of snow when thirst took him.

He could sleep now.

And dream.

9

The Dream

HERE NOW was a village.

The man drove his dogs out of the fog, the great gray dogs out of the gray fog, as if the dogs were not animals but fog that had come alive. Out they came onto a clearing on top of a bluff overlooking a coastal village, and the man set his bone snow-hook.

There were many skin tents along the beach-ice, each tent by a meat rack filled with black blood-meat from walrus and seal. Steam from the heat was coming from the breathing holes on the tents, and though it was dim he saw children playing with puppies near the tents. It was a good camp. All the puppies were fat, and the dogs had good hair and were fat.

In the dream Russel could see over the man, could see how his mind was working and he knew that the man was holding back above the village out of sadness.

The camp was nothing he knew but the playing children and the sounds of women calling to each other through the tent walls made him think of the family he had left when he'd gone to hunt.

He was in a new land but the people were known to him as all people are known to all other people and their words made him think of his own family and he missed them, and for a moment Russel thought he might turn the team and head for home with the red meat and yellow fat.

But the dogs were excited and they jerked the snowhook free and tore down the hill with the ivory and bone sled flying behind like a feather in the wind. They wanted to meet the new dogs and perhaps fight and breed and eat and rest and they pulled the man down into the settlement on the beach.

Everybody came running out of the tents, half-dressed, yelling at the dogs to stop them from fighting, for the man's dogs were among the loose village dogs, snapping and barking, the sled behind them. After much whipping and yelling the dogs were separated.

There was great joy in the village. Visitors came very seldom and strangers almost never. The man had come from far away—they knew that from his dogs which were of a strange bloodline—and he was surely a mighty hunter because his sled was full of meat and his dogs were sleek and well fed even though they had come a long distance.

The new man would have stories to tell, wonderful stories of taking the large beast and traveling through strange lands. They would show the stranger their hospitality by feeding him much fat meat and feeding his dogs until they threw the meat up to eat it again.

Then they would take him into the main tent and they would talk and talk and perhaps later they would sing and dance to the drum and make up songs. Perhaps the stranger would sing his song.

It would be a night to last many days, with eating and eating until nothing more could be put down. A great time.

A new folding.

When it cleared Russel was inside a great tent. There were many people in the tent, sitting around the outside in a circle with the women back on a ledge.

There were a dozen or so lamps burning so that their light made the tent bright, hot-yellow with hazy smoke, and in the middle of the tent with his back to Russel stood the man who had come on the sled with the great gray dogs.

He wore only a breechclout held by a thin leather thong and Russel could see the knotted muscles in his back and down his legs, cords of power. His skin shone with sweat and grease from rubbing his hands on his body to clean them while he ate and his hair hung down in straight lines, heavy with grease.

He is not a man standing on the ground, Russel thought—he is growing up *from* the ground. His legs are the earth and they take strength from it, up through his ankles and into his muscles so that he grows with what he takes from it. More than strength, more than substance—all that the man would be is growing up from the earth through his legs and into his body.

Strong.

Strong beyond what he was merely, the man

had grown strong from the dogs and the wind and the winter and strong from the people around in a circle who watched now, watched and waited.

The man kept his back to Russel but Russel knew why and didn't care. He knew that he was the man, knew it and let that knowledge carry him into the man.

And now the man started to move.

His legs shuffled and his head swung from side to side and his hair moved with his body and he was not a man anymore.

He was the mammoth. It was more than a dance, more than a story, he *became* the mammoth, down to the smell, the foul smell that came from the beast.

The man moved and the mammoth moved and the people swept back to avoid being trampled, moved back in fear and some children who had no manners cried out in fear that the beast would see them.

But there was sadness here. For the mammoth knew that he must die, knew that he must furnish meat for the man. And so he knew he must run down the lance and give his death for food. There was sadness in his dance. In his movement.

The man sang and Russel could not understand the words but he knew their meaning: it was the song of the beast, the mammoth's song as he moved to his death at the hands of the puny man with the dogs. It was a noble song, a song to proclaim that he did not really have to die but chose to because it was his time and he would die with rightness, die correctly.

Sadness.

A rich sadness that took the man and made everybody watching feel deeply for the plight of the mammoth, cursed to death to make meat.

But now there was something new.

Now the mammoth grew, took strength and rage. Around the circle the man moved-danced, his voice growing through the song of the mammoth as it first saw the dogs and man.

And in the way of such things it had to attack. There was no sense to it because the mammoth could have kept going away. But the beast turned. In rage it attacked the dogs and turned its head to hit them and ran upon the lance.

Sometimes a man would be wrong and the lance would miss or hit the shoulder and slide off to the side and the man would die, would be trampled to death. Then it was not the time for the mammoth to die but time for the man to die and Russel knew this, knew all of this because of the movements of the man in the dream.

Now he changed again and now he was himself, the man, dancing and moving to kill the mammoth.

And now the beast charged.

And now he ran on the lance.

And now he died.

And it was all in the man and all in the people who watched and all in the small space in the council tent, all of it.

When the song was done the children screamed for joy and hunger at the meat he had brought and the men nodded and grunted approval at his mighty hunting and the women moved for him to attract his eye, because he was a hunter of such stature.

The man fell to the floor exhausted and they left him there, at the side, while somebody else rose to dance his song of a kayak and a walrus and near-death in the water.

And when he was done another got up, and then another, and so the songs soared on and on through day and night as the dream folded back into the fog.

10

The Run

When the storm hit his shelter it awakened him and he listened for a time. But he was secure and had fat for the lamp and he went back to sleep—the best way to ride storms out in the arctic.

When he awakened the next time—perhaps twenty hours later—he was ravenous and thirsty, and outside it was still. He looked from the shelter and saw that the dogs were still sleeping, resting, and would remain so until he called them up. He was learning. If they worked hard they might sleep for three days, getting up just to relieve themselves and change position—not even that if the wind was bad and they had good snow caves made for shelter.

Russel took snow in and ate from it, mourning once more his lack of a pot for cooking and boiling and making water from the snow. He fashioned a ladle from a leg bone but got only sips for his work.

He added fat chips to the lamp, which was halfway empty, and they melted and he found that by pushing the wick further into the fluid fat the flame rose.

He used the expanded flame to heat a piece of loin from the deer and when it was warm ate it in large mouthfuls.

It didn't fill him and he ate some warm fat, then more meat and yet more fat until his stomach bulged and he was again full.

But this time sleep didn't come. He had slept the better part of two days now and no part of his body was tired enough to sleep more.

He looked out of the tent again and saw that daylight was coming.

He shrugged away the camp as he would shrug

away light snow. It was time to leave, time to head north again to see the father of ice. He brought his parka in, brushed off the frozen sweat and put it on. Then he pinched the flame out with his fingers and slid his mukluks on and stepped into the darkness. It took him just a few moments to take down the skins, softened now from the heat of the lamp, and fold them in the sled bottom, then the lamp in the sled bag, and finally the rest of the meat on top of the skins and, lastly, his weapons: the lance and harpoon shafts on top of the skins, then his bow and the quiver of arrows. None of the deer had broken arrows when they fell and he had cleaned the points of the bubbled blood that comes from a kill and put them back in the quiver.

Still the dogs weren't moving.

When everything was lashed down to the sled, Russel went up the line and jerked the team out of the snow.

Two of them growled and he slapped them with a mitten across their noses to get their attention.

When they were all up and standing he got on the sled and called them up.

They started slowly, two of them holding back until he yelled at them again. Then they went to work and headed away from the camp.

Light came gently, but the sky was clear and cold and clean and he let the dogs seek their own pace. Once they had shaken out their legs they began an easy lope that covered miles at a fierce clip.

They ran into light, then all through the day, easily pulling the sled on the fast snow, grabbing a mouthful when they got thirsty, and Russel watched the new country come.

There were few hills now. The land was very flat, and there were no trees of any kind. If he kept going this way for a long time—he was not sure how long it would take with dogs but it took all day with an airplane—he would come to mountains. He thought.

But before the mountains he believed the sea came back in again. In the school he had seen a map that showed the sea coming back into the land but he was not sure if that was straight north or north and west and he was not sure how long it would take to get to the sea by dog sled. He did not know how far dogs traveled in a day.

Yet it didn't matter.

Oogruk had said, "It isn't the destination that counts. It is the journey. That is what life is. A journey. Make it the right way and you will fill it correctly with days. Pay attention to the journey."

So Russel ran the team and now the land was so flat that it seemed to rise around him like a great lamp bowl sloping up to the sky.

Looking ahead, he could feel a small grit coming to his eyes, sensed the first stages of snow blindness—caused when the light comes from all directions, from the white snow and the flat blue sky. When it is very bad it's as if someone has poured sand in the eyes and it's impossible to open them to see. More often snow blindness just irritates.

Russel rubbed his eyes. He knew if he had wood he could make a pair of snow goggles, with small slits to cut out the light from the sides. But he didn't have wood, so he rubbed his eyes now and then and pulled his hood tighter.

When the short day was gone the dogs didn't seem to want to stop. He let them run. There was no place to camp anyway and his mind looked now to the run.

He had come north a long way but was not sure how long. In the dark they kept up the pace, increased it, and they could cover many more miles before he had to rest them again, running on fresh meat as they were.

He sensed in the night that he was passing a large herd of deer and the dogs started for them but he had meat and called them back to the north. They obeyed instantly and he felt good.

They were his now. They were his dogs and they would run to him. He made the meat for them and they would run to him—just as the dogs in the dream ran to the man. Just as they ran, his dogs would run.

Out into the night he ran, and through the other side of darkness.

It was coming into first light when he saw the snowmachine tracks.

They started as if by magic. Suddenly the snow bore the small ridges that come from a snowmachine.

They headed off to the north.

The dogs dropped into the line of the tracks easily, as they dropped into any trail, which surprised Russel. Given a chance they seemed to follow the path of least resistance as if they expected something.

Russel let them run and thought for a time. He knew quite an area, had once flown to a northern settlement, a village three hundred miles up the coast from his own.

But he could not think of a settlement that fit

with the tracks. There was nothing straight north. If the tracks were a hunting party from the village, it was way out of the normal hunting territory—and besides, Russel thought, anybody hunting now would be working the sea ice for seals.

He did not want to see anybody, especially somebody on a snowmachine. The idea of a snowmachine was out of place, opposite, wrong.

But.

It was possible that whoever it was might have an extra pot or can he could use. He sorely missed having a way to boil meat or make water from snow and his lips were starting to crack and bleed from the snow's sharpness. If he did not find a way to melt snow his lips would soon go to sores.

Oogruk had talked of using stone bowls to melt snow but Russel couldn't find the right kind of soft stone and so he hoped to find a pot or a can.

And there was the other thing. He was starting to notice the dogs, notice that they seemed to be an extension of his thoughts. Now they ran to the trail and perhaps that was because he wanted them to run to the trail.

Perhaps he wanted to see whoever it was, see where the tracks led. So he let them run the snowmachine trail and they lasted through that day and into the night and still he ran. The tracks led steadily to the north, the line moving out to the rim of the white saucer into dark and then out of sight into the blackness.

Always north.

He let the dogs run, stopping in the cold dawn to feed them some meat, taking a cold mouthful for himself, then eating some snow, wincing in pain from his cracked lips, and moving them on.

He saw no game that day, no other sign but the snowmachine tracks with the slight dusting of snow on the edges, filling in as the wind blew, and he debated stopping.

But the dogs wanted to run and he let them.

They ran the second night, and he did not sleep but his mind circled and slipped down as he rode the runners, tired but not tired. He quit thinking, quit being anything but part of the sled, part of the dogs. At one time he began to hallucinate and thought somebody was riding the sled in front of him, sitting in the basket. A blurred idea of someone.

But then the hallucination was gone and another one came; he saw lights on all the dogs' feet, small lights, and then they disappeared and he felt somehow that the opening of his parka hood was a mirror and everything he saw in front of him was somehow in back of him, and then, driving on into the night, the mirror vanished and he had the dream.

The dream again.

But darker.

II

The Dream

THE MAN WAS no longer in the settlement on the edge of the sea, fat with walrus and seal oil, among fat puppies and round dogs and round faces.

Now there was not a fog, but a slashing gray storm that took everything.

He was trying to drive his dogs in the storm and there was an air of madness to it. The wind tore at them, lifted their hair and drove the snow underneath it to freeze on their skin until the dogs were coated in ice. Icedogs. They shone through the snow as they tried to drive forward.

But the wind tore at them. The dogs were blown sideways so hard that they leaned to stand and when they hit patches of ice or frozen snow they went down, staggering.

Yet the man drove them.

He stood on the runners, screamed blindly at them, let the long whip go out to tear at their flanks. His will flew along the line to the dogs, pushing them fiercely into the roaring storm.

Russel could see no sense to it. The sled was full of the red meat, the man could stop and make a shelter and eat and feed the dogs and wait for the storm.

But there was terrible worry in the man, fear and worry that Russel could feel, up from the dream into his mind, into his soul, and when he let his mind go into the dream, into the man, he knew the reason.

He had stayed long at the village with the fat of seal and walrus. Perhaps too long. And now the journey home was taking too long, too long for the family that waited back in the skin tent for the red meat and fat.

The storm was stopping him. He could fight

and fight, whip the dogs until they ran red with blood, but the storm was stopping him.

It was too fierce. Now it blew the dogs sideways, and now it blew them backward and they felt the frustration of the man and it became anger and they fought among themselves, tearing and slashing.

The man used his whip handle like a club and beat them apart and settled them and admitted defeat, fell in the wind, fell next to the sled and huddled in his parka as the gray blasts of snow took him down and down . . .

The wind took the dream with snow as the fog had once taken it, closed on it. But now the dream wasn't finished . . .

From Russel's mind came the tent with the woman and the two children. But now they were not the same . . . Now the lamp flickers with the last of the oil and the faces are thin. Worse than thin, the children's faces have the deep lines and dark shades that come from starvation.

Both children lie quietly on the sleeping bench, end to end, their heads together. They are very weak, weak perhaps beyond coming back.

The mother sits by the lamp, fingering the strangulation cord. There are no skins left. They have eaten them all. They have eaten all the skin clothing and the soles from their mukluks and the leather lines cut to use for tying dogs.

They have cut the mittens into small squares to chew on the skin, spitting the hair out, and now those are gone.

Everything is gone.

And outside, the storm still tears and rips the earth, drives the snow sideways, guts the land.

She would eat the skin of the tent but that is the same as dying. With the tent gone the wind and cold would have them. They have no clothing left, will have no oil left when the lamp goes out.

Nothing.

The mother is weaker than the children but she takes a finger now and wipes it in the small bit of rancid oil in the lamp and wipes the finger across the lips of each child, leaving a thin film of grease on each lip.

One child licks the grease off.

The other does not.

And outside, the wind slashes and looks for their lives.

The hungry wind.

12

The Run

HE CAME upon the snowmachine in the flat white light of the arctic dawn. It was sitting on its skis, just squatting in the middle of the great sweeps.

Nobody was near it. Russel stopped when the dogs were next to it and set his hook. On the back of the seat was a box and he opened it, hoping to find a coffee can or pot but there was nothing but an empty plastic gas jug.

He felt the engine with a bare hand. It was cold, still cold, dead cold.

It was a fairly new machine and while it was true that snowmachines broke down, the newer ones tended to last a bit longer. He opened the gas tank and found it bone dry.

A smile cut his lips and made them bleed.

"They are not of the land," he said to the dogs. "They need fuel that is not part of the land. They cannot run on fat and meat."

A small set of footprints led off ahead of the machine but there were also snowmachine tracks. It was as if another snowmachine had gone ahead, but left the person to walk. It made no sense.

Or. Perhaps the snowmachine had come out this way and the rider was headed back when the machine ran out of gas.

That made more sense to Russel, considering the tracks.

But there was nothing, no village, where the footprints were leading. Nothing that Russel knew about at any rate, and if whoever left the tracks was heading for help on foot he had almost no chance of getting anywhere. There were no settlements within walking distance of the snowmachine.

And the tracks were small enough to belong to a child. Or a girl.

He pulled the hook and the team started off silently. They had run steadily now for two days and needed rest. They could sleep running, a doze-sleep, but they needed real rest after the hard work of a long run.

But with the full light Russel could see the high wisps of clouds that meant a storm was coming.

He wanted to try to catch whoever was ahead before the storm hit. On foot he could not be carrying much of a shelter, nor could he be carrying much food. And if it was a child he would probably not survive a bad storm.

Russel let the dogs adopt a slower trot, but he kept them going steadily, watching the tracks ahead.

At first they didn't seem very fresh. The rising wind had blown them in so that some of them were filled completely. But as the hours passed they seemed to be getting cleaner, newer. Now and then the lead dog dropped his nose to smell them, looking for scent, and Russel could see his ears jerk forward whenever he got a bit.

And when the darkness came again the leader started to run with his nose down all the time, following the smell of the trail that must be fresh, Russel knew, to hold for the dogs.

But now there was wind and more wind. Not

as bad as the dreamwind, but getting worse all the time so that the dogs had to lean slightly left into it to keep their balance. And snow.

There was a driving sharp snow with the wind. Not heavy snow, but small and mean and it worked with the force of the wind to get inside clothing, in the eyes, even blow up into the nostrils.

And finally, when he could no longer see the trail, no longer see the front end of the team, could barely make out the two wheel-dogs directly in front of the sled, finally he came to that time when he should stop and hole up in the storm.

And he did not.

He drove them on. They wanted to stop, twice the leader did stop, but Russel used words as a whip and drove them.

The leader was all important now. The trail was gone, wiped away by the wind and snow in the dark, but the dog sensed with his nose and his feet where the tracks lay and he followed them. Russel almost did not believe the dog could do this—almost, but not quite. Had it happened earlier, when he first started to run the team, back at Oogruk's, he would not have believed. But now he understood more of the dogs, knew that they had understanding he did not have. Yet.

And he believed in the dogs.

The only advantage they had was that the storm was almost straight out of the north. They could fight dead against the wind and that was a bit easier than going side-on where the team would have been blown over.

But it was hard. And the storm, it seemed, worsened by the minute. At length Russel sensed that they were going up a slight incline, not a hill so much as a gradual upgrade, and at the top the dogs stopped dead in the wind.

He yelled at them, swore at them, finally began slamming the sled with his mittened hand and threatened to come up to the unseen dogs and beat them into submission.

But they would not move.

So they are done, he thought. He would have to make a shelter and ride the storm out. But first he would walk to the front of the team and bring the leader back around and use the dogs to form a part of a shelter.

He staggered against the wind to the front of the line and as he reached down for the collar on the lead dog he tripped and fell on something in the trail.

When he had recovered he saw that it was a booted foot, attached to a leg, and by moving up along the leg he found a person with a parka lying curled up, face away from the wind, extremely still.

He shook the figure with his hand but there was no response and he thought the person must be dead.

So much death, he thought. Oogruk and now this person. So much death given in this hard place.

But as he turned away he saw the arm move, or thought he saw some movement, and when he looked back he was sure of it—the bulky form had some life. Somewhere inside the round shape huddled on the trail there was a living person.

There was little time now. Whoever it was, the life was almost gone. There had to be a place to live now, a warm place, and Russel worked as fast as he could without sweating. Sweat, of all things, could kill. Steadily, evenly, he brought the dogs around and placed them down with his hands in a living screen across the face of the wind. They would soon be covered with snow and warm in their small igloos.

Then he took the skins from the sled and using the sled basket as one wall made a tent lean-to of two skins, folding one with the hair in to make a floor. The wind took the tent down twice, pulling the skins out and away so that he had to fight hard to keep them. But at last, using some bits of cord from the sled bag, he tied the skins down at the corners to the sled and packed snow around them and they held. The wind would blow more snow in and pack them still further.

Then he put the lamp and a partial carcass into the lean-to and went back for the figure in the snow. It took much heaving, pulling on the feet, to get the unconscious person into the lean-to and reclose the flap so the wind wouldn't tear it open. But he succeeded at last and fumbled with matches to get the lamp going. It started slowly, casting only a tiny flicker of light, until the fat around the wick began to melt and when it was going at last and he could feel some heat coming from it he turned to his companion.

When he pushed the hood back he was stunned to see that it was a girl. Woman, he thought—girl-woman. She had a round face with the white spots that come from freezing, and pitch-black thick hair pulled back in a bun and held with a leather thong.

He rubbed her cheeks but there was no response and yet he could see that she was breathing. Small spurts of steam came up in the cold yellow air in the lean-to. There was life inside the frozen shell.

He tore off her outerparka. Really it was a light

anorak made of canvas, and underneath she had on a vest. When the parka was off he realized that she was not only a young woman but that she was pregnant.

This realization stopped him and he settled back on his haunches to think of it. There were so many strange things here. She was where she couldn't possibly be, riding a snowmachine that had run out of gas, with no supplies, coming from nowhere and going nowhere.

She couldn't be.

And yet she was.

And she was pregnant and nearly dead.

He chipped some pieces of fat off the deer carcass and added them to the lamp. He did it several times while he thought on what to do. Soon the lamp was full of fat and he remembered the dream, remembered the woman trying to save the children from starvation.

He took his finger and dipped it in the fat of the lamp and wiped it across the blue lips. There was no indication from the woman-girl at all. He did it again, and again, until some of the fat had worked into her mouth and then he saw the jaw move. Not a swallowing, not a chewing, but a ripple in the jaw muscle.

She was coming back.

Soon the pain would hit her. When somebody has gotten close to death by freezing and he comes back, Russel knew, there is terrible pain. Sometimes it was possible to relieve the pain by rubbing snow on the frozen parts but when it was the whole body nothing helped.

The pain had to be. It was considered by some—by Oogruk—to be the same pain as birth. To have been close to death and come back could not be done without the pain of birth.

Russel sat back again, then cut some meat and held it over the flame. After the pain would come hunger. She would want to eat. As he wanted to eat.

The meat softened with the flame and when it had taken on some warmth he ate part of it. Doing so made him think of the dogs and he considered cutting them food but decided to let them sleep for a time first. They had run long and were probably too tired to eat.

Instead he ate some more meat and watched the woman-girl he had rescued. He did not think anything, left his mind blank. There was nothing to think. Just the storm outside and the girl-woman who had almost died but who had come back.

He was extremely tired and as soon as the shelter—drummed into noise by the wind and blown snow—had warmed and the meat had reached his stomach he couldn't hold his eyes open.

He slept sitting up—or didn't sleep so much as close his eyes—and ceased to be in the tent.

His mind slid sideways into the dream.

13

The Dream

THE STORM had cleared but it had taken days, many days. Too many days.

The man got the dogs up, up out of stiffness and the frozen positions they had taken in ice. One got up and fell over, too far gone to live. The man used his spear and the quick thrust to the back of the head to kill the dog. Its feet were frozen and it would have been in agony if he had tried to keep it alive. When it was dead he threw the carcass on the sled to feed the other dogs later.

Then he made them go. They did not want to leave, they were stiff with cold, but he whipped them and made them go.

Across the strange dreamgrass and dreamsnow they moved, the bone and ivory sled starting slow and pulling hard. He stopped and urinated on the runners, using a piece of hide with hair on it to smooth the new ice, and the sled pulled much easier.

And now, where the land had been open and barren, there was much game for the man. He passed herds of caribou, once another mammoth which had died and was frozen, with giant wolves tearing at it.

The wolves watched him pass. Two of them made a small sweep toward the sled and the man—there were times when they would have killed and eaten both the man and the dogs—but there was much easy meat on the mammoth. They turned away without making an open threat but it wouldn't have mattered.

The man almost did not see them. He had one purpose now, driving the lined-out team in front of him. Down to four stiff dogs, but loosening by the mile, he ran them out. The whip cracked and cracked again, reaching out to flick meat from their backs, meat and tufts of hair that flew into the cold, and they ran for him.

They ran for home.

Across the white land they ran, across the whiteness that was so bright in the dream it turned at last into light. Whitelight with the dogs churning through the brightness, legs slamming forward and down, feet kicking up snow, day into night into day into night into day . . .

The dreamdogs ran in the dreamworld across the whitelight until finally in the great distance they disappeared and out in front of what they were, what they had become, Russel could see the space where the tent was in the dream.

But it was the tent space only.

Torn leather, ripped skins that flew and flapped, tattered banners in the never-ending arctic dreamwind.

Where there had been a place of life, a place of laughter and round fat faces, where there had been a place of things that meant home and living, there was only the bleak shreds of flapping leather and the signs of death.

An end to things.

No, Russel thought—out of the dream but still in it in some way he did not understand. No, that cannot be.

But it was. In the dream it was. There was an

end that came in the north, an end that came to all things, the same end that came to Oogruk. The wolves had come, and when they were done, the small white foxes had come, and where there had been a woman and two children, where they had ended their lives, there was nothing.

Two bones.

Neither of them was identifiable except as bones, but they were human because they had not been cracked for the marrow and if they had been left from meat the woman would have cracked them to eat of the marrow—one small and the other large and long.

Two bones.

They were in the space that used to be tent but they were all. Everything else, every little thing that would have meant life and home was gone.

Even the lamp.

But only a small distance to the north, under an overhanging ledge, the lamp lay. Russel saw it. A fox had taken it there; drawn by the smell of fat that for years had soaked into the stone, it had taken the lamp under the ledge to get away from the other foxes and had licked the fat-smell until even that smell was gone.

Then it had left the lamp and trotted away.

It was a shallow stone lamp, with a flat bottom

and a groove in the edge where the moss wick would lie.

The dreamlamp lay where the fox had dropped it, lay until the blowing wind would cover it with snow and the snow would make grass and the grass would cover it still more, and then the snow and grass would, each after the other, time after time, mat the lamp down where it would lie forever. Or until somebody came to move it.

The lamp, Russel dreamthought. Not all that was left . . .

Another shift came; the dream moved sideways once more and he saw the man. Into the night and back to day the man had driven the sled until the dogs were staggering, falling. They were run down so far they would die surely. There would not be a team when the man was done—there would be only dead dogs.

Nothing but the man would be left.

They had run through the light, through the dreamlight the dreamdogs had run until they were no more.

Until there was only the man and the sled and where the tent had been flapping in the wind, only tattered pieces of tent.

And the man was Russel and Russel was the man. He knew that the woman and two children were no more and that the dogs would be no more and that's when Russel awakened in his own tent and saw the lamp.

Saw the flickering lamp and felt himself bathed in the stink-sweat of fear and knew, knew in his center, that it was the same lamp and that it was all there was left of what had been.

That's when Russel awakened in his own tent and knew that there was not a line any longer between the dream and the run.

That's when Russel awakened in his own tent stinking of fear and sweat, knowing that the dream had become his life and his life and the run had become the dream and the woman was looking at him.

The woman-girl, girl-woman sat staring at him past the flickering yellow of the lamp.

And she was the same woman as the woman in the dream. The same round face of the girl-woman in the dream, the same hair, the same even mouth of the dreamwoman-girl, with the same wide nose and clear eyes staring at him through the flamelight.

The dreamflame.

From the dreamlamp.

14

The Dreamrun

At the other end of the dreamrun nothing was the same as when he started. At the other end, Russel was no longer young but he wasn't old, either. He wasn't afraid, but he wasn't brave. He wasn't smart, but he wasn't a fool. He wasn't as strong as he would be, but he wasn't ever going to be as weak as he was.

When he thought of what happened, later, when he wasn't what he would be but wasn't what he had been, he thought that in some mysterious way a great folding had happened.

The dream had folded into his life and his life had folded back into the dream so many times that it was not possible for him to find which was real and which was dream.

Nor did he feel that it was important to decide. In its way the dream was more real than the run, than his life.

These things happened. Either in the dream or the run, either in one fold or another fold, these things happened:

He came to know the woman-girl. She was named Nancy. She had become pregnant without meaning to, without being married, and because the missionaries had told her that it was a sin she had been driven by her mind, driven out into the tundra to die on the snowmachine.

But fear had taken her. She had been afraid to die and she had turned to go back—she did not know how far she had come—and she had run out of gas. She had started to walk, had gone down with the cold, was going to die and Russel saved her.

She had gone first out to sea and then turned inland so they would think she'd gone through the ice and would not look for her inland. She did not have parents to worry for her. Her baby was not due for four months but she had pain in the tent that first night and Russel worried, though there was nothing he could do for her.

They could not leave. The storm was too strong for them to leave. He fed her meat and fat from a caribou carcass, watching her eat and talk between mouthfuls, heating the pieces of meat and putting them in her mouth, holding back when she winced with pain as she came back from freezing, handing her the next piece when she was ready for it. He let her talk and talk, now that he was rested.

When at last she had settled and had stopped talking about herself she stared at him.

"What is the matter?" Russel asked. "Have you never seen people before?"

Nancy looked down, suddenly shy. "It isn't that. It just came to me that you were out here with a dog team. There is nothing out here. How did you come to be here?"

Russel thought of telling her of Oogruk, of the dream, of the run, but held back. That was part of his song and it wouldn't be good to talk about it before it was ready to sing.

Then he thought he might tell her of the lamp, but decided against that for the same reason. Finally he shrugged. "I am a person who is running north and came upon your machine. That is all." He did not tell her about following the tracks for so long.

"How far north?"

It was an impertinent question but he ignored the discourtesy. "Until I run to the end of where I am going."

And then she did a strange thing. She nodded, almost wisely. "I understand. But tell me, is it possible for a person to be with you when you run north to the end?"

It was a hard question to answer. In this run, Russel thought, in this run I thought I would be alone but it was perhaps not supposed to be so. It may be that is what the dream is telling me. That I am not supposed to be alone. If the dream is telling me anything.

Or another way of thinking: Is it possible to leave her out here? No. And still a third way: Would it be possible to take her home?

"There is nothing for me there," she said, shaking her head when he asked. "I have done wrong. There is not a way to live there. I will stay out here."

"And die," Russel finished for her.

"Yes."

"No." He shook his head. "You tried that and it didn't work. You became afraid and tried to get home."

"Not home," she corrected. "Back. I have no home."

"So."

"So."

"What am I to do?"

"Take me with you. I will earn my way. I can scrape the skins and sew them. I can make camp. I can feed dogs."

"Do you know dogs?"

"No. There were none left in my village. But I can learn."

And in that way she came to be with him when his life folded into the dream and the dream folded into his life.

In that way she came to be with him on the run.

Again during that long storm-night she slept and he dozed, but did not dream, and when he awakened this time there was light outside the tent and the wind had stopped. He reached outside and brought his parka in, scraped the ice off, slid it over his underparka and stood outside. He was stiff, worse than he'd ever been, so he stretched, felt his bones crack and creak.

The woman-girl put her anorak on and came out.

"It is cold," she said.

"Cold is our friend."

"I know. But I am not dressed as you. I feel it more."

"We will wrap you in skins in the sled. You will be all right."

She said nothing but nodded and began taking the tent down while he hacked meat off the carcass for the dogs. She put one skin on the bottom of the sled, curved up on the sides, with the hair in. The other three she put on top as a kind of blanket, with the fur inside. When it came time to go—after he had fed and brought the dogs up—she got in between the hides.

"There is comfort here."

He misunderstood. "I have never hauled anybody who is going to have a baby."

"I meant it is warm. There is nothing comfortable about having a baby."

"Ahh. I see."

The dogs were rested but stiff and it took them a mile or so to loosen up. But they settled into the routine of running; the leader knew that Russel wanted to cover distance and they ran.

The land was new. White-new with snow from

the storm and drifts from the wind and after a time the dogs were running up the sides of a white saucer into the light, running out and out until their legs vanished in light and the steam came back to Russel across their backs and turned them into part of the wind, turned them into ghost-dogs.

He stood the sled loosely, proud of the team, and he could tell that the woman-girl thought highly of them.

Out, he thought. Out before me they go. Out before me I go, they go . . .

They ran north, now two where there was one, ran north for the mother of wind and the father of ice.

And these things happened when Russel's life folded into the dream and the dream folded into his life:

It came that they ran past their food.

It was true that he perhaps fed the dogs a bit too much, but they were working hard and it took meat and fat to drive them. Three, four, seven more days of running north, stopping at night in the skins with the lamp and the chips of fat and the yellow glow while they ate much and talked little; sat in their own minds until they dozed and he came to know the woman-girl—eight, nine, ten days and nights they ran north toward the mother of wind, and they ran past their food.

The first and second day without food there was no trouble. The dogs grew weak, but when they didn't get fed they went back to work and began to use of the stored fat and meat of their bodies.

"They will run to death," Oogruk had said. "You must not let them."

At the end of the second day Russel's stomach demanded food and when he didn't feed it and ignored it his body finally quit asking for food and he went to work and began using the meat and fat of his body.

The woman-girl grew weak rapidly because her body fed the baby within. Russel saved the last of the food for her and when that was gone and it was obvious that the dogs could not go much further he stopped.

There had been no game. No sign. They had seen nothing and he was worried. No, more than worried—he had been worried when the first two days with no game sighted had come. Now he was afraid.

He had to make meat.

"I will leave you in the tent and take the team for meat. They will run lighter with only one person."

Nancy agreed, nodding. She got slowly out of the sled and pulled the skins out to make the shelter. They were near the side of a cut bank where a creek had long ago run. They used the dirt bank for one wall and made a lean-to.

There were some chips for the lamp, and a long strip of fat that he had been saving for fuel—pictures from the dream haunted him and he did not want to leave her without heat.

When the shelter was up he returned to the sled. "I'll be back."

It was as close as he would come to a goodbye and he made the dogs leave. They did not want to go. They thought they should sleep in camp and eat and saw no reason to go out again. But he forced them and when they were away from camp he made them run to the east, up the old creekbed. If there is game, he thought, it will be up the creek run.

But they went all of that day into the dark and he saw nothing. No hare, no ptarmigan, no tracks of anything.

With dark he stopped and lay on the sled in his parka. There was light wind, but not the vicious cold of the previous days of running. He tried to sleep but it did not come.

Instead he lay awake all night thinking of the woman-girl back in the tent. If he did not find game she would die.

She would die.

He would die.

The dogs would die.

Perhaps I ought to run back to her and kill and eat the dogs, he thought, over and over. If he kept running away from the shelter until the dogs went down he would not get back to her. If there was not game out ahead of him he would not get back to her. If he saw game but his mind was not true and the arrow flew wrong he would not get back. She would die.

She would die.

He would die.

The dogs would die.

But if he went back and they ate the dogs they would not be able to leave and they would die anyway.

And now when he thought, there was nothing from the ghost of Oogruk. No help. Nothing. Nothing from the trance or the time when they turned to yellow smoke.

Whatever decision he made, when the light came

back, it was *his* decision, just as going back to live the old way must have been *his* decision.

And when the light came across the snow he made the decision to go ahead to find game, knowing that if he was wrong they would all be wrong, the woman-girl, the dogs and all would be wrong and gone. Gone and gone.

In the second day he found nothing. Nor did he on the third day and now they had gone six days without eating and he felt weak. His eyes worked poorly and he ate snow so often that his lips were sore. Twice, then several more times, he thought he saw deer but when he got to where they had been there was nothing. Never had been anything. It was the hunger in his eyes, he found, that made him see things.

Finally the dogs stopped. They could pull no more, or so they thought. But now he remembered one more thing from Oogruk.

"The dogs run because they want to run," the old man had told him, "or because they *think* they want to run, or because you *make* them think they want to run. That is how to drive dogs."

And so now Russel drove them. He cut a whip from some willows in the old streambed and he laid it on their backs and they ran for him but it was wrong, wrong to drive them down that way and he knew that when he had whipped them and made them run and they went down there would be nothing left.

He would not get back to Nancy. His mind took that and made it part of him—he was failing. He would not get back. As in the dream, he would not get back and there would be only two bones left by the foxes.

Two bones.

And so he drove the dogs down, drove them the way the man in the dream had driven them and when his mind was gone, when there was nothing left of his thinking and nothing left of the dogs, he came around a bend in the old streambed and saw tracks.

At first he didn't believe them. They came off the left side of the bank and tore down into the snow at the bottom, breaking through the hard pack that had held the dogs and sled. He thought they were from the hunger in his eyes but when he got closer they did not go away.

They were huge.

And when he got still closer he saw that they were tracks of a great polar bear and that he did not believe, either, because the bear were hunted out for their white fur. Men used snowmachines and hunted them out and there were no bears.

But there were the tracks. And they were tracks of a great bear. And they had to be real because now the dogs caught the smell and took excitement. They increased speed but he knew that they could not last now.

And how to kill a bear?

Oogruk had said nothing.

The arrow would not be enough. He had the killing lance on the sled and he would have to use that somehow. He would have to catch the bear and use the lance to kill it.

A polar bear that was bigger than he, the team, the sled, the woman-girl and the tent combined—he had to take it with the small killing lance in the old way that nobody had used for so long that he didn't think there was a memory of it. Oogruk had never done it, or he would have told him.

The dogs went faster still and he was afraid that he would burn them out. He stopped them and let the right point dog loose—the one just in back of the leader on the right. He seemed to be the strongest dog and the most excited by the smell of the bear tracks. Perhaps he would catch the bear and keep it busy until Russel could get there and bring it down. Or try.

There was much doubt in him now about the bear, some fear, and more doubt. But the dog tore away up the streambed and Russel took the killing lance from the tie-down on the sled and loosened the bow case and quiver.

Then he let the dogs take the sled after the loose dog. They were clamoring to run—even though weakened by hunger. They smelled it now, saw him take up the weapons and knew that he would try to kill soon and the sight made them crazy.

Up the old stream they wound, following the tracks, faster and faster until at last they came around a corner and there it was.

The bear had his rear back against the bank, his head low and teeth bared. He was immense, the largest bear Russel had ever seen, even in pictures. The fur was dirty white, almost yellow. It was an old male, with his teeth worn down, but full of the winter death that makes a polar bear so awesome. When he saw the sled coming he raised on his hind legs and Russel's heart almost stopped. The bear was a tower, a white-yellow tower standing over the loose dog. The dog had been dodging back and forth, trying to worry the bear, but when the bear raised he went in to bite at the white back leg. It was his last act.

The bear's head snaked down in a great curve of power and his jaws closed on the back of the dog and broke its back in a bite so savage that the dog was dead before it could scream. Then the bear shook its head—a tearing shake—and the dead dog flew sideways in a spray of gore.

All in silence.

But now the bear rumbled in its throat and turned to Russel and the sled and the team. Here was an enemy, a thing to face, and it would face it and kill it.

But wait, Russel thought. But wait, bear. It is the same as the mammoth. There is sadness here for the same reason. A dog is dead. You will want the other dogs and you will turn your head sideways and the lance will enter you like light. But wait, bear. Wait for me. Wait for the sadness of your life that you must die to feed the man. Not all the time. But wait for the sadness this time, bear.

Russel took the lance and stood away from the sled and let the dogs go. They went for the bear in a pummeling scream, and with the same sharp movement the bear lowered on all fours and came for Russel.

The bear did not want the dogs. He wanted Russel. He wanted to kill the enemy standing with the little stick, kill the man. Kill the man-thing.

Russel felt a great calmness. He wasn't Russel. He was the man in the dream and the bear wasn't a bear but the great stinking beast and Russel set the shaft of the killing lance in the ground and held the wide-ivory point at the right height to take the bear at the base of his throat and now the bear came and now the dogs swerved in to take him and the bear's head went sideways for the dogs and the bear, stinking with the same smell as the beast in the dream, and now the bear had his head sideways and now the lance entered.

Like light. It slid through the hair and the fat and into the center of the bear, into the center of the center of the bear and Russel screamed a savage roar of triumph and the bear was on him.

On him and over him, hitting him with a stunning blow of his right paw even as the lance took his life. Russel knew he had killed the bear, but felt the pain and saw the flash as his own life seemed to fly from him and he thought with a violent clarity: but wait, bear.

But wait, bear.

And then he saw nothing.

And these things happened when Russel's life folded into the dream and the dream folded into his life:

When he came back into his life from where the

bear had knocked him away the bear was dead and the dogs were chewing at his rear end and Russel was underneath his left front shoulder, the blood dripping down on him from where the lance shaft had entered the bear.

He fought to get from under and crawl to the side. When he could stand, his head aching and dizzy, he looked down on the bear and felt his heart go out of him and into the bear.

"Thank you. The meat will be welcome."

A sadness took him, because he had no food for the bear. Such a bear it was, so big, but he had nothing for him but the thought of food. It would have to be enough.

The bear was a mountain of meat. It weighed close to three quarters of a ton. More meat than he could eat, than the dogs could eat in a month. More even than the woman-girl . . .

He remembered her suddenly.

He would feed the dogs and take some meat and go back for her. As fast as possible.

He used his knife to lift the back-end hide and took a large chunk of meat from the rear leg. This he fed to the dogs, who ate and puked and ate again. Then he took another large chunk of fat meat, which he put in the sled, and he turned them and started back.

They didn't want to leave the bear. The meat had given them strength almost miraculously fast, but they didn't want to leave the kill. He finally had to get in front and drag the leader back down the streambed until they had gone around two bends and were well away from the dead bear. Even then they worked reluctantly for a time.

But he let them seek their own pace and kept them going and in two days—feeding them liberally from the meat as he drove them—they had come within sight of the tent.

It was day—clear and cold—and he saw the lean-to half a mile before they got to it. It was not tattered, but there was no steam coming from the opening at the top and he feared for her.

"Nancy!" He called her name when he came near the tent. "I am back . . ."

But there was no answer. He set the hook and grabbed the meat and ran for the tent. It took him just a second to lift a corner and get inside but he felt the cold immediately.

She was lying on her side, the end of a skin wrapped around her as a sleeping bag and she was either sleeping or dead or in a coma.

The lamp was out. The fat was gone. He took some from the bear, rich yellow fat, and cut pieces into the lamp. He found some moss and got the lamp going—as the first time, only with great difficulty.

The warmth came out from the flame at once and he opened the skin around the woman-girl to let the heat reach her.

When he moved her he saw her eye flicker and he thought: twice. Twice she has come back from death.

But this time she was not frozen, as she had been the first time, or not frozen to such depth. There was not that wrong with her. She smiled at him.

"I did not think you were coming back." She spoke in a whisper that was almost a hiss.

"I said I would be back."

She said nothing more. He cut meat in small pieces and heated them on the lamp and put them in her mouth and she chewed and swallowed and where there had been an end there was once more a beginning.

But worse was wrong. Worse than he thought could be.

Even with the meat she did not revive. She ate, but when he thought she should eat more she held back and she did not come up and because he had come to know the woman-girl he worried.

"You are sick," he said. Outside it was dark and

the wind was blowing again. Or still. "What makes you sick?"

She didn't answer at first. Then she grunted. "It is the baby. The baby is coming early. I cannot stop it."

"Ahh. That is not good, is it?"

"No." She turned away from him, face to the back of the tent. "Maybe you should leave me alone."

But he had run once, left her to go for meat and he would not leave her again. Leaving had torn him and he still thought of the dream and the tattered tent with the foxes. "I will stay."

She said nothing to this and he took that as acceptance—or perhaps she was too sick to argue.

"Is there a thing I can do?" he asked.

But again she did not answer. He put more fat in the lamp, pulled the wick up to make more heat, then went outside and fed the dogs. They would sleep for days now, he knew, and that was fine. He had enough meat to last a long time and by then they would be able to travel. If not, he could just go back to the carcass and get more. With a strong team it was only a day and a half away.

With food anything was possible.

When the dogs were fed and the meat pulled

back in the shelter, he felt the exhaustion come down on him and it was not possible for him to stay awake.

In the warmth of the lean-to he slept, the ringing, deep sleep of the utterly tired when it seems as if nothing can awaken the mind. His head lay back against her feet and he slept and thought he would not dream.

But a thing came. He could not say if it was a dream or if it was real. But a thing came to happen in that night that he knew—and if he knew it sleeping or knew it awake it did not matter.

Foldings:

The woman-girl became a woman in the night. She was quiet at first, but moving and throwing her body back and forth and then in the yellow of the lamp she gave short-sharp sounds, sounds from the center of her center.

And he saw-felt that.

She strained and heaved and pushed and in the folds of the skin and the agony of it was not something he understood but he knew the sadness because it was the same sadness somehow that killing the bear had been.

In his mind he tried to help her but he was not sure if he really did or only wished that he could.

And still she worked. The cries became closer

together, and shorter, and deeper, and then she screamed, and then a time, a lifetime of almost animal whimpers and another scream and the thing had happened and it was in his hands and there was not life in it.

"Take it away!" she screamed. "Take it away now. Before I see it. Put it away from me. Outside."

And either he did or dreamed he did or wished he did—he went from the tent with the baby and up on the hill in back of the tent and he walked in the cold and put it on the hill and he thought that he had never been so sad. A tearing sadness.

But there was not life in it. There was not life.

And when he got back to the lean-to or thought he did or wished he did she was either asleep or unconscious and he fell back on the skin and slept with her.

And he wished then that he had stayed in his village.

And these things happened when Russel's life folded into the dream and the dream folded into his life:

Nancy lay for five days in the lean-to while Russel fed her meat from the bear, warming small pieces on the end of a willow and handing them to her.

But there was some trouble he did not understand with the woman and soon she went back to being a girl-woman, looking small and pale, and when those five days had passed he knew they would have to go.

"You need help," he said. "From a doctor. We will have to go to a settlement."

She said nothing. Her face had taken on the yellow of the lamp but it was the wrong yellow, the kind of yellow that stayed even when he opened the tent flap and let the daylight in.

"Here is the way it is," he told her, though he was not sure she knew what he meant, or even that she listened. "I do not know for sure where we are or how far we've come. But I think it is closer to the north coast and a village there than it would be to try to get back to your village. We came a long way. My dogs are strong." Even now, he thought, even now it is hard to keep pride away. "So I think we will go to the carcass of the bear and get meat and fat and then run for the north. As before. It should not be far to the edge of the land and there will be a village as there are villages along the coast everywhere and there will be help for you." It was the longest talk he had made since finding her. "That is the way it is."

Still she said nothing. But she nodded so he knew that even weak she understood and had been listening and he felt better for that.

So began the race.

The dogs were strong almost past measuring. Though there were only four left they had been fed meat and run so their legs rippled and were hard to the touch. Their heads were also hard. They had seen and done much and now they knew the man on the sled, knew that he was part of them, knew that no matter what happened he would be there and that made them stronger still. The strength in them came back to Russel and he fed on it and returned it as more strength still.

We have fire, he thought as they left the camp and went for meat to begin the final leg of the run. We have fire between us that grows and grows. Fire that will take us north to safety, fire that will save Nancy.

So began the race.

They took meat from the bear, as much as Russel thought they could carry, but had to leave the hide, the beautiful hide, because it was too heavy. He took the skin from the front legs to make pants, but the rest had to stay.

She brightened when they reached the dead bear. "You did this," she whispered. "With a spear you did this?"

He looked away. "And with the dogs. A man does not kill a bear alone. The dogs helped."

"Still. It is a huge thing, is it not?"

And now he chose not to answer. The dead bear made him sad, doubly so because they had to leave so much behind. It seemed wrong to talk of it as being a big thing—killing the bear with the lance. He did not wish to speak cheaply of it, or brag of it.

So began the race.

They left the bear and headed north again, running in sun and light wind. In the dark and some gentle snow they ran; up the edge of the saucer of light they ran, day into day they ran for six days, stopping only to feed the dogs and rest them in three- and four-hour naps, sleeping on the sled—or Russel sleeping next to it and Nancy on the skins—then up and gone again.

I must win this race, Russel thought. I must win. The girl-woman named Nancy got worse, grew weaker, but his strength grew with her weakness, his strength grew and went into the dogs.

Now they had more light. Winter was still there,

but the sun was coming back and he ran through the sun, grateful for the warmth. Even the nights were not so cold.

The dogs did not go down now. They were everything he would have wanted them to be and he drove them with his mind, drove them to the edge of the land, drove them until he felt the land start to tip down and then he smelled it, finally saw the sea ice out ahead.

When he got them to the edge of the sea he stopped and leaned over.

"See? We are north. We have come to the edge of the land."

She was still, but the edges of her eyes were glowing with life, with happiness, with the pride in his voice at what his dogs had done. She was weak, weak and down, but there was still life, enough life, and the corners of her mouth turned up in a smile, a smile that went into Russel.

"See?" he said, raising the team. "We will be in a village soon."

And he brought them up and ran them with his thoughts and on the ice they cut a snowmachine trail and he followed it to the left because that is what his leader said to do and he was the leader and the leader was him.

They drove down the coast, drove on the edge

of the sea-ice and land-snow, drove into the soft light of the setting spring sun, drove for the coastal village that had to be soon; the man-boy and the woman-girl and the driving mind-dogs that came from Russel's thoughts and went out and out and came from the dreamfold back.

Back.

PART THREE

DOGSONG

Come, see my dogs.

Out before me
they go,
in the long line to the sea.
Out they go.

Come, see my dogs.

They carry me
into all things, all things I will be;
all things that will come to me
will come to my dogs.
I stand on the earth and I sing.

Come, see my dogs.

See them, see them
in the smoke of my life,
in the eyes of my children,
in the sound of my feet,
in the dance of my words.
I stand on the earth and I sing.

Come, see my dogs.

My dogs are what lead me,
they are what move me.
See my dogs in the steam,
in the steam of my life.
They are me.

Come, see my dogs.

I was nothing before them,
no man
and no wife.
Without them, no life,
no girl-woman breathing
no song.

Come, see my dogs.

With them I ran,
ran north to the sea.
I stand by the sea and I sing.
I sing of my hunts
and of Oogruk.

Come, see my dogs.

Out before me they go.
Out before me they curve
in the long line out
before me
they go, I go, we go. They are me.

Hatchet

Also by Gary Paulsen

DANCING CARL
DOGSONG
SENTRIES
TRACKER

Hatchet

GARY PAULSEN

A Richard Jackson Book
Atheneum Books for Young Readers

ATHENEUM BOOKS FOR YOUNG READERS
An imprint of Simon & Schuster Children's Publishing Division
1230 Avenue of the Americas
New York, New York 10020

Printed and bound in the United States of America
30 29 28

The text of this book is set in 12 pt ITC Garamond Book.

Library of Congress Cataloging-in-Publication Data

Paulsen, Gary.
Hatchet.

Summary: After a plane crash, thirteen-year-old Brian spends fifty-four days in the wilderness, learning to survive initially with only the aid of a hatchet given by his mother, and learning also to survive his parents' divorce.
[1. Survival—Fiction. 2. Divorce—Fiction]
I. Title.
PZ7.P2843Hat 1987 [Fic] 87-6416
ISBN 0-689-84092-6

To the students of the
Hershey Middle School

Hatchet

1

BRIAN ROBESON stared out the window of the small plane at the endless green northern wilderness below. It was a small plane, a Cessna 406—a bushplane—and the engine was so loud, so roaring and consuming and loud, that it ruined any chance for conversation.

Not that he had much to say. He was thirteen and the only passenger on the plane with a pilot named—what was it? Jim or Jake or something—who was in his mid-forties and who had been silent as he worked to prepare for take-off. In fact since Brian had come to the small airport in Hampton, New York to meet the plane—driven by his mother—the pilot had spoken only five words to him.

"Get in the copilot's seat."

Which Brian had done. They had taken off and that was the last of the conversation. There had been the initial excitement, of course. He had never flown in a single-engine plane before and to be sitting in the copilot's seat with all the controls right there in front of him, all the instruments in his face as the plane clawed for altitude, jerking and sliding on the wind currents as the pilot took off, had been interesting and exciting. But in five minutes they had leveled off at six thousand feet and headed northwest and from then on the pilot had been silent, staring out the front, and the drone of the engine had been all that was left. The drone and the sea of green trees that lay before the plane's nose and flowed to the horizon, spread with lakes, swamps, and wandering streams and rivers.

Now Brian sat, looking out the window with the roar thundering through his ears, and tried to catalog what had led up to his taking this flight.

The thinking started.

Always it started with a single word.

Divorce.

It was an ugly word, he thought. A tearing, ugly word that meant fights and yelling, lawyers—God, he thought, how he hated lawyers who sat with their comfortable smiles and tried to explain to him in legal terms how all that he lived in was coming apart—and the breaking and shattering of all the solid things. His home, his life—all the solid things. Divorce. A breaking word, an ugly breaking word.

Divorce.

Secrets.

No, not secrets so much as just the Secret. What he knew and had not told anybody, what he knew about his mother that had caused the divorce, what he knew, what he knew—the Secret.

Divorce.

The Secret.

Brian felt his eyes beginning to burn and knew there would be tears. He had cried for a time, but that was gone now. He didn't cry now. Instead his eyes burned and tears came, the seeping tears that burned, but he didn't cry. He wiped his eyes with a finger and looked at the pilot out of the corner of his eye to make sure he hadn't noticed the burning and tears.

The pilot sat large, his hands lightly on the wheel, feet on the rudder pedals. He seemed more a machine than a man, an extension of the plane. On the dashboard in front of him Brian saw dials, switches, meters, knobs, levers, cranks, lights, handles that were wiggling and flickering, all indicating nothing that he understood and the pilot seemed the same way. Part of the plane, not human.

When he saw Brian look at him, the pilot seemed

to open up a bit and he smiled. "Ever fly in the copilot's seat before?" He leaned over and lifted the headset off his right ear and put it on his temple, yelling to overcome the sound of the engine.

Brian shook his head. He had never been in any kind of plane, never seen the cockpit of a plane except in films or on television. It was loud and confusing. "First time."

"It's not as complicated as it looks. Good plane like this almost flies itself." The pilot shrugged. "Makes my job easy." He took Brian's left arm. "Here, put your hands on the controls, your feet on the rudder pedals, and I'll show you what I mean."

Brian shook his head. "I'd better not."

"Sure. Try it . . . "

Brian reached out and took the wheel in a grip so tight his knuckles were white. He pushed his feet down on the pedals. The plane slewed suddenly to the right.

"Not so hard. Take her light, take her light."

Brian eased off, relaxed his grip. The burning in his eyes was forgotten momentarily as the vibration of the plane came through the wheel and the pedals. It seemed almost alive.

"See?" The pilot let go of his wheel, raised his hands in the air and took his feet off the pedals to show Brian he was actually flying the plane alone.

"Simple. Now turn the wheel a little to the right and push on the right rudder pedal a small amount."

Brian turned the wheel slightly and the plane immediately banked to the right, and when he pressed on the right rudder pedal the nose slid across the horizon to the right. He left off on the pressure and straightened the wheel and the plane righted itself.

"Now you can turn. Bring her back to the left a little."

Brian turned the wheel left, pushed on the left pedal, and the plane came back around. "It's easy." He smiled. "At least this part."

The pilot nodded. "All of flying is easy. Just takes learning. Like everything else. Like everything else." He took the controls back, then reached up and rubbed his left shoulder. "Aches and pains—must be getting old."

Brian let go of the controls and moved his feet away from the pedals as the pilot put his hands on the wheel. "Thank you . . . "

But the pilot had put his headset back on and the gratitude was lost in the engine noise and things went back to Brian looking out the window at the ocean of trees and lakes. The burning eyes did not come back, but memories did, came flooding in. The words. Always the words.

Divorce.

The Secret.

Fights.

Split.

The big split. Brian's father did not understand as Brian did, knew only that Brian's mother wanted to break the marriage apart. The split had come and then the divorce, all so fast, and the court had left him with his mother except for the summers and what the judge called "visitation rights." So formal. Brian hated judges as he hated lawyers. Judges that leaned over the bench and asked Brian if he understood where he was to live and why. Judges who did not know what had really happened. Judges with the caring look that meant nothing as lawyers said legal phrases that meant nothing.

In the summer Brian would live with his father. In the school year with his mother. That's what the judge said after looking at papers on his desk and listening to the lawyers talk. Talk. Words.

Now the plane lurched slightly to the right and Brian looked at the pilot. He was rubbing his shoulder again and there was the sudden smell of body gas in the plane. Brian turned back to avoid embarrassing the pilot, who was obviously in some discomfort. Must have stomach troubles.

So this summer, this first summer when he was

allowed to have "visitation rights" with his father, with the divorce only one month old, Brian was heading north. His father was a mechanical engineer who had designed or invented a new drill bit for oil drilling, a self-cleaning, self-sharpening bit. He was working in the oil fields of Canada, up on the tree line where the tundra started and the forests ended. Brian was riding up from New York with some drilling equipment—it was lashed down in the rear of the plane next to a fabric bag the pilot had called a survival pack, which had emergency supplies in case they had to make an emergency landing—that had to be specially made in the city, riding in a bushplane with the pilot named Jim or Jake or something who had turned out to be an all right guy, letting him fly and all.

Except for the smell. Now there was a constant odor, and Brian took another look at the pilot, found him rubbing the shoulder and down the arm now, the left arm, letting go more gas and wincing. Probably something he ate, Brian thought.

His mother had driven him from the city to meet the plane at Hampton where it came to pick up the drilling equipment. A drive in silence, a long drive in silence. Two and a half hours of sitting in the car, staring out the window just as he was now staring out the window of the plane. Once, after an hour, when they were out of the city she turned to him.

"Look, can't we talk this over? Can't we talk this out? Can't you tell me what's bothering you?"

And there were the words again. Divorce. Split. The Secret. How could he tell her what he knew? So he had remained silent, shook his head and continued to stare unseeing at the countryside, and his mother had gone back to driving only to speak to him one more time when they were close to Hampton.

She reached over the back of the seat and brought up a paper sack. "I got something for you, for the trip."

Brian took the sack and opened the top. Inside there was a hatchet, the kind with a steel handle and a rubber handgrip. The head was in a stout leather case that had a brass-riveted belt loop.

"It goes on your belt." His mother spoke now without looking at him. There were some farm trucks on the road now and she had to weave through them and watch traffic. "The man at the store said you could use it. You know. In the woods with your father."

Dad, he thought. Not "my father." My dad. "Thanks. It's really nice." But the words sounded hollow, even to Brian.

"Try it on. See how it looks on your belt."

And he would normally have said no, would normally have said no that it looked too hokey to have a hatchet on your belt. Those were the normal things he would say. But her voice was thin, had a sound like something thin that would break if you touched it, and he felt bad for not speaking to her. Knowing what he knew, even with the anger, the hot white hate of his anger at her, he still felt bad for not speaking to her, and so to humor her he loosened his belt and pulled the right side out and put the hatchet on and rethreaded the belt.

"Scootch around so I can see."

He moved around in the seat, feeling only slightly ridiculous.

She nodded. "Just like a scout. My little scout." And there was the tenderness in her voice that she had when he was small, the tenderness that she had when he was small and sick, with a cold, and she put her hand on his forehead, and the burning came into his eyes again and he had turned away from her and looked out the window, forgotten the hatchet on his belt and so arrived at the plane with the hatchet still on his belt.

Because it was a bush flight from a small airport there had been no security and the plane had been waiting, with the engine running when he arrived and he had grabbed his suitcase and pack bag and run for the plane without stopping to remove the hatchet.

So it was still on his belt. At first he had been embarrassed but the pilot had said nothing about it and Brian forgot it as they took off and began flying.

More smell now. Bad. Brian turned again to glance at the pilot, who had both hands on his stomach and was grimacing in pain, reaching for the left shoulder again as Brain watched.

"Don't know, kid . . ." The pilot's words were a hiss, barely audible. "Bad aches here. Bad aches. Thought it was something I ate but . . ."

He stopped as a fresh spasm of pain hit him. Even Brian could see how bad it was—the pain drove the pilot back into the seat, back and down.

"I've never had anything like this . . ."

The pilot reached for the switch on his mike cord, his hand coming up in a small arc from his stomach, and he flipped the switch and said, "This is flight four six . . ."

And now a jolt took him like a hammerblow, so forcefully that he seemed to crush back into the seat, and Brian reached for him, could not understand at first what it was, could not know.

And then knew.

Brian knew. The pilot's mouth went rigid, he swore and jerked a short series of slams into the seat, holding his shoulder now. Swore and hissed, "Chest! Oh God, my chest is coming apart!"

Brian knew now.

The pilot was having a heart attack. Brian had been in the shopping mall with his mother when a man in front of Paisley's store had suffered a heart attack. He had gone down and screamed about his chest. An old man. Much older than the pilot.

Brian knew.

The pilot was having a heart attack and even as the knowledge came to Brian he saw the pilot slam into the seat one more time, one more awful time he slammed back into the seat and his right leg jerked, pulling the plane to the side in a sudden twist and his head fell forward and spit came. Spit came from the corners of his mouth and his legs contracted up, up into the seat, and his eyes rolled back in his head until there was only white.

Only white for his eyes and the smell became worse, filled the cockpit, and all of it so fast, so incredibly fast that Brian's mind could not take it in at first. Could only see it in stages.

The pilot had been talking, just a moment ago, complaining of the pain. He had been talking.

Then the jolts had come.

The jolts that took the pilot back had come, and now Brian sat and there was a strange feeling of silence in the thrumming roar of the engine—a strange feeling of silence and being alone. Brian was stopped.

He was stopped. Inside he was stopped. He could not think past what he saw, what he felt. All was stopped. The very core of him, the very center of Brian Robeson was stopped and stricken with a white-flash of horror, a terror so intense that his breathing, his thinking, and nearly his heart had stopped.

Stopped.

Seconds passed, seconds that became all of his life, and he began to know what he was seeing, began to understand what he saw and that was worse, so much worse that he wanted to make his mind freeze again.

He was sitting in a bushplane roaring seven thousand feet above the northern wilderness with a pilot who had suffered a massive heart attack and who was either dead or in something close to a coma.

He was alone.

In the roaring plane with no pilot he was alone.

Alone.

2

For a Time that he could not understand Brian could do nothing. Even after his mind began working and he could see what had happened he could do nothing. It was as if his hands and arms were lead.

Then he looked for ways for it not to have happened. Be asleep, his mind screamed at the pilot. Just be asleep and your eyes will open now and your hands will take the controls and your feet will move to the pedals—but it did not happen.

The pilot did not move except that his head rolled on a neck impossibly loose as the plane hit a small bit of turbulence.

The plane.

Somehow the plane was still flying. Seconds had

passed, nearly a minute, and the plane flew on as if nothing had happened and he had to do something, had to do something but did not know what.

Help.

He had to help.

He stretched one hand toward the pilot, saw that his fingers were trembling, and touched the pilot on the chest. He did not know what to do. He knew there were procedures, that you could do mouth-to-mouth on victims of heart attacks and push their chests—C.P.R.—but he did not know how to do it and in any case could not do it with the pilot, who was sitting up in the seat and still strapped in with his seatbelt. So he touched the pilot with the tips of his fingers, touched him on the chest and could feel nothing, no heartbeat, no rise and fall of breathing. Which meant that the pilot was almost certainly dead.

"Please," Brian said. But did not know what or who to ask. "Please . . ."

The plane lurched again, hit more turbulence, and Brian felt the nose drop. It did not dive, but the nose went down slightly and the down-angle increased the speed, and he knew that at this angle, this slight angle down, he would ultimately fly into the trees. He could see them ahead on the horizon where before he could see only sky.

He had to fly it somehow. Had to fly the plane. He had to help himself. The pilot was gone, beyond anything he could do. He had to try and fly the plane.

He turned back in the seat, facing the front, and put his hands—still trembling—on the control wheel, his feet gently on the rudder pedals. You pulled back on the stick to raise the plane, he knew that from reading. You always pulled back on the wheel. He gave it a tug and it slid back toward him easily. Too easily. The plane, with the increased speed from the tilt down, swooped eagerly up and drove Brian's stomach down. He pushed the wheel back in, went too far this time, and the plane's nose went below the horizon and the engine speed increased with the shallow dive.

Too much.

He pulled back again, more gently this time, and the nose floated up again, too far but not as violently as before, then down a bit too much, and up again, very easily, and the front of the engine cowling settled. When he had it aimed at the horizon and it seemed to be steady, he held the wheel where it was, let out his breath—which he had been holding all this time—and tried to think what to do next.

It was a clear, blue-sky day with fluffy bits of clouds here and there and he looked out the window for a moment, hoping to see something, a town or village, but there was nothing. Just the green of the trees, endless green, and lakes scattered more and more thickly as the plane flew—where?

He was flying but did not know where, had no idea where he was going. He looked at the dashboard of the plane, studied the dials and hoped to get some help, hoped to find a compass, but it was all so confusing, a jumble of numbers and lights. One lighted display in the top center of the dashboard said the number 342, another next to it said 22. Down beneath that were dials with lines that seemed to indicate what the wings were doing, tipping or moving, and one dial with a needle pointing to the number 70, which he thought—only thought—might be the altimeter. The device that told him his height above the ground. Or above sea level. Somewhere he had read something about altimeters but he couldn't remember what, or where, or anything about them.

Slightly to the left and below the altimeter he saw a small rectangular panel with a lighted dial and two knobs. His eyes had passed over it two or three times before he saw what was written in tiny letters on top of the panel. TRANSMITTER 221, was stamped in the metal and it hit him, finally, that this was the radio.

The radio. Of course. He had to use the radio. When the pilot had—had been hit that way (he couldn't bring himself to say that the pilot was dead, couldn't think it), he had been trying to use the radio.

Brian looked to the pilot. The headset was still on his head, turned sideways a bit from his jamming back into the seat, and the microphone switch was clipped into his belt.

Brian had to get the headset from the pilot. Had to reach over and get the headset from the pilot or he would not be able to use the radio to call for help. He had to reach over...

His hands began trembling again. He did not want to touch the pilot, did not want to reach for him. But he had to. Had to get the radio. He lifted his hands from the wheel, just slightly, and held them waiting to see what would happen. The plane flew on normally, smoothly.

All right, he thought. Now. Now to do this thing. He turned and reached for the headset, slid it from the pilot's head, one eye on the plane, waiting for it to dive. The headset came easily, but the microphone switch at the pilot's belt was jammed in and he had to pull to get it loose. When he pulled, his elbow bumped the wheel and pushed it in and the plane started down in a shallow dive. Brian grabbed the wheel and pulled it back, too hard again, and the plane went through another series of stomach-wrenching swoops up and down before he could get it under control.

When things had settled again he pulled at the mike cord once more and at last jerked the cord free. It took him another second or two to place the headset on his own head and position the small microphone tube in front of his mouth. He had seen the pilot use it, had seen him depress the switch at his belt, so Brian pushed the switch in and blew into the mike.

He heard the sound of his breath in the headset. "Hello! Is there anybody listening on this? Hello . . . "

He repeated it two or three times and then waited but heard nothing except his own breathing.

Panic came then. He had been afraid, had been stopped with the terror of what was happening, but now panic came and he began to scream into the microphone, scream over and over.

"Help! Somebody help me! I'm in this plane and don't know . . . don't know . . . don't know . . . "

And he started crying with the screams, crying and slamming his hands against the wheel of the plane, causing it to jerk down, then back up. But again, he heard nothing but the sound of his own sobs in the microphone, his own screams mocking him, coming back into his ears.

The microphone. Awareness cut into him. He had used a CB radio in his uncle's pickup once. You had to turn the mike switch off to hear anybody else. He reached to his belt and released the switch.

For a second all he heard was the *whusssh* of the empty air waves. Then, through the noise and static he heard a voice.

"Whoever is calling on this radio net, I repeat, release your mike switch—you are covering me. You are covering me. Over."

It stopped and Brian hit his mike switch. "I hear you! I hear you. This is me . . . !" He released the switch.

"Roger. I have you now." The voice was very faint and breaking up. "Please state your difficulty and location. And say *over* to signal end of transmission. Over."

Please state my difficulty, Brian thought. God. My difficulty. "I am in a plane with a pilot who is—who has had a heart attack or something. He is—he can't fly. And I don't know how to fly. Help me. Help . . . " He turned his mike off without ending transmission properly.

There was a moment's hesitation before the answer. "Your signal is breaking up and I lost most of it. Understand . . . pilot . . . you can't fly. Correct? Over."

Brian could barely hear him now, heard mostly

noise and static. "That's right. I can't fly. The plane is flying now but I don't know how much longer. Over."

"... lost signal. Your location please. Flight number ... location ... ver."

"I don't know my flight number or location. I don't know anything. I told you that, over."

He waited now, waited but there was nothing. Once, for a second, he thought he heard a break in the noise, some part of a word, but it could have been static. Two, three minutes, ten minutes, the plane roared and Brian listened but heard no one. Then he hit the switch again.

"I do not know the flight number. My name is Brian Robeson and we left Hampton, New York headed for the Canadian oil fields to visit my father and I do not know how to fly an airplane and the pilot ..."

He let go of the mike. His voice was starting to rattle and he felt as if he might start screaming at any second. He took a deep breath. "If there is anybody listening who can help me fly a plane, please answer."

Again he released the mike but heard nothing but the hissing of noise in the headset. After half an hour of listening and repeating the cry for help he tore the headset off in frustration and threw it to the floor. It all seemed so hopeless. Even if he did get somebody, what could anybody do? Tell him to be careful?

All so hopeless.

He tried to figure out the dials again. He thought he might know which was speed—it was a lighted number that read 160—but he didn't know if that was actual miles an hour, or kilometers, or if it just meant how fast the plane was moving through the air and not over the ground. He knew airspeed was different from groundspeed but not by how much.

Parts of books he'd read about flying came to him. How wings worked, how the propellor pulled the plane through the sky. Simple things that wouldn't help him now.

Nothing could help him now.

An hour passed. He picked up the headset and tried again—it was, he knew, in the end all he had—but there was no answer. He felt like a prisoner, kept in a small cell that was hurtling through the sky at what he thought to be 160 miles an hour, headed—he didn't know where—just headed somewhere until...

There it was. Until what? Until he ran out of fuel. When the plane ran out of fuel it would go down.

Period.

Or he could pull the throttle out and make it go

down now. He had seen the pilot push the throttle in to increase speed. If he pulled the throttle back out, the engine would slow down and the plane would go down.

Those were his choices. He could wait for the plane to run out of gas and fall or he could push the throttle in and make it happen sooner. If he waited for the plane to run out of fuel he would go farther—but he did not know which way he was moving. When the pilot had jerked he had moved the plane, but Brian could not remember how much or if it had come back to its original course. Since he did not know the original course anyway and could only guess at which display might be the compass—the one reading 342—he did not know where he had been or where he was going, so it didn't make much difference if he went down now or waited.

Everything in him rebelled against stopping the engine and falling now. He had a vague feeling that he was wrong to keep heading as the plane was heading, a feeling that he might be going off in the wrong direction, but he could not bring himself to stop the engine and fall. Now he was safe, or safer than if he went down—the plane was flying, he was still breathing. When the engine stopped he would go down.

So he left the plane running, holding altitude, and

kept trying the radio. He worked out a system. Every ten minutes by the small clock built into the dashboard he tried the radio with a simple message: "I need help. Is there anybody listening to me?"

In the times between transmissions he tried to prepare himself for what he knew was coming. When he ran out of fuel the plane would start down. He guessed that without the propellor pulling he would have to push the nose down to keep the plane flying—he thought he may have read that somewhere, or it just came to him. Either way it made sense. He would have to push the nose down to keep flying speed and then, just before he hit, he would have to pull the nose back up to slow the plane as much as possible.

It all made sense. Glide down, then slow the plane and hit.

Hit.

He would have to find a clearing as he went down. The problem with that was he hadn't seen one clearing since they'd started flying over the forest. Some swamps, but they had trees scattered through them. No roads, no trails, no clearings.

Just the lakes, and it came to him that he would have to use a lake for landing. If he went down in the trees he was certain to die. The trees would tear the plane to pieces as it went into them.

He would have to come down in a lake. No. On

the edge of a lake. He would have to come down near the edge of a lake and try to slow the plane as much as possible just before he hit the water.

Easy to say, he thought, hard to do.

Easy say, hard do. Easy say, hard do. It became a chant that beat with the engine. Easy say, hard do.

Impossible to do.

He repeated the radio call seventeen times at the ten-minute intervals, working on what he would do between transmissions. Once more he reached over to the pilot and touched him on the face, but the skin was cold, hard cold, death cold, and Brian turned back to the dashboard. He did what he could, tightened his seatbelt, positioned himself, rehearsed mentally again and again what his procedure should be.

When the plane ran out of gas he should hold the nose down and head for the nearest lake and try to fly the plane kind of onto the water. That's how he thought of it. Kind of fly the plane onto the water. And just before it hit he should pull back on the wheel and slow the plane down to reduce the impact.

Over and over his mind ran the picture of how it would go. The plane running out of gas, flying the plane onto the water, the crash—from pictures he'd seen on television. He tried to visualize it. He tried to be ready.

But between the seventeenth and eighteenth radio transmissions, without a warning, the engine coughed, roared violently for a second and died. There was sudden silence, cut only by the sound of the windmilling propellor and the wind past the cockpit.

Brian pushed the nose of the plane down and threw up.

3

GOING TO DIE, Brian thought. Going to die, gonna die, gonna die—his whole brain screamed it in the sudden silence.

Gonna die.

He wiped his mouth with the back of his arm and held the nose down. The plane went into a glide, a very fast glide that ate altitude, and suddenly there weren't any lakes. All he'd seen since they started flying over the forest was lakes and now they were gone. Gone. Out in front, far away at the horizon, he could see lots of them, off to the right and left more of them, glittering blue in the late afternoon sun.

But he needed one right in front. He desperately

needed a lake right in front of the plane and all he saw through the windshield were trees, green death trees. If he had to turn—if he had to turn he didn't think he could keep the plane flying. His stomach tightened into a series of rolling knots and his breath came in short bursts...

There!

Not quite in front but slightly to the right he saw a lake. L-shaped, with rounded corners, and the plane was nearly aimed at the long part of the L, coming from the bottom and heading to the top. Just a tiny bit to the right. He pushed the right rudder pedal gently and the nose moved over.

But the turn cost him speed and now the lake was above the nose. He pulled back on the wheel slightly and the nose came up. This caused the plane to slow dramatically and almost seem to stop and wallow in the air. The controls became very loose-feeling and frightened Brian, making him push the wheel back in. This increased the speed a bit but filled the windshield once more with nothing but trees, and put the lake well above the nose and out of reach.

For a space of three or four seconds things seemed to hang, almost to stop. The plane was flying, but so slowly, so slowly... it would never reach the lake. Brian looked out to the side and saw a small pond and at the edge of the pond some large animal—he thought a moose—standing out in the water. All so still looking, so stopped, the pond and the moose and the trees, as he slid over them now only three or four hundred feet off the ground—all like a picture.

Then everything happened at once. Trees suddenly took on detail, filled his whole field of vision with green, and he knew he would hit and die, would die, but his luck held and just as he was to hit he came into an open lane, a channel of fallen trees, a wide place leading to the lake.

The plane, committed now to landing, to crashing, fell into the wide place like a stone, and Brian eased back on the wheel and braced himself for the crash. But there was a tiny bit of speed left and when he pulled on the wheel the nose came up and he saw in front the blue of the lake and at that instant the plane hit the trees.

There was a great wrenching as the wings caught the pines at the side of the clearing and broke back, ripping back just outside the main braces. Dust and dirt blew off the floor into his face so hard he thought there must have been some kind of explosion. He was momentarily blinded and slammed forward in the seat, smashing his head on the wheel.

Then a wild crashing sound, ripping of metal, and

the plane rolled to the right and blew through the trees, out over the water and down, down to slam into the lake, skip once on water as hard as concrete, water that tore the windshield out and shattered the side windows, water that drove him back into the seat. Somebody was screaming, screaming as the plane drove down into the water. Someone screamed tight animal screams of fear and pain and he did not know that it was his sound, that he roared against the water that took him and the plane still deeper, down in the water. He saw nothing but sensed blue, cold blue-green, and he raked at the seatbelt catch, tore his nails loose on one hand. He ripped at it until it released and somehow—the water trying to kill him, to end him—somehow he pulled himself out of the shattered front window and clawed up into the blue, felt something hold him back, felt his windbreaker tear and he was free. Tearing free. Ripping free.

But so far! So far to the surface and his lungs could not do this thing, could not hold and were through, and he sucked water, took a great pull of water that would—finally—win, finally take him, and his head broke into light and he vomited and swam, pulling without knowing what he was, what he was doing. Without knowing anything. Pulling until his hands caught at weeds and muck, pulling and screaming until his hands caught at last in grass and brush and he felt his chest on land, felt his face in the coarse blades of grass and he stopped, everything stopped. A color came that he had never seen before, a color that exploded in his mind with the pain and he was gone, gone from it all, spiraling out into the world, spiraling out into nothing.

Nothing.

4

THE MEMORY was like a knife cutting into him. Slicing deep into him with hate.

The Secret.

He had been riding his ten-speed with a friend named Terry. They had been taking a run on a bike trail and decided to come back a different way, a way that took them past the Amber Mall. Brian remembered everything in incredible detail. Remembered the time on the bank clock in the mall, flashing 3:31, then the temperature, 82, and the date. All the numbers were part of the memory, all of his life was part of the memory.

Terry had just turned to smile at him about something and Brian looked over Terry's head and saw her.

His mother.

She was sitting in a station wagon, a strange wagon. He saw her and she did not see him. Brian was going to wave or call out, but something stopped him. There was a man in the car.

Short blond hair, the man had. Wearing some kind of white pullover tennis shirt.

Brian saw this and more, saw the Secret and saw more later, but the memory came in pieces, came in scenes like this—Terry smiling, Brian looking over his head to see the station wagon and his mother sitting with the man, the time and temperature clock, the front wheel of his bike, the short blond hair of the man, the white shirt of the man, the hot-hate slices of the memory were exact.

The Secret.

Brian opened his eyes and screamed.

For seconds he did not know where he was, only that the crash was still happening and he was going to die, and he screamed until his breath was gone.

Then silence, filled with sobs as he pulled in air, half crying. How could it be so quiet? Moments ago there was nothing but noise, crashing and tearing, screaming, now quiet.

Some birds were singing.

How could birds be singing?

His legs felt wet and he raised up on his hands and looked back down at them. They were in the lake. Strange. They went down into the water. He tried to move, but pain hammered into him and made his breath shorten into gasps and he stopped, his legs still in the water.

Pain.

Memory.

He turned again and sun came across the water, late sun, cut into his eyes and made him turn away.

It was over then. The crash.

He was alive.

The crash is over and I am alive, he thought. Then his eyes closed and he lowered his head for minutes that seemed longer. When he opened them again it was evening and some of the sharp pain had abated—there were many dull aches—and the crash came back to him fully.

Into the trees and out onto the lake. The plane had crashed and sunk in the lake and he had somehow pulled free.

He raised himself and crawled out of the water, grunting with the pain of movement. His legs were on fire, and his forehead felt as if somebody had been pounding on it with a hammer, but he could move. He pulled his legs out of the lake and crawled on his hands and knees until he was away from the wet-soft shore and near a small stand of brush of some kind.

Then he went down, only this time to rest, to save something of himself. He lay on his side and put his head on his arm and closed his eyes because that was all he could do now, all he could think of being able to do. He closed his eyes and slept, dreamless, deep and down.

There was almost no light when he opened his eyes again. The darkness of night was thick and for a moment he began to panic again. To see, he thought. To see is everything. And he could not see. But he turned his head without moving his body and saw that across the lake the sky was a light gray, that the sun was starting to come up, and he remembered that it had been evening when he went to sleep.

"Must be morning now..." He mumbled it, almost in a hoarse whisper. As the thickness of sleep left him the world came back.

He was still in pain, all-over pain. His legs were cramped and drawn up, tight and aching, and his back hurt when he tried to move. Worst was a keening throb in his head that pulsed with every beat of his heart. It seemed that the whole crash had happened to his head.

He rolled on his back and felt his sides and his legs, moving things slowly. He rubbed his arms; nothing seemed to be shattered or even sprained all that badly. When he was nine he had plowed his small dirt bike into a parked car and broken his ankle, had to wear a cast for eight weeks, and there was nothing now like that. Nothing broken. Just battered around a bit.

His forehead felt massively swollen to the touch, almost like a mound out over his eyes, and it was so tender that when his fingers grazed it he nearly cried. But there was nothing he could do about it and, like the rest of him, it seemed to be bruised more than broken.

I'm alive, he thought. I'm alive. It could have been different. There could have been death. I could have been done.

Like the pilot, he thought suddenly. The pilot in the plane, down into the water, down into the blue water strapped in the seat . . .

He sat up—or tried to. The first time he fell back. But on the second attempt, grunting with the effort, he managed to come to a sitting position and scrunched sideways until his back was against a small tree where he sat facing the lake, watching the sky get lighter and lighter with the coming dawn.

His clothes were wet and clammy and there was a faint chill. He pulled the torn remnants of his windbreaker, pieces really, around his shoulders and tried to hold what heat his body could find. He could not think, could not make thought patterns work right. Things seemed to go back and forth between reality and imagination—except that it was all reality. One second he seemed only to have imagined that there was a plane crash, that he had fought out of the sinking plane and swum to shore; that it had all happened to some other person or in a movie playing in his mind. Then he would feel his clothes, wet and cold, and his forehead would slash a pain through his thoughts and he would know it was real, that it had really happened. But all in a haze, all in a haze-world. So he sat and stared at the lake, felt the pain come and go in waves, and watched the sun come over the end of the lake.

It took an hour, perhaps two—he could not measure time yet and didn't care—for the sun to get halfway up. With it came some warmth, small bits of it at first, and with the heat came clouds of insects—thick, swarming hordes of mosquitos that flocked to his body, made a living coat on his exposed skin, clogged his nostrils when he inhaled, poured into his mouth when he opened it to take a breath.

It was not possibly believable. Not this. He had

come through the crash, but the insects were not possible. He coughed them up, spat them out, sneezed them out, closed his eyes and kept brushing his face, slapping and crushing them by the dozens, by the hundreds. But as soon as he cleared a place, as soon as he killed them, more came, thick, whining, buzzing masses of them. Mosquitos and some small black flies he had never seen before. All biting, chewing, taking from him.

In moments his eyes were swollen shut and his face puffy and round to match his battered forehead. He pulled the torn pieces of his windbreaker over his head and tried to shelter in it but the jacket was full of rips and it didn't work. In desperation he pulled his T-shirt up to cover his face, but that exposed the skin of his lower back and the mosquitos and flies attacked the new soft flesh of his back so viciously that he pulled the shirt down.

In the end he sat with the windbreaker pulled up, brushed with his hands and took it, almost crying in frustration and agony. There was nothing left to do. And when the sun was fully up and heating him directly, bringing steam off of his wet clothes and bathing him with warmth, the mosquitos and flies disappeared. Almost that suddenly. One minute he was sitting in the middle of a swarm; the next, they were gone and the sun was on him.

Vampires, he thought. Apparently they didn't like

the deep of night, perhaps because it was too cool, and they couldn't take the direct sunlight. But in that gray time in the morning, when it began to get warm and before the sun was full up and hot—he couldn't believe them. Never, in all the reading, in the movies he had watched on television about the outdoors, never once had they mentioned the mosquitos or flies. All they ever showed on the naturalist shows was beautiful scenery or animals jumping around having a good time. Nobody ever mentioned mosquitos and flies.

"Unnnhhh." He pulled himself up to stand against the tree and stretched, bringing new aches and pains. His back muscles must have been hurt as well—they almost seemed to tear when he stretched—and while the pain in his forehead seemed to be abating somewhat, just trying to stand made him weak enough to nearly collapse.

The backs of his hands were puffy and his eyes were almost swollen shut from the mosquitos, and he saw everything through a narrow squint.

Not that there was much to see, he thought, scratching the bites. In front of him lay the lake, blue and deep. He had a sudden picture of the plane, sunk in the lake, down and down in the blue with the pilot's body still strapped in the seat, his hair waving...

He shook his head. More pain. That wasn't something to think about.

He looked at his surroundings again. The lake stretched out slightly below him. He was at the base of the L, looking up the long part with the short part out to his right. In the morning light and calm the water was absolutely, perfectly still. He could see the reflections of the trees at the other end of the lake. Upside down in the water they seemed almost like another forest, an upside-down forest to match the real one. As he watched, a large bird—he thought it looked like a crow but it seemed larger—flew from the top, real forest, and the reflection-bird matched it, both flying out over the water.

Everything was green, so green it went into him. The forest was largely made up of pines and spruce, with stands of some low brush smeared here and there and thick grass and some other kind of very small brush all over. He couldn't identify most of it—except the evergreens—and some leafy trees he thought might be aspen. He'd seen pictures of aspens in the mountains on television. The country around the lake was moderately hilly, but the hills were small—almost hummocks—and there were very few rocks except to his left. There lay a rocky ridge that stuck out overlooking the lake, about twenty feet high.

If the plane had come down a little to the left it would have hit the rocks and never made the lake. He would have been smashed.

Destroyed.

The word came. I would have been destroyed and torn and smashed. Driven into the rocks and destroyed.

Luck, he thought. I have luck, I had good luck there. But he knew that was wrong. If he had had good luck his parents wouldn't have divorced because of the Secret and he wouldn't have been flying with a pilot who had a heart attack and he wouldn't be here where he had to have good luck to keep from being destroyed.

If you keep walking back from good luck, he thought, you'll come to bad luck.

He shook his head again—wincing. Another thing not to think about.

The rocky ridge was rounded and seemed to be of some kind of sandstone with bits of darker stone layered and stuck into it. Directly across the lake from it, at the inside corner of the L, was a mound of sticks and mud rising up out of the water a good eight or ten feet. At first Brian couldn't place it but knew that he somehow knew what it was—had seen it in films. Then a small brown head popped to the surface of the water near the mound and began swimming off down the short leg of the L leaving a V of ripples behind and he remembered where he'd seen it. It was a beaver house, called a beaver lodge in a special he'd seen on the public channel.

A fish jumped. Not a large fish, but it made a big splash near the beaver, and as if by a signal there were suddenly little splops all over the sides of the lake—along the shore—as fish began jumping. Hundreds of them, jumping and slapping the water. Brian watched them for a time, still in the half-daze, still not thinking well. The scenery was very pretty, he thought, and there were new things to look at, but it was all a green and blue blur and he was used to the gray and black of the city, the sounds of the city. Traffic, people talking, sounds all the time—the hum and whine of the city.

Here, at first, it was silent, or he thought it was silent, but when he started to listen, really listen, he heard thousands of things. Hisses and blurks, small sounds, birds singing, hum of insects, splashes from the fish jumping—there was great noise here, but a noise he did not know, and the colors were new to him, and the colors and noise mixed in his mind to make a green-blue blur that he could hear, hear as a hissing pulse-sound and he was still tired.

So tired.

So awfully tired, and standing had taken a lot of

energy somehow, had drained him. He supposed he was still in some kind of shock from the crash and there was still the pain, the dizziness, the strange feeling.

He found another tree, a tall pine with no branches until the top, and sat with his back against it looking down on the lake with the sun warming him, and in a few moments he scrunched down and was asleep again.

5

HIS EYES snapped open, hammered open, and there were these things about himself that he knew, instantly.

He was unbelievably, viciously thirsty. His mouth was dry and tasted foul and sticky. His lips were cracked and felt as if they were bleeding and if he did not drink some water soon he felt that he would wither up and die. Lots of water. All the water he could find.

He knew the thirst and felt the burn on his face. It was midafternoon and the sun had come over him and cooked him while he slept and his face was on fire, would blister, would peel. Which did not help the thirst, made it much worse. He stood, using the tree to pull himself up because there was still some pain and much stiffness, and looked down at the lake.

It was water. But he did not know if he could drink it. Nobody had ever told him if you could or could not drink lakes. There was also the thought of the pilot.

Down in the blue with the plane, strapped in, the body . . .

Awful, he thought. But the lake was blue, and wet-looking, and his mouth and throat raged with the thirst and he did not know where there might be another form of water he could drink. Besides, he had probably swallowed a ton of it while he was swimming out of the plane and getting to shore. In the movies they always showed the hero finding a clear spring with pure sweet water to drink but in the movies they didn't have plane wrecks and swollen foreheads and aching bodies and thirst that tore at the hero until he couldn't think.

Brian took small steps down the bank to the lake. Along the edge there were thick grasses and the water looked a little murky and there were small things swimming in the water, small bugs. But there was a log extending about twenty feet out into the water of the lake—a beaver drop from some time before—with old limbs sticking up, almost like handles. He balanced on the log, holding himself up with the limbs, and teetered out past the weeds and murky water.

When he was out where the water was clear and he could see no bugs swimming he kneeled on the log to drink. A sip, he thought, still worrying about the lake water—I'll just take a sip.

But when he brought a cupped hand to his mouth and felt the cold lake water trickle past his cracked lips and over his tongue he could not stop. He had never, not even on long bike trips in the hot summer, been this thirsty. It was as if the water were more than water, as if the water had become all of life, and he could not stop. He stooped and put his mouth to the lake and drank and drank, pulling it deep and swallowing great gulps of it. He drank until his stomach was swollen, until he nearly fell off the log with it, then he rose and stagger-tripped his way back to the bank.

Where he was immediately sick and threw up most of the water. But his thirst was gone and the water seemed to reduce the pain in his head as well—although the sunburn still cooked his face.

"So." He almost jumped with the word, spoken aloud. It seemed so out of place, the sound. He tried it again. "So. So. So here I am."

And there it is, he thought. For the first time since

the crash his mind started to work, his brain triggered and he began thinking.

Here I am—and where is that?

Where am I?

He pulled himself once more up the bank to the tall tree without branches and sat again with his back against the rough bark. It was hot now, but the sun was high and to his rear and he sat in the shade of the tree in relative comfort. There were things to sort out.

Here I am and that is nowhere. With his mind opened and thoughts happening it all tried to come in with a rush, all of what had occurred and he could not take it. The whole thing turned into a confused jumble that made no sense. So he fought it down and tried to take one thing at a time.

He had been flying north to visit his father for a couple of months, in the summer, and the pilot had had a heart attack and had died, and the plane had crashed somewhere in the Canadian north woods but he did not know how far they had flown or in what direction or where he was...

Slow down, he thought. Slow down more.

My name is Brian Robeson and I am thirteen years old and I am alone in the north woods of Canada.

All right, he thought, that's simple enough.

I was flying to visit my father and the plane crashed and sank in a lake.

There, keep it that way. Short thoughts.

I do not know where I am.

Which doesn't mean much. More to the point, *they* do not know where I am—*they* meaning anybody who might be wanting to look for me. The searchers.

They would look for him, look for the plane. His father and mother would be frantic. They would tear the world apart to find him. Brian had seen searches on the news, seen movies about lost planes. When a plane went down they mounted extensive searches and almost always they found the plane within a day or two. Pilots all filed flight plans—a detailed plan for where and when they were going to fly, with all the courses explained. They would come, they would look for him. The searchers would get government planes and cover both sides of the flight plan filed by the pilot and search until they found him.

Maybe even today. They might come today. This was the second day after the crash. No. Brian frowned. Was it the first day or the second day? They had gone down in the afternoon and he had spent the whole night out cold. So this was the first real day. But they could still come today. They would have started the search immediately when Brian's plane did not arrive.

Yeah, they would probably come today.

Probably come in here with amphibious planes, small bushplanes with floats that could land right here on the lake and pick him up and take him home.

Which home? The father home or the mother home. He stopped the thinking. It didn't matter. Either on to his dad or back to his mother. Either way he would probably be home by late night or early morning, home where he could sit down and eat a large, cheesy, juicy burger with tomatoes and double fries with ketchup and a thick chocolate shake.

And there came hunger.

Brian rubbed his stomach. The hunger had been there but something else—fear, pain—had held it down. Now, with the thought of the burger, the emptiness roared at him. He could not believe the hunger, had never felt it this way. The lake water had filled his stomach but left it hungry, and now it demanded food, screamed for food.

And there was, he thought, absolutely nothing to eat.

Nothing.

What did they do in the movies when they got

stranded like this? Oh, yes, the hero usually found some kind of plant that he knew was good to eat and that took care of it. Just ate the plant until he was full or used some kind of cute trap to catch an animal and cook it over a slick little fire and pretty soon he had a full eight-course meal.

The trouble, Brian thought, looking around, was that all he could see was grass and brush. There was nothing obvious to eat and aside from about a million birds and the beaver he hadn't seen animals to trap and cook, and even if he got one somehow he didn't have any matches so he couldn't have a fire...

Nothing.

It kept coming back to that. He had nothing.

Well, almost nothing. As a matter of fact, he thought, I don't know what I've got or haven't got. Maybe I should try and figure out just how I stand. It will give me something to do—keep me from thinking of food. Until they come to find me.

Brian had once had an English teacher, a guy named Perpich, who was always talking about being positive, thinking positive, staying on top of things. That's how Perpich had put it—stay positive and stay on top of things. Brian thought of him now—wondered how to stay positive and stay on top of this. All Perpich would say is that I have to get motivated. He was always telling kids to get motivated.

Brian changed position so he was sitting on his knees. He reached into his pockets and took out everything he had and laid it on the grass in front of him.

It was pitiful enough. A quarter, three dimes, a nickel, and two pennies. A fingernail clipper. A bill-fold with a twenty dollar bill—"In case you get stranded at the airport in some small town and have to buy food," his mother had said—and some odd pieces of paper.

And on his belt, somehow still there, the hatchet his mother had given him. He had forgotten it and now reached around and took it out and put it in the grass. There was a touch of rust already forming on the cutting edge of the blade and he rubbed it off with his thumb.

That was it.

He frowned. No, wait—if he was going to play the game, might as well play it right. Perpich would tell him to quit messing around. Get motivated. Look at *all* of it, Robeson.

He had on a pair of good tennis shoes, now almost dry. And socks. And jeans and underwear and a thin leather belt and a T-shirt with a windbreaker so torn it hung on him in tatters.

And a watch. He had a digital watch still on his wrist but it was broken from the crash—the little screen blank—and he took it off and almost threw it away but stopped the hand motion and lay the watch on the grass with the rest of it.

There. That was it.

No, wait. One other thing. Those were all the things he had, but he also had himself. Perpich used to drum that into them—"You are your most valuable asset. Don't forget that. *You* are the best thing you have."

Brian looked around again. I wish you were here, Perpich. I'm hungry and I'd trade everything I have for a hamburger.

"I'm hungry." He said it aloud. In normal tones at first, then louder and louder until he was yelling it. "I'm hungry, I'm hungry, I'm hungry!"

When he stopped there was sudden silence, not just from him but the clicks and blurps and bird sounds of the forest as well. The noise of his voice had startled everything and it was quiet. He looked around, listened with his mouth open, and realized that in all his life he had never heard silence before. Complete silence. There had always been some sound, some kind of sound.

It lasted only a few seconds, but it was so intense that it seemed to become part of him. Nothing.

There was no sound. Then the bird started again, and some kind of buzzing insect, and then a chattering and a cawing, and soon there was the same background of sound.

Which left him still hungry.

Of course, he thought, putting the coins and the rest back in his pocket and the hatchet in his belt—of course if they come tonight or even if they take as long as tomorrow the hunger is no big thing. People have gone for many days without food as long as they've got water. Even if they don't come until late tomorrow I'll be all right. Lose a little weight, maybe, but the first hamburger and a malt and fries will bring it right back.

A mental picture of a hamburger, the way they showed it in the television commercials, thundered into his thoughts. Rich colors, the meat juicy and hot...

He pushed the picture away. So even if they didn't find him until tomorrow, he thought, he would be all right. He had plenty of water, although he wasn't sure if it was good and clean or not.

He sat again by the tree, his back against it. There was a thing bothering him. He wasn't quite sure what it was but it kept chewing at the edge of his thoughts. Something about the plane and the pilot that would change things...

Ahh, there it was—the moment when the pilot

had his heart attack his right foot had jerked down on the rudder pedal and the plane had slewed sideways. What did that mean? Why did that keep coming into his thinking that way, nudging and pushing?

It means, a voice in his thoughts said, that they might not be coming for you tonight or even tomorrow. When the pilot pushed the rudder pedal the plane had jerked to the side and assumed a new course. Brian could not remember how much it had pulled around, but it wouldn't have had to be much because after that, with the pilot dead, Brian had flown for hour after hour on the new course.

Well away from the flight plan the pilot had filed. Many hours, at maybe 160 miles an hour. Even if it was only a little off course, with that speed and time Brian might now be sitting several hundred miles off to the side of the recorded flight plan.

And they would probably search most heavily at first along the flight plan course. They might go out to the side a little, but he could easily be three, four hundred miles to the side. He could not know, could not think of how far he might have flown wrong because he didn't know the original course and didn't know how much they had pulled sideways.

Quite a bit—that's how he remembered it. Quite a jerk to the side. It pulled his head over sharply when the plane had swung around.

They might not find him for two or three days.

He felt his heartbeat increase as the fear started. The thought was there but he fought it down for a time, pushed it away, then it exploded out.

They might not find him for a long time.

And the next thought was there as well, that they might never find him, but that was panic and he fought it down and tried to stay positive. They searched hard when a plane went down, they used many men and planes and they would go to the side, they would know he was off from the flight path, he had talked to the man on the radio, they would somehow know...

It would be all right.

They would find him. Maybe not tomorrow, but soon. Soon. Soon.

They would find him soon.

Gradually, like sloshing oil his thoughts settled back and the panic was gone. Say they didn't come for two days—no, say they didn't come for three days, even push that to four days—he could live with that. He would have to live with that. He didn't want to think of them taking longer. But say four days. He had to do something. He couldn't just sit at the bottom of this tree and stare down at the lake for four days.

And nights. He was in deep woods and didn't have any matches, couldn't make a fire. There were large things in the woods. There were wolves, he thought, and bears—other things. In the dark he would be in the open here, just sitting at the bottom of a tree.

He looked around suddenly, felt the hair on the back of his neck go up. Things might be looking at him right now, waiting for him—waiting for dark so they could move in and take him.

He fingered the hatchet at his belt. It was the only weapon he had, but it was something.

He had to have some kind of shelter. No, make that more: He had to have some kind of shelter and he had to have something to eat.

He pulled himself to his feet and jerked the back of his shirt down before the mosquitos could get at it. He had to do something to help himself.

I have to get motivated, he thought, remembering Perpich. Right now I'm all I've got. I have to do something.

6

Two Years before he and Terry had been fooling around down near the park, where the city seemed to end for a time and the trees grew thick and came down to the small river that went through the park. It was thick there and seemed kind of wild, and they had been joking and making things up and they pretended that they were lost in the woods and talked in the afternoon about what they would do. Of course they figured they'd have all sorts of goodies like a gun and a knife and fishing gear and matches so they could hunt and fish and have a fire.

I wish you were here, Terry, he thought. With a gun and a knife and some matches...

In the park that time they had decided the best

shelter was a lean-to and Brian set out now to make one up. Maybe cover it with grass or leaves or sticks, he thought, and he started to go down to the lake again, where there were some willows he could cut down for braces. But it struck him that he ought to find a good place for the lean-to and so he decided to look around first. He wanted to stay near the lake because he thought the plane, even deep in the water, might show up to somebody flying over and he didn't want to diminish any chance he might have of being found.

His eyes fell upon the stone ridge to his left and he thought at first he should build his shelter against the stone. But before that he decided to check out the far side of the ridge and that was where he got lucky.

Using the sun and the fact that it rose in the east and set in the west, he decided that the far side was the northern side of the ridge. At one time in the far past it had been scooped by something, probably a glacier, and this scooping had left a kind of sideways bowl, back in under a ledge. It wasn't very deep, not a cave, but it was smooth and made a perfect roof and he could almost stand in under the ledge. He had to hold his head slightly tipped forward at the front to keep it from hitting the top. Some of the rock that had been scooped out had also been pulverized by the glacial action, turned into sand, and now made a small sand beach that went down to the edge of the water in front and to the right of the overhang.

It was his first good luck.

No, he thought. He had good luck in the landing. But this was good luck as well, luck he needed.

All he had to do was wall off part of the bowl and leave an opening as a doorway and he would have a perfect shelter—much stronger than a lean-to and dry because the overhang made a watertight roof.

He crawled back in, under the ledge, and sat. The sand was cool here in the shade, and the coolness felt wonderful to his face, which was already starting to blister and get especially painful on his forehead, with the blisters on top of the swelling.

He was also still weak. Just the walk around the back of the ridge and the slight climb over the top had left his legs rubbery. It felt good to sit for a bit under the shade of the overhang in the cool sand.

And now, he thought, if I just had something to eat.

Anything.

When he had rested a bit he went back down to the lake and drank a couple of swallows of water. He wasn't all that thirsty but he thought the water might help to take the edge off his hunger. It didn't.

Somehow the cold lake water actually made it worse, sharpened it.

He thought of dragging in wood to make a wall on part of the overhang, and picked up one piece to pull up, but his arms were too weak and he knew then that it wasn't just the crash and injury to his body and head, it was also that he was weak from hunger.

He would have to find something to eat. Before he did anything else he would have to have something to eat.

But what?

Brian leaned against the rock and stared out at the lake. What, in all of this, was there to eat? He was so used to having food just be there, just always being there. When he was hungry he went to the icebox, or to the store, or sat down at a meal his mother cooked.

Oh, he thought, remembering a meal now—oh. It was the last Thanksgiving, last year, the last Thanksgiving they had as a family before his mother demanded the divorce and his father moved out in the following January. Brian already knew the Secret but did not know it would cause them to break up and thought it might work out, the Secret that his father still did not know but that he would try to tell him. When he saw him.

The meal had been turkey and they cooked it in the back yard in the barbecue over charcoal with the lid down tight. His father had put hickory chips on the charcoal and the smell of the cooking turkey and the hickory smoke had filled the yard. When his father took the lid off, smiling, the smell that had come out was unbelievable, and when they sat to eat the meat was wet with juice and rich and had the taste of the smoke in it...

He had to stop this. His mouth was full of saliva and his stomach was twisting and growling.

What was there to eat?

What had he read or seen that told him about food in the wilderness? Hadn't there been something? A show, yes, a show on television about air force pilots and some kind of course they took. A survival course. All right, he had the show coming into his thoughts now. The pilots had to live in the desert. They put them in the desert down in Arizona or someplace and they had to live for a week. They had to find food and water for a week.

For water they had made a sheet of plastic into a dew-gathering device and for food they ate lizards.

That was it. Of course Brian had lots of water and there weren't too many lizards in the Canadian woods, that he knew. One of the pilots had used a watch crystal as a magnifying glass to focus the sun and start a fire so they didn't have to eat the lizards raw. But Brian had a digital watch, without a crystal, broken at that. So the show didn't help him much.

Wait, there was one thing. One of the pilots, a woman, had found some kind of beans on a bush and she had used them with her lizard meat to make a little stew in a tin can she had found. Bean lizard stew. There weren't any beans here, but there must be berries. There had to be berry bushes around. Sure, the woods were full of berry bushes. That's what everybody always said. Well, he'd actually never heard anybody *say* it. But he felt that it should be true.

There must be berry bushes.

He stood and moved out into the sand and looked up at the sun. It was still high. He didn't know what time it must be. At home it would be one or two if the sun were that high. At home at one or two his mother would be putting away the lunch dishes and getting ready for her exercise class. No, that would have been yesterday. Today she would be going to see *him*. Today was Thursday and she always went to see him on Thursdays. Wednesday was the exercise class and Thursdays she went to see him. Hot little jets of hate worked into his thoughts, pushed once, moved back. If his mother hadn't begun to see *him* and forced the divorce, Brian wouldn't be here now.

He shook his head. Had to stop that kind of thinking. The sun was still high and that meant that he had some time before darkness to find berries. He didn't want to be away from his—he almost thought of it as home—shelter when it came to be dark.

He didn't want to be anywhere in the woods when it came to be dark. And he didn't want to get lost—which was a real problem. All he knew in the world was the lake in front of him and the hill at his back and the ridge—if he lost sight of them there was a really good chance that he would get turned around and not find his way back.

So he had to look for berry bushes, but keep the lake or the rock ridge in sight at all times.

He looked up the lake shore, to the north. For a good distance, perhaps two hundred yards, it was fairly clear. There were tall pines, the kind with no limbs until very close to the top, with a gentle breeze sighing in them, but not too much low brush. Two hundred yards up there seemed to be a belt of thick, lower brush starting—about ten or twelve feet high—and that formed a wall he could not see through. It seemed to go on around the lake, thick and lushly green, but he could not be sure.

If there were berries they would be in that brush, he felt, and as long as he stayed close to the lake, so he could keep the water on his right and know it was there, he wouldn't get lost. When he was done or found berries, he thought, he would just turn around so the water was on his left and walk back until he came to the ridge and his shelter.

Simple. Keep it simple. I am Brian Robeson. I have been in a plane crash. I am going to find some food. I am going to find berries.

He walked slowly—still a bit pained in his joints and weak from hunger—up along the side of the lake. The trees were full of birds singing ahead of him in the sun. Some he knew, some he didn't. He saw a robin, and some kind of sparrows, and a flock of reddish orange birds with thick beaks. Twenty or thirty of them were sitting in one of the pines. They made much noise and flew away ahead of him when he walked under the tree. He watched them fly, their color a bright slash in solid green, and in this way he found the berries. The birds landed in some taller willow type of undergrowth with wide leaves and started jumping and making noise. At first he was too far away to see what they were doing, but their color drew him and he moved toward them, keeping the lake in sight on his right, and when he got closer he saw they were eating berries.

He could not believe it was that easy. It was as if the birds had taken him right to the berries. The slender branches went up about twenty feet and were heavy, drooping with clusters of bright red berries. They were half as big as grapes but hung in bunches much like grapes and when Brian saw them, glistening red in the sunlight, he almost yelled.

His pace quickened and he was in them in moments, scattering the birds, grabbing branches, stripping them to fill his mouth with berries.

He almost spit them out. It wasn't that they were bitter so much as that they lacked any sweetness, had a tart flavor that left his mouth dry feeling. And they were like cherries in that they had large pits, which made them hard to chew. But there was such a hunger on him, such an emptiness, that he could not stop and kept stripping branches and eating berries by the handful, grabbing and jamming them into his mouth and swallowing them pits and all.

He could not stop and when, at last, his stomach was full he was still hungry. Two days without food must have shrunken his stomach, but the drive of hunger was still there. Thinking of the birds, and how they would come back into the berries when he left, he made a carrying pouch of his torn windbreaker and kept picking. Finally, when he judged he had close to four pounds in the jacket he stopped and went back to his camp by the ridge.

Now, he thought. Now I have some food and I

can do something about fixing this place up. He glanced at the sun and saw he had some time before dark.

If only I had matches, he thought, looking ruefully at the beach and lakeside. There was driftwood everywhere, not to mention dead and dry wood all over the hill and dead-dry branches hanging from every tree. All firewood. And no matches. How did they used to do it? he thought. Rub two sticks together?

He tucked the berries in the pouch back in under the overhang in the cool shade and found a couple of sticks. After ten minutes of rubbing he felt the sticks and they were almost cool to the touch. Not that, he thought. They didn't do fire that way. He threw the sticks down in disgust. So no fire. But he could still fix the shelter and make it—here the word "safer" came into his mind and he didn't know why—more livable.

Kind of close in it, he thought. I'll just close it in a bit.

He started dragging sticks up from the lake and pulling long dead branches down from the hill, never getting out of sight of the water and the ridge. With these he interlaced and wove a wall across the opening of the front of the rock. It took over two hours, and he had to stop several times because he still felt a bit weak and once because he felt a strange new twinge in his stomach. A tightening, rolling. Too many berries, he thought. I ate too many of them.

But it was gone soon and he kept working until the entire front of the overhang was covered save for a small opening at the right end, nearest the lake. The doorway was about three feet, and when he went in he found himself in a room almost fifteen feet long and eight to ten feet deep, with the rock wall sloping down at the rear.

"Good," he said, nodding. "Good . . ."

Outside the sun was going down, finally, and in the initial coolness the mosquitos came out again and clouded in on him. They were thick, terrible, if not quite as bad as in the morning, and he kept brushing them off his arms until he couldn't stand it and then dumped the berries and put the torn windbreaker on. At least the sleeves covered his arms.

Wrapped in the jacket, with darkness coming down fast now, he crawled back in under the rock and huddled and tried to sleep. He was deeply tired, and still aching some, but sleep was slow coming and did not finally settle in until the evening cool turned to night cool and the mosquitos slowed.

Then, at last, with his stomach turning on the berries, Brian went to sleep.

7

"MOTHER!"

He screamed it and he could not be sure if the scream awakened him or the pain in his stomach. His whole abdomen was torn with great rolling jolts of pain, pain that doubled him in the darkness of the little shelter, put him over and face down in the sand to moan again and again: "Mother, mother, mother . . ."

Never anything like this. Never. It was as if all the berries, all the pits had exploded in the center of him, ripped and tore at him. He crawled out the doorway and was sick in the sand, then crawled still farther and was sick again, vomiting and with terrible diarrhea for over an hour, for over a year he thought, until he was at last empty and drained of all strength.

Then he crawled back into the shelter and fell again to the sand but could not sleep at first, could do nothing except lie there, and his mind decided then to bring the memory up again.

In the mall. Every detail. His mother sitting in the station wagon with the man. And she had leaned across and kissed him, kissed the man with the short blond hair, and it was not a friendly peck, but a kiss. A kiss where she turned her head over at an angle and put her mouth against the mouth of the blond man who was not his father and kissed, mouth to mouth, and then brought her hand up to touch his cheek, his forehead, while they were kissing. And Brian saw it.

Saw this thing that his mother did with the blond man. Saw the kiss that became the Secret that his father still did not know about, know all about.

The memory was so real that he could feel the heat in the mall that day, could remember the worry that Terry would turn and see his mother, could remember the worry of the shame of it and then the memory faded and he slept again...

Awake.

For a second, perhaps two, he did not know

where he was, was still in his sleep somewhere. Then he saw the sun streaming in the open doorway of the shelter and heard the close, vicious whine of the mosquitos and knew. He brushed his face, completely welted now with two days of bites, completely covered with lumps and bites, and was surprised to find the swelling on his forehead had gone down a great deal, was almost gone.

The smell was awful and he couldn't place it. Then he saw the pile of berries at the back of the shelter and remembered the night and being sick.

"Too many of them," he said aloud. "Too many gut cherries . . ."

He crawled out of the shelter and found where he'd messed the sand. He used sticks and cleaned it as best he could, covered it with clean sand and went down to the lake to wash his hands and get a drink.

It was still very early, only just past true dawn, and the water was so calm he could see his reflection. It frightened him—the face was cut and bleeding, swollen and lumpy, the hair all matted, and on his forehead a cut had healed but left the hair stuck with blood and scab. His eyes were slits in the bites and he was—somehow—covered with dirt. He slapped the water with his hand to destroy the mirror.

Ugly, he thought. Very, very ugly.

And he was, at that moment, almost overcome with self-pity. He was dirty and starving and bitten and hurt and lonely and ugly and afraid and so completely miserable that it was like being in a pit, a dark, deep pit with no way out.

He sat back on the bank and fought crying. Then let it come and cried for perhaps three, four minutes. Long tears, self-pity tears, wasted tears.

He stood, went back to the water, and took small drinks. As soon as the cold water hit his stomach he felt the hunger sharpen, as it had before, and he stood and held his abdomen until the hunger cramps receded.

He had to eat. He was weak with it again, down with the hunger, and he had to eat.

Back at the shelter the berries lay in a pile where he had dumped them when he grabbed his windbreaker—gut cherries he called them in his mind now—and he thought of eating some of them. Not such a crazy amount, as he had, which he felt brought on the sickness in the night—but just enough to stave off the hunger a bit.

He crawled into the shelter. Some flies were on the berries and he brushed them off. He selected only the berries that were solidly ripe—not the light red ones, but the berries that were dark, maroon red to black and swollen in ripeness. When he had a small handful of them he went back down to the lake and washed them in the water—small fish scattered away when he splashed the water up and he wished he had a fishing line and hook—then he ate them carefully, spitting out the pits. They were still tart, but had a sweetness to them, although they seemed to make his lips a bit numb.

When he finished he was still hungry, but the edge was gone and his legs didn't feel as weak as they had.

He went back to the shelter. It took him half an hour to go through the rest of the berries and sort them, putting all the fully ripe ones in a pile on some leaves, the rest in another pile. When he was done he covered the two piles with grass he tore from the lake shore to keep the flies off and went back outside.

They were awful berries, those gut cherries, he thought. But there was food there, food of some kind, and he could eat a bit more later tonight if he had to.

For now he had a full day ahead of him. He looked at the sky through the trees and saw that while there were clouds they were scattered and did not seem to hold rain. There was a light breeze that seemed to keep the mosquitos down and, he thought, looking up along the lake shore, if there was one kind of berry there should be other kinds. Sweeter kinds.

If he kept the lake in sight as he had done yesterday he should be all right, should be able to find home again—and it stopped him. He had actually thought it that time.

Home. Three days, no, two—or was it three? Yes, this was the third day and he had thought of the shelter as home.

He turned and looked at it, studied the crude work. The brush made a fair wall, not weathertight but it cut most of the wind off. He hadn't done so badly at that. Maybe it wasn't much, but also maybe it was all he had for a home.

All right, he thought, so I'll call it home.

He turned back and set off up the side of the lake, heading for the gut cherry bushes, his windbreaker-bag in his hand. Things were bad, he thought, but maybe not that bad.

Maybe he could find some better berries.

When he came to the gut cherry bushes he paused. The branches were empty of birds but still had many berries, and some of those that had been merely red yesterday were now a dark maroon to black. Much riper. Maybe he should stay and pick them to save them.

But the explosion in the night was still much in his memory and he decided to go on. Gut cherries were food, but tricky to eat. He needed something better.

Another hundred yards up the shore there was a place where the wind had torn another path. These must have been fierce winds, he thought, to tear places up like this—as they had the path he had found with the plane when he crashed. Here the trees were not all the way down but twisted and snapped off halfway up from the ground, so their tops were all down and rotted and gone, leaving the snags poking into the sky like broken teeth. It made for tons of dead and dry wood and he wished once more he could get a fire going. It also made a kind of clearing—with the tops of the trees gone the sun could get down to the ground—and it was filled with small thorny bushes that were covered with berries.

Raspberries.

These he knew because there were some raspberry bushes in the park and he and Terry were always picking and eating them when they biked past.

The berries were full and ripe, and he tasted one to find it sweet, and with none of the problems of the gut cherries. Although they did not grow in clusters, there were many of them and they were easy to pick and Brian smiled and started eating.

Sweet juice, he thought. Oh, they were sweet

with just a tiny tang and he picked and ate and picked and ate and thought that he had never tasted anything this good. Soon, as before, his stomach was full, but now he had some sense and he did not gorge or cram more down. Instead he picked more and put them in his windbreaker, feeling the morning sun on his back and thinking he was rich, rich with food now, just rich, and he heard a noise to his rear, a slight noise, and he turned and saw the bear.

He could do nothing, think nothing. His tongue, stained with berry juice, stuck to the roof of his mouth and he stared at the bear. It was black, with a cinnamon-colored nose, not twenty feet from him and big. No, huge. It was all black fur and huge. He had seen one in the zoo in the city once, a black bear, but it had been from India or somewhere. This one was wild, and much bigger than the one in the zoo and it was right there.

Right there.

The sun caught the ends of the hairs along his back. Shining black and silky the bear stood on its hind legs, half up, and studied Brian, just studied him, then lowered itself and moved slowly to the left, eating berries as it rolled along, wuffling and delicately using its mouth to lift each berry from the stem, and in seconds it was gone. Gone, and

Brian still had not moved. His tongue was stuck to the top of his mouth, the tip half out, his eyes were wide and his hands were reaching for a berry.

Then he made a sound, a low: "Nnnnnnggg." It made no sense, was just a sound of fear, of disbelief that something that large could have come so close to him without his knowing. It just walked up to him and could have eaten him and he could have done nothing. Nothing. And when the sound was half done a thing happened with his legs, a thing he had nothing to do with, and they were running in the opposite direction from the bear, back toward the shelter.

He would have run all the way, in panic, but after he had gone perhaps fifty yards his brain took over and slowed and, finally, stopped him.

If the bear had wanted you, his brain said, he would have taken you. It is something to understand, he thought, not something to run away from. The bear was eating berries.

Not people.

The bear made no move to hurt you, to threaten you. It stood to see you better, study you, then went on its way eating berries. It was a big bear, but it did not want you, did not want to cause you harm, and that is the thing to understand here.

He turned and looked back at the stand of raspberries. The bear was gone, the birds were singing, he saw nothing that could hurt him. There was no danger here that he could sense, could feel. In the city, at night, there was sometimes danger. You could not be in the park at night, after dark, because of the danger. But here, the bear had looked at him and had moved on and—this filled his thoughts—the berries were so good.

So good. So sweet and rich and his body was so empty.

And the bear had almost indicated that it didn't mind sharing—had just walked from him.

And the berries were so good.

And, he thought, finally, if he did not go back and get the berries he would have to eat the gut cherries again tonight.

That convinced him and he walked slowly back to the raspberry patch and continued picking for the entire morning, although with great caution, and once when a squirrel rustled some pine needles at the base of a tree he nearly jumped out of his skin.

About noon—the sun was almost straight overhead—the clouds began to thicken and look dark. In moments it started to rain and he took what he had picked and trotted back to the shelter. He had eaten probably two pounds of raspberries and had maybe another three pounds in his jacket, rolled in a pouch.

He made it to the shelter just as the clouds completely opened and the rain roared down in sheets. Soon the sand outside was drenched and there were rivulets running down to the lake. But inside he was dry and snug. He started to put the picked berries back in the sorted pile with the gut cherries but noticed that the raspberries were seeping through the jacket. They were much softer than the gut cherries and apparently were being crushed a bit with their own weight.

When he held the jacket up and looked beneath it he saw a stream of red liquid. He put a finger in it and found it to be sweet and tangy, like pop without the fizz, and he grinned and lay back on the sand, holding the bag up over his face and letting the seepage drip into his mouth.

Outside the rain poured down, but Brian lay back, drinking the syrup from the berries, dry and with the pain almost all gone, the stiffness also gone, his belly full and a good taste in his mouth.

For the first time since the crash he was not thinking of himself, of his own life. Brian was wondering if the bear was as surprised as he to find another being in the berries.

Later in the afternoon, as evening came down, he

went to the lake and washed the sticky berry juice from his face and hands, then went back to prepare for the night.

While he had accepted and understood that the bear did not want to hurt him, it was still much in his thoughts and as darkness came into the shelter he took the hatchet out of his belt and put it by his head, his hand on the handle, as the day caught up with him and he slept.

8

AT FIRST he thought it was a growl. In the still darkness of the shelter in the middle of the night his eyes came open and he was awake and he thought there was a growl. But it was the wind, a medium wind in the pines had made some sound that brought him up, brought him awake. He sat up and was hit with the smell.

It terrified him. The smell was one of rot, some musty rot that made him think only of graves with cobwebs and dust and old death. His nostrils widened and he opened his eyes wider but he could see nothing. It was too dark, too hard dark with clouds covering even the small light from the stars, and he could not see. But the smell was alive, alive and full and in the shelter. He thought of the bear, thought of Bigfoot and every monster he had ever seen in every fright movie he had ever watched, and his heart hammered in his throat.

Then he heard the slithering. A brushing sound, a slithering brushing sound near his feet—and he kicked out as hard as he could, kicked out and threw the hatchet at the sound, a noise coming from his throat. But the hatchet missed, sailed into the wall where it hit the rocks with a shower of sparks, and his leg was instantly torn with pain, as if a hundred needles had been driven into it. "Unnnngh!"

Now he screamed, with the pain and fear, and skittered on his backside up into the corner of the shelter, breathing through his mouth, straining to see, to hear.

The slithering moved again, he thought toward him at first, and terror took him, stopping his breath. He felt he could see a low dark form, a bulk in the darkness, a shadow that lived, but now it moved away, slithering and scraping it moved away and he saw or thought he saw it go out of the door opening.

He lay on his side for a moment, then pulled a rasping breath in and held it, listening for the attacker to return. When it was apparent that the shadow wasn't coming back he felt the calf of his leg, where the pain was centered and spreading to fill the whole leg.

His fingers gingerly touched a group of needles that had been driven through his pants and into the fleshy part of his calf. They were stiff and very sharp on the ends that stuck out, and he knew then what the attacker had been. A porcupine had stumbled into his shelter and when he had kicked it the thing had slapped him with its tail of quills.

He touched each quill carefully. The pain made it seem as if dozens of them had been slammed into his leg, but there were only eight, pinning the cloth against his skin. He leaned back against the wall for a minute. He couldn't leave them in, they had to come out, but just touching them made the pain more intense.

So fast, he thought. So fast things change. When he'd gone to sleep he had satisfaction and in just a moment it was all different. He grasped one of the quills, held his breath, and jerked. It sent pain signals to his brain in tight waves, but he grabbed another, pulled it, then another quill. When he had pulled four of them he stopped for a moment. The pain had gone from being a pointed injury pain to spreading in a hot smear up his leg and it made him catch his breath.

Some of the quills were driven in deeper than others and they tore when they came out. He breathed deeply twice, let half of the breath out, and went back to work. Jerk, pause, jerk—and three more times before he lay back in the darkness, done. The pain filled his leg now, and with it came new waves of self-pity. Sitting alone in the dark, his leg aching, some mosquitos finding him again, he started crying. It was all too much, just too much, and he couldn't take it. Not the way it was.

I can't take it this way, alone with no fire and in the dark, and next time it might be something worse, maybe a bear, and it wouldn't be just quills in the leg, it would be worse. I can't do this, he thought, again and again. I can't. Brian pulled himself up until he was sitting upright back in the corner of the cave. He put his head down on his arms across his knees, with stiffness taking his left leg, and cried until he was cried out.

He did not know how long it took, but later he looked back on this time of crying in the corner of the dark cave and thought of it as when he learned the most important rule of survival, which was that feeling sorry for yourself didn't work. It wasn't just that it was wrong to do, or that it was considered incorrect. It was more than that—it didn't work. When he sat alone in the darkness and cried and was done, was all done with it, nothing had changed. His leg still hurt, it was still dark, he was still alone and the self-pity had accomplished nothing.

At last he slept again, but already his patterns

were changing and the sleep was light, a resting doze more than a deep sleep, with small sounds awakening him twice in the rest of the night. In the last doze period before daylight, before he awakened finally with the morning light and the clouds of new mosquitos, he dreamed. This time it was not of his mother, not of the Secret, but of his father at first and then of his friend Terry.

In the initial segment of the dream his father was standing at the side of a living room looking at him and it was clear from his expression that he was trying to tell Brian something. His lips moved but there was no sound, not a whisper. He waved his hands at Brian, made gestures in front of his face as if he were scratching something, and he worked to make a word with his mouth but at first Brian could not see it. Then the lips made an *mmmmm* shape but no sound came. *Mmmmm—maaaa.* Brian could not hear it, could not understand it and he wanted to so badly; it was so important to understand his father, to know what he was saying. He was trying to help, trying so hard, and when Brian couldn't understand he looked cross, the way he did when Brian asked questions more than once, and he faded. Brian's father faded into a fog place Brian could not see and the dream was almost over, or seemed to be, when Terry came.

He was not gesturing to Brian but was sitting in the park at a bench looking at a barbecue pit and for a time nothing happened. Then he got up and poured some charcoal from a bag into the cooker, then some starter fluid, and he took a flick type of lighter and lit the fluid. When it was burning and the charcoal was at last getting hot he turned, noticing Brian for the first time in the dream. He turned and smiled and pointed to the fire as if to say, see, a fire.

But it meant nothing to Brian, except that he wished he had a fire. He saw a grocery sack on the table next to Terry. Brian thought it must contain hot dogs and chips and mustard and he could think only of the food. But Terry shook his head and pointed again to the fire, and twice more he pointed to the fire, made Brian see the flames, and Brian felt his frustration and anger rise and he thought all right, all right, I see the fire but so what? I don't have a fire. I know about fire; I know I need a fire.

I know that.

His eyes opened and there was light in the cave, a gray dim light of morning. He wiped his mouth and tried to move his leg, which had stiffened like wood. There was thirst, and hunger, and he ate some raspberries from the jacket. They had spoiled a bit, seemed softer and mushier, but still had a rich sweetness. He crushed the berries against the roof of his mouth with his tongue and drank the sweet juice as it ran down his throat. A flash of metal caught his eye and he saw his hatchet in the sand where he had thrown it at the porcupine in the dark.

He scootched up, wincing a bit when he bent his stiff leg, and crawled to where the hatchet lay. He picked it up and examined it and saw a chip in the top of the head.

The nick wasn't large, but the hatchet was important to him, was his only tool, and he should not have thrown it. He should keep it in his hand, and make a tool of some kind to help push an animal away. Make a staff, he thought, or a lance, and save the hatchet. Something came then, a thought as he held the hatchet, something about the dream and his father and Terry, but he couldn't pin it down.

"Ahhh . . ." He scrambled out and stood in the morning sun and stretched his back muscles and his sore leg. The hatchet was still in his hand, and as he stretched and raised it over his head it caught the first rays of the morning sun. The first faint light hit the silver of the hatchet and it flashed a brilliant gold in the light. Like fire. That is it, he thought. What they were trying to tell me.

Fire. The hatchet was the key to it all. When he

threw the hatchet at the porcupine in the cave and missed and hit the stone wall it had showered sparks, a golden shower of sparks in the dark, as golden with fire as the sun was now.

The hatchet was the answer. That's what his father and Terry had been trying to tell him. Somehow he could get fire from the hatchet. The sparks would make fire.

Brian went back into the shelter and studied the wall. It was some form of chalky granite, or a sandstone, but imbedded in it were large pieces of a darker stone, a harder and darker stone. It only took him a moment to find where the hatchet had struck. The steel had nicked into the edge of one of the darker stone pieces. Brian turned the head backward so he would strike with the flat rear of the hatchet and hit the black rock gently. Too gently, and nothing happened. He struck harder, a glancing blow, and two or three weak sparks skipped off the rock and died immediately.

He swung harder, held the hatchet so it would hit a longer, sliding blow, and the black rock exploded in fire. Sparks flew so heavily that several of them skittered and jumped on the sand beneath the rock and he smiled and stuck again and again.

There could be fire here, he thought. I will have a fire here, he thought, and struck again—I will have fire from the hatchet.

9

BRIAN FOUND it was a long way from sparks to fire.

Clearly there had to be something for the sparks to ignite, some kind of tinder or kindling—but what? He brought some dried grass in, tapped sparks into it and watched them die. He tried small twigs, breaking them into little pieces, but that was worse than the grass. Then he tried a combination of the two, grass and twigs.

Nothing. He had no trouble getting sparks, but the tiny bits of hot stone or metal—he couldn't tell which they were—just sputtered and died.

He settled back on his haunches in exasperation, looking at the pitiful clump of grass and twigs.

He needed something finer, something soft and fine and fluffy to catch the bits of fire.

Shredded paper would be nice, but he had no paper.

"So close," he said aloud, "so close . . ."

He put the hatchet back in his belt and went out of the shelter, limping on his sore leg. There had to be something, had to be. Man had made fire. There had been fire for thousands, millions of years. There had to be a way. He dug in his pockets and found the twenty-dollar bill in his wallet. Paper. Worthless paper out here. But if he could get a fire going . . .

He ripped the twenty into tiny pieces, made a pile of pieces, and hit sparks into them. Nothing happened. They just wouldn't take the sparks. But there had to be a way—some way to do it.

Not twenty feet to his right, leaning out over the water were birches and he stood looking at them for a full half-minute before they registered on his mind. They were a beautiful white with bark like clean, slightly speckled paper.

Paper.

He moved to the trees. Where the bark was peeling from the trunks it lifted in tiny tendrils, almost fluffs. Brian plucked some of them loose, rolled them in his fingers. They seemed flammable, dry and nearly powdery. He pulled and twisted bits off the trees, packing them in one hand while he picked them with the other, picking and gathering until he had a wad close to the size of a baseball.

Then he went back into the shelter and arranged the ball of birchbark peelings at the base of the black rock. As an afterthought he threw in the remains of the twenty-dollar bill. He struck and a stream of sparks fell into the bark and quickly died. But this time one spark fell on one small hair of dry bark—almost a thread of bark—and seemed to glow a bit brighter before it died.

The material had to be finer. There had to be a soft and incredibly fine nest for the sparks.

I must make a home for the sparks, he thought. A perfect home or they won't stay, they won't make fire.

He started ripping the bark, using his fingernails at first, and when that didn't work he used the sharp edge of the hatchet, cutting the bark in thin slivers, hairs so fine they were almost not there. It was painstaking work, slow work, and he stayed with it for over two hours. Twice he stopped for a handful of berries and once to go to the lake for a drink. Then back to work, the sun on his back, until at last he had a ball of fluff as big as a grapefruit—dry birchbark fluff.

He positioned his spark nest—as he thought of it—at the base of the rock, used his thumb to make a small depression in the middle, and slammed the back of the hatchet down across the black rock. A cloud of sparks rained down, most of them missing the nest, but some, perhaps thirty or so, hit in the depression and of those six or seven found fuel and grew, smoldered and caused the bark to take on the red glow.

Then they went out.

Close—he was close. He repositioned the nest, made a new and smaller dent with his thumb, and struck again.

More sparks, a slight glow, then nothing.

It's me, he thought. I'm doing something wrong. I do not know this—a cave dweller would have had a fire by now, a Cro-Magnon man would have a fire by now—but I don't know this. I don't know how to make a fire.

Maybe not enough sparks. He settled the nest in place once more and hit the rock with a series of blows, as fast as he could. The sparks poured like a golden waterfall. At first they seemed to take, there were several, many sparks that found life and took briefly, but they all died.

Starved.

He leaned back. They are like me. They are starving. It wasn't quantity, there were plenty of sparks, but they needed more.

I would kill, he thought suddenly, for a book of matches. Just one book. Just one match. I would kill.

What makes fire? He thought back to school. To all those science classes. Had he ever learned what made a fire? Did a teacher ever stand up there and say, "This is what makes a fire . . ."

He shook his head, tried to focus his thoughts. What did it take? You have to have fuel, he thought—and he had that. The bark was fuel. Oxygen—there had to be air.

He needed to add air. He had to fan on it, blow on it.

He made the nest ready again, held the hatchet backward, tensed, and struck four quick blows. Sparks came down and he leaned forward as fast as he could and blew.

Too hard. There was a bright, almost intense glow, then it was gone. He had blown it out.

Another set of strikes, more sparks. He leaned and blew, but gently this time, holding back and aiming the stream of air from his mouth to hit the brightest spot. Five or six sparks had fallen in a tight mass of bark hair and Brian centered his efforts there.

The sparks grew with his gentle breath. The red glow moved from the sparks themselves into the bark, moved and grew and became worms, glowing red worms that crawled up the bark hairs and caught other threads of bark and grew until there was a pocket of red as big as a quarter, a glowing red coal of heat.

And when he ran out of breath and paused to inhale, the red ball suddenly burst into flame.

"Fire!" He yelled. "I've got fire! I've got it, I've got it, I've got it . . ."

But the flames were thick and oily and burning fast, consuming the ball of bark as fast as if it were gasoline. He had to feed the flames, keep them going. Working as fast as he could he carefully placed the dried grass and wood pieces he had tried at first on top of the bark and was gratified to see them take.

But they would go fast. He needed more, and more. He could not let the flames go out.

He ran from the shelter to the pines and started breaking off the low, dead small limbs. These he threw in the shelter, went back for more, threw those in, and squatted to break and feed the hungry flames. When the small wood was going well he went out and found larger wood and did not relax until that was going. Then he leaned back against the wood brace of his door opening and smiled.

I have a friend, he thought—I have a friend now.

A hungry friend, but a good one. I have a friend named fire.

"Hello, fire..."

The curve of the rock back made an almost perfect drawing flue that carried the smoke up through the cracks of the roof but held the heat. If he kept the fire small it would be perfect and would keep anything like the porcupine from coming through the door again.

A friend and a guard, he thought.

So much from a little spark. A friend and a guard from a tiny spark.

He looked around and wished he had somebody to tell this thing, to show this thing he had done. But there was nobody.

Nothing but the trees and the sun and the breeze and the lake.

Nobody.

And he thought, rolling thoughts, with the smoke curling up over his head and the smile still half on his face he thought: I wonder what they're doing now.

I wonder what my father is doing now.

I wonder what my mother is doing now.

I wonder if she is with him.

10

He Could Not at first leave the fire.

It was so precious to him, so close and sweet a thing, the yellow and red flames brightening the dark interior of the shelter, the happy crackle of the dry wood as it burned, that he could not leave it. He went to the trees and brought in as many dead limbs as he could chop off and carry, and when he had a large pile of them he sat near the fire—though it was getting into the warm middle part of the day and he was hot—and broke them in small pieces and fed the fire.

I will not let you go out, he said to himself, to the flames—not ever. And so he sat through a long part of the day, keeping the flames even, eating from his stock of raspberries, leaving to drink from the lake when he was thirsty. In the afternoon, toward evening, with his face smoke smeared and his skin red from the heat, he finally began to think ahead to what he needed to do.

He would need a large woodpile to get through the night. It would be almost impossible to find wood in the dark so he had to have it all in and cut and stacked before the sun went down.

Brian made certain the fire was banked with new wood, then went out of the shelter and searched for a good fuel supply. Up the hill from the campsite the same windstorm that left him a place to land the plane—had that only been three, four days ago?—had dropped three large white pines across each other. They were dead now, dry and filled with weathered dry dead limbs—enough for many days. He chopped and broke and carried wood back to the camp, stacking the pieces under the overhang until he had what he thought to be an enormous pile, as high as his head and six feet across the base. Between trips he added small pieces to the fire to keep it going and on one of the trips to get wood he noticed an added advantage of the fire. When he was in the shade of the trees breaking limbs the mosquitos swarmed on him, as usual, but when he came to the fire, or just near the shelter where the smoke eddied and swirled, the insects were gone.

It was a wonderful discovery. The mosquitos had

nearly driven him mad and the thought of being rid of them lifted his spirits. On another trip he looked back and saw the smoke curling up through the trees and realized, for the first time, that he now had the means to make a signal. He could carry a burning stick and build a signal fire on top of the rock, make clouds of smoke and perhaps attract attention.

Which meant more wood. And still more wood. There did not seem to be an end to the wood he would need and he spent all the rest of the afternoon into dusk making wood trips.

At dark he settled in again for the night, next to the fire with the stack of short pieces ready to put on, and he ate the rest of the raspberries. During all the work of the day his leg had loosened but it still ached a bit, and he rubbed it and watched the fire and thought for the first time since the crash that he might be getting a handle on things, might be starting to do something other than just sit.

He was out of food, but he could look tomorrow and he could build a signal fire tomorrow and get more wood tomorrow . . .

The fire cut the night coolness and settled him back into sleep, thinking of tomorrow.

He slept hard and wasn't sure what awakened him but his eyes came open and he stared into the darkness. The fire had burned down and looked out but he stirred with a piece of wood and found a bed of coals still glowing hot and red. With small pieces of wood and careful blowing he soon had a blaze going again.

It had been close. He had to be sure to try and sleep in short intervals so he could keep the fire going, and he tried to think of a way to regulate his sleep but it made him sleepy to think about it and he was just going under again when he heard the sound outside.

It was not unlike the sound of the porcupine, something slithering and being dragged across the sand, but when he looked out the door opening it was too dark to see anything.

Whatever it was it stopped making that sound in a few moments and he thought he heard something sloshing into the water at the shoreline, but he had the fire now and plenty of wood so he wasn't as worried as he had been the night before.

He dozed, slept for a time, awakened again just at dawn-gray light, and added wood to the still-smoking fire before standing outside and stretching. Standing with his arms stretched over his head and the tight knot of hunger in his stomach, he looked toward the lake and saw the tracks.

They were strange, a main center line up from the lake in the sand with claw marks to the side leading to a small pile of sand, then going back down to the water.

He walked over and squatted near them, studied them, tried to make sense of them.

Whatever had made the tracks had some kind of flat dragging bottom in the middle and was apparently pushed along by the legs that stuck out to the side.

Up from the water to a small pile of sand, then back down into the water. Some animal. Some kind of water animal that came up to the sand to . . . to do what?

To do something with the sand, to play and make a pile in the sand?

He smiled. City boy, he thought. Oh, you city boy with your city ways—he made a mirror in his mind, a mirror of himself, and saw how he must look. City boy with your city ways sitting in the sand trying to read the tracks and not knowing, not understanding. Why would anything wild come up from the water to play in the sand? Not that way, animals weren't that way. They didn't waste time that way.

It had come up from the water for a reason, a good reason, and he must try to understand the reason, he must change to fully understand the reason himself or he would not make it.

It had come up from the water for a reason, and

the reason, he thought, squatting, the reason had to do with the pile of sand.

He brushed the top off gently with his hand but found only damp sand. Still, there must be a reason and he carefully kept scraping and digging until, about four inches down, he suddenly came into a small chamber in the cool-damp sand and there lay eggs, many eggs, almost perfectly round eggs the size of table tennis balls, and he laughed then because he knew.

It had been a turtle. He had seen a show on television about sea turtles that came up onto beaches and laid their eggs in the sand. There must be freshwater lake turtles that did the same. Maybe snapping turtles. He had heard of snapping turtles. They became fairly large, he thought. It must have been a snapper that came up in the night when he heard the noise that awakened him; she must have come then and laid the eggs.

Food.

More than eggs, more than knowledge, more than anything this was food. His stomach tightened and rolled and made noise as he looked at the eggs, as if his stomach belonged to somebody else or had seen the eggs with its own eyes and was demanding food. The hunger, always there, had been somewhat controlled and dormant when there was nothing to eat but with the eggs came the scream to eat. His whole body craved food with such an intensity that it quickened his breath.

He reached into the nest and pulled the eggs out one at a time. There were seventeen of them, each as round as a ball, and white. They had leathery shells that gave instead of breaking when he squeezed them.

When he had them heaped on the sand in a pyramid—he had never felt so rich somehow—he suddenly realized that he did not know how to eat them.

He had a fire but no way to cook them, no container, and he had never thought of eating a raw egg. He had an uncle named Carter, his father's brother, who always put an egg in a glass of milk and drank it in the morning. Brian had watched him do it once, just once, and when the runny part of the white left the glass and went into his uncle's mouth and down the throat in a single gulp Brian almost lost everything he had ever eaten.

Still, he thought. Still. As his stomach moved toward his backbone he became less and less fussy. Some natives in the world ate grasshoppers and ants and if they could do that he could get a raw egg down.

He picked one up and tried to break the shell

and found it surprisingly tough. Finally, using the hatchet he sharpened a stick and poked a hole in the egg. He widened the hole with his finger and looked inside. Just an egg. It had a dark yellow yolk and not so much white as he thought there would be.

Just an egg.

Food.

Just an egg he had to eat.

Raw.

He looked out across the lake and brought the egg to his mouth and closed his eyes and sucked and squeezed the egg at the same time and swallowed as fast as he could.

"Ecch . . . "

It had a greasy, almost oily taste, but it was still an egg. His throat tried to throw it back up, his whole body seemed to convulse with it, but his stomach took it, held it, and demanded more.

The second egg was easier, and by the third one he had no trouble at all—it just slid down. He ate six of them, could have easily eaten all of them and not been full, but a part of him said to hold back, save the rest.

He could not now believe the hunger. The eggs had awakened it fully, roaringly, so that it tore at him. After the sixth egg he ripped the shell open and licked the inside clean, then went back and ripped the other five open and licked them out as well and wondered if he could eat the shells. There must be some food value in them. But when he tried they were too leathery to chew and he couldn't get them down.

He stood away from the eggs for a moment, literally stood and turned away so that he could not see them. If he looked at them he would have to eat more.

He would store them in the shelter and eat only one a day. He fought the hunger down again, controlled it. He would take them now and store them and save them and eat one a day, and he realized as he thought it that he had forgotten that *they* might come. The searchers. Surely, they would come before he could eat all the eggs at one a day.

He had forgotten to think about them and that wasn't good. He had to keep thinking of them because if he forgot them and did not think of them they might forget about him.

And he had to keep hoping.

He had to keep hoping.

11

THERE WERE these things to do.

He transferred all the eggs from the small beach into the shelter, reburying them near his sleeping area. It took all his will to keep from eating another one as he moved them, but he got it done and when they were out of sight again it was easier. He added wood to the fire and cleaned up the camp area.

A good laugh, that—cleaning the camp. All he did was shake out his windbreaker and hang it in the sun to dry the berry juice that had soaked in, and smooth the sand where he slept.

But it was a mental thing. He had gotten depressed thinking about how they hadn't found him yet, and when he was busy and had something to do the depression seemed to leave.

So there were things to do.

With the camp squared away he brought in more wood. He had decided to always have enough on hand for three days and after spending one night with the fire for a friend he knew what a staggering amount of wood it would take. He worked all through the morning at the wood, breaking down dead limbs and breaking or chopping them in smaller pieces, storing them neatly beneath the overhang. He stopped once to take a drink at the lake and in his reflection he saw that the swelling on his head was nearly gone. There was no pain there so he assumed that had taken care of itself. His leg was also back to normal, although he had a small pattern of holes—roughly star-shaped—where the quills had nailed him, and while he was standing at the lake shore taking stock he noticed that his body was changing.

He had never been fat, but he had been slightly heavy with a little extra weight just above his belt at the sides.

This was completely gone and his stomach had caved in to the hunger and the sun had cooked him past burning so he was tanning, and with the smoke from the fire his face was starting to look like leather. But perhaps more than his body was the change in his mind, or in the way he was—was becoming.

I am not the same, he thought. I see, I hear differently. He did not know when the change started, but it was there; when a sound came to him now he didn't just hear it but would know the sound. He would swing and look at it—a breaking twig, a movement of air—and know the sound as if he somehow could move his mind back down the wave of sound to the source.

He could know what the sound was before he quite realized he had heard it. And when he saw something—a bird moving a wing inside a bush or a ripple on the water—he would truly see that thing, not just notice it as he used to notice things in the city. He would see all parts of it; see the whole wing, the feathers, see the color of the feathers, see the bush, and the size and shape and color of its leaves. He would see the way the light moved with the ripples on the water and see that the wind made the ripples and which way that wind had to blow to make the ripples move in that certain way.

None of that used to be in Brian and now it was a part of him, a changed part of him, a grown part of him, and the two things, his mind and his body, had come together as well, had made a connection with each other that he didn't quite understand. When his ears heard a sound or his eyes saw a sight his mind took control of his body. Without his thinking, he moved to face the sound or sight, moved to make ready for it, to deal with it.

There were these things to do.

When the wood was done he decided to get a signal fire ready. He moved to the top of the rock ridge that comprised the bluff over his shelter and was pleased to find a large, flat stone area.

More wood, he thought, moaning inwardly. He went back to the fallen trees and found more dead limbs, carrying them up on the rock until he had enough for a bonfire. Initially he had thought of making a signal fire every day but he couldn't—he would never be able to keep the wood supply going. So while he was working he decided to have the fire ready and if he heard an engine, or even thought he heard a plane engine, he would run up with a burning limb and set off the signal fire.

Things to do.

At the last trip to the top of the stone bluff with wood he stopped, sat on the point overlooking the lake, and rested. The lake lay before him, twenty or so feet below, and he had not seen it this way since he had come in with the plane. Remembering the crash he had a moment of fear, a breath-tightening little rip of terror, but it passed and he was quickly caught up in the beauty of the scenery.

It was so incredibly beautiful that it was almost unreal. From his height he could see not just the lake but across part of the forest, a green carpet, and it was full of life. Birds, insects—there was a constant hum and song. At the other end of the bottom of the L there was another large rock sticking out over the water and on top of the rock a snaggly pine had somehow found food and grown, bent and gnarled. Sitting on one limb was a blue bird with a crest and sharp beak, a kingfisher—he thought of a picture he had seen once—which left the branch while he watched and dove into the water. It emerged a split part of a second later. In its mouth was a small fish, wiggling silver in the sun. It took the fish to a limb, juggled it twice, and swallowed it whole.

Fish.

Of course, he thought. There were fish in the lake and they were food. And if a bird could do it . . .

He scrambled down the side of the bluff and trotted to the edge of the lake, looking down into the water. Somehow it had never occurred to him to look *inside* the water—only at the surface. The sun was flashing back up into his eyes and he moved off to the side and took his shoes off and waded out fifteen feet. Then he turned and stood still, with the sun at his back, and studied the water again.

It was, he saw after a moment, literally packed with life. Small fish swam everywhere, some narrow and long, some round, most of them three or four inches long, some a bit larger and many smaller. There was a patch of mud off to the side, leading into deeper water, and he could see old clam shells there, so there must be clams. As he watched, a crayfish, looking like a tiny lobster, left one of the empty clam shells and went to another looking for something to eat, digging with its claws.

While he stood some of the small, roundish fish came quite close to his legs and he tensed, got ready, and made a wild stab at grabbing one of them. They exploded away in a hundred flicks of quick light, so fast that he had no hope of catching them that way. But they soon came back, seemed to be curious about him, and as he walked from the water he tried to think of a way to use that curiosity to catch them.

He had no hooks or string but if he could somehow lure them into the shallows—and make a spear, a small fish spear—he might be able to strike fast enough to get one.

He would have to find the right kind of wood, slim and straight—he had seen some willows up along the lake that might work—and he could use the hatchet to sharpen it and shape it while he was sitting by the fire tonight. And that brought up the fire, which he had to feed again. He looked at the sun and saw it was getting late in the afternoon, and when he thought of how late it was he thought that he ought to reward all his work with another egg and that made him think that some kind of dessert would be nice—he smiled when he thought of dessert, so fancy—and he wondered if he should move up the lake and see if he could find some raspberries after he banked the fire and while he was looking for the right wood for a spear. Spearwood, he thought, and it all rolled together, just rolled together and rolled over him...

There were these things to do.

12

THE FISH SPEAR didn't work.

He stood in the shallows and waited, again and again. The small fish came closer and closer and he lunged time after time but was always too slow. He tried throwing it, jabbing it, everything but flailing with it, and it didn't work. The fish were just too fast.

He had been so sure, so absolutely certain that it would work the night before. Sitting by the fire he had taken the willow and carefully peeled the bark until he had a straight staff about six feet long and just under an inch thick at the base, the thickest end.

Then, propping the hatchet in a crack in the rock

wall, he had pulled the head of his spear against it, carving a thin piece off each time, until the thick end tapered down to a needle point. Still not satisfied—he could not imagine hitting one of the fish with a single point—he carefully used the hatchet to split the point up the middle for eight or ten inches and jammed a piece of wood up into the split to make a two-prong spear with the points about two inches apart. It was crude, but it looked effective and seemed to have good balance when he stood outside the shelter and hefted the spear.

He had worked on the fish spear until it had become more than just a tool. He'd spent hours and hours on it, and now it didn't work. He moved into the shallows and stood and the fish came to him. Just as before they swarmed around his legs, some of them almost six inches long, but no matter how he tried they were too fast. At first he tried throwing it but that had no chance. As soon as he brought his arm back—well before he threw—the movement frightened them. Next he tried lunging at them, having the spear ready just above the water and thrusting with it. Finally he actually put the spear in the water and waited until the fish were right in front of it, but still somehow he telegraphed his motion before he thrust and they saw it and flashed away.

He needed something to spring the spear forward, some way to make it move faster than the fish—some motive force. A string that snapped—or a bow. A bow and arrow. A thin, long arrow with the point in the water and the bow pulled back so that all he had to do was release the arrow . . . yes. That was it.

He had to "invent" the bow and arrow—he almost laughed as he moved out of the water and put his shoes on. The morning sun was getting hot and he took his shirt off. Maybe that was how it really happened, way back when—some primitive man tried to spear fish and it didn't work and he "invented" the bow and arrow. Maybe it was always that way, discoveries happened because they needed to happen.

He had not eaten anything yet this morning so he took a moment to dig up the eggs and eat one. then he reburied them, banked the fire with a couple of thicker pieces of wood, settled the hatchet on his belt and took the spear in his right hand and set off up the lake to find wood to make a bow. He went without a shirt but something about the wood smoke smell on him kept the insects from bothering him as he walked to the berry patch. The raspberries were starting to become overripe, just in two days, and he would have to pick as many as possible after he found the wood but he did take a little time now to pick a few and eat them. They were full and sweet and when he picked one, two others would fall off the limbs into the grass and soon his hands and cheeks were covered with red berry juice and he was full. That surprised him—being full.

He hadn't thought he would ever be full again, knew only the hunger, and here he was full. One turtle egg and a few handfuls of berries and he felt full. He looked down at his stomach and saw that it was still caved in—did not bulge out as it would have with two hamburgers and a freezy slush. It must have shrunk. And there was still hunger there, but not like it was—not tearing at him. This was hunger that he knew would be there always, even when he had food—a hunger that made him look for things, see things. A hunger to make him hunt.

He swung his eyes across the berries to make sure the bear wasn't there, at his back, then he moved down to the lake. The spear went out before him automatically, moving the brush away from his face as he walked, and when he came to the water's edge he swung left. Not sure what he was looking for, not knowing what wood might be best for a bow—he had never made a bow, never shot a bow in his life—but it seemed that it would be along the lake, near the water.

He saw some young birch, and they were springy, but they lacked snap somehow, as did the willows. Not enough whip-back.

Halfway up the lake, just as he started to step over a log, he was absolutely terrified by an explosion under his feet. Something like a feathered bomb blew up and away in flurry of leaves and thunder. It frightened him so badly that he fell back and down and then it was gone, leaving only an image in his mind.

A bird, it had been, about the size of a very small chicken only with a fantail and stubby wings that slammed against its body and made loud noise. Noise there and gone. He got up and brushed himself off. The bird had been speckled, brown and gray, and it must not be very smart because Brian's foot had been nearly on it before it flew. Half a second more and he would have stepped on it.

And caught it, he thought, and eaten it. He might be able to catch one, or spear one. Maybe, he thought, maybe it tasted like chicken. Maybe he could catch one or spear one and it probably did taste just like chicken. Just like chicken when his mother baked it in the oven with garlic and salt and it turned golden brown and crackled....

He shook his head to drive the picture out and moved down to the shore. There was a tree there with long branches that seemed straight and when he pulled on one of them and let go it had an almost vicious snap to it. He picked one of the limbs that seemed right and began chopping where the limb joined the tree.

The wood was hard and he didn't want to cause it to split so he took his time, took small chips and concentrated so hard that at first he didn't hear it.

A persistent whine, like the insects only more steady with an edge of a roar to it, was in his ears and he chopped and cut and was thinking of a bow, how he would make a bow, how it would be when he shaped it with the hatchet and still the sound did not cut through until the limb was nearly off the tree and the whine was inside his head and he knew it then.

A plane! It was a motor, far off but seeming to get louder. They were coming for him!

He threw down the limb and his spear and, holding the hatchet, he started to run for camp. He had to get fire up on the bluff and signal them, get fire and smoke up. He put all of his life into his legs, jumped logs and moved through brush like a light ghost, swiveling and running, his lungs filling and blowing and now the sound was louder, coming in his direction.

If not right at him, at least closer. He could see

it all in his mind now, the picture, the way it would be. He would get the fire going and the plane would see the smoke and circle, circle once, then again, and waggle its wings. It would be a float plane and it would land on the water and come across the lake and the pilot would be amazed that he was alive after all these days.

All this he saw as he ran for the camp and the fire. They would take him from here and this night, this very night, he would sit with his father and eat and tell him all the things. He could see it now. Oh, yes, all as he ran in the sun, his legs liquid springs. He got to the camp still hearing the whine of the engine, and one stick of wood still had good flame.

He dove inside and grabbed the wood and ran around the edge of the ridge, scrambled up like a cat and blew and nearly had the flame feeding, growing, when the sound moved away.

It was abrupt, as if the plane had turned. He shielded the sun from his eyes and tried to see it, tried to make the plane become real in his eyes. But the trees were so high, so thick, and now the sound was still fainter. He kneeled again to the flames and blew and added grass and chips and the flames fed and grew and in moments he had a bonfire as high as his head but the sound was gone now.

Look back, he thought. Look back and see the smoke now and turn, please turn.

"Look back," he whispered, feeling all the pictures fade, seeing his father's face fade like the sound, like lost dreams, like an end to hope. Oh, turn now and come back, look back and see the smoke and turn for me. . . .

But it kept moving away until he could not hear it even in his imagination, in his soul. Gone. He stood on the bluff over the lake, his face cooking in the roaring bonfire, watching the clouds of ash and smoke going into the sky and thought—no, more than thought—he knew then that he would not get out of this place. Not now, not ever.

That had been a search plane. He was sure of it. That must have been them and they had come as far off to the side of the flight plan as they thought they would have to come and then turned back. They did not see his smoke, did not hear the cry from his mind.

They would not return. He would never leave now, never get out of here. He went down to his knees and felt the tears start, cutting through the smoke and ash on his face, silently falling onto the stone.

Gone, he thought finally, it was all gone. All silly and gone. No bows, no spears, or fish or berries, it was all silly anyway, all just a game. He could do a day, but not forever—he could not make it if they did not come for him someday.

He could not play the game without hope; could not play the game without a dream. They had taken it all away from him now, they had turned away from him and there was nothing for him now. The plane gone, his family gone, all of it gone. They would not come. He was alone and there was nothing for him.

13

BRIAN STOOD at the end of the long part of the L of the lake and watched the water, smelled the water, listened to the water, was the water.

A fish moved and his eyes jerked sideways to see the ripples but he did not move any other part of his body and did not raise the bow or reach into his belt pouch for a fish arrow. It was not the right kind of fish, not a food fish.

The food fish stayed close in, in the shallows, and did not roll that way but made quicker movements, small movements, food movements. The large fish rolled and stayed deep and could not be taken. But it didn't matter. This day, this morning, he was not looking for fish. Fish was light meat and he was sick of them.

He was looking for one of the foolish birds—he called them foolbirds—and there was a flock that lived near the end of the long part of the lake. But something he did not understand had stopped him and he stood, breathing gently through his mouth to keep silent, letting his eyes and ears go out and do the work for him.

It had happened before this way, something had come into him from outside to warn him and he had stopped. Once it had been the bear again. He had been taking the last of the raspberries and something came inside and stopped him, and when he looked where his ears said to look there was a female bear with cubs.

Had he taken two more steps he would have come between the mother and her cubs and that was a bad place to be. As it was the mother had stood and faced him and made a sound, a low sound in her throat to threaten and warn him. He paid attention to the feeling now and he stood and waited, patiently, knowing he was right and that something would come.

Turn, smell, listen, feel and then a sound, a small sound, and he looked up and away from the lake and saw the wolf. It was halfway up the hill from the lake, standing with its head and shoulders sticking out into a small opening, looking down on him with wide yellow eyes. He had never seen a wolf and the size threw him—not as big as a bear but somehow seeming that large. The wolf claimed all that was below him as his own, took Brian as his own.

Brian looked back and for a moment felt afraid because the wolf was so . . . so right. He knew Brian, knew him and owned him and chose not to do anything to him. But the fear moved then, moved away, and Brian knew the wolf for what it was—another part of the woods, another part of all of it. Brian relaxed the tension on the spear in his hand, settled the bow in his other hand from where it had started to come up. He knew the wolf now, as the wolf knew him, and he nodded to it, nodded and smiled.

The wolf watched him for another time, another part of his life, then it turned and walked effortlessly up the hill and as it came out of the brush it was followed by three other wolves, all equally large and gray and beautiful, all looking down on him as they trotted past and away and Brian nodded to each of them.

He was not the same now—the Brian that stood and watched the wolves move away and nodded to them was completely changed. Time had come, time that he measured but didn't care about; time had come into his life and moved out and left him different.

In measured time forty-seven days had passed since the crash. Forty-two days, he thought, since he had died and been born as the new Brian.

When the plane had come and gone it had put him down, gutted him and dropped him and left him with nothing. The rest of that first day he had gone down and down until dark. He had let the fire go out, had forgotten to eat even an egg, had let his brain take him down to where he was done, where he wanted to be done and done.

To where he wanted to die. He had settled into the gray funk deeper and still deeper until finally, in the dark, he had gone up on the ridge and taken the hatchet and tried to end it by cutting himself.

Madness. A hissing madness that took his brain. There had been nothing for him then and he tried to become nothing but the cutting had been hard to do, impossible to do, and he had at last fallen to his side, wishing for death, wishing for an end, and slept only didn't sleep.

With his eyes closed and his mind open he lay on the rock through the night, lay and hated and wished for it to end and thought the word *Clouddown, Clouddown* through that awful night. Over and over the word, wanting all his clouds to come down, but in the morning he was still there.

Still there on his side and the sun came up and when he opened his eyes he saw the cuts on his arm, the dry blood turning black; he saw the blood and hated the blood, hated what he had done to himself when he was the old Brian and was weak, and two things came into his mind—two true things.

He was not the same. The plane passing changed him, the disappointment cut him down and made him new. He was not the same and would never be again like he had been. That was one of the true things, the new things. And the other one was that he would not die, he would not let death in again.

He was new.

Of course he had made a lot of mistakes. He smiled now, walking up the lake shore after the wolves were gone, thinking of the early mistakes; the mistakes that came before he realized that he had to find new ways to be what he had become.

He had made new fire, which he now kept going using partially rotten wood because the punky wood would smolder for many hours and still come back with fire. But that had been the extent of doing things right for a while. His first bow was a disaster that almost blinded him.

He had sat a whole night and shaped the limbs carefully until the bow looked beautiful. Then he had spent two days making arrows. The shafts were willow, straight and with the bark peeled, and he fire-hardened the points and split a couple of them to make forked points, as he had done with the spear. He had no feathers so he just left them bare, figuring for fish they only had to travel a few inches. He had no string and that threw him until he looked down at his tennis shoes. They had long laces, too long, and he found that one lace cut in half would take care of both shoes and that left the other lace for a bowstring.

All seemed to be going well until he tried a test shot. He put an arrow to the string, pulled it back to his cheek, pointed it at a dirt hummock, and at that precise instant the bow wood exploded in his hands sending splinters and chips of wood into his face. Two pieces actually stuck into his forehead, just above his eyes, and had they been only slightly lower they would have blinded him.

Too stiff.

Mistakes. In his mental journal he listed them to tell his father, listed all the mistakes. He had made a new bow, with slender limbs and a more fluid, gentle pull, but could not hit the fish though he sat in the water and was, in the end, surrounded by a virtual cloud of small fish. It was infuriating. He would pull the bow back, set the arrow just above the water, and when the fish was no more than an inch away release the arrow.

Only to miss. It seemed to him that the arrow had gone right through the fish, again and again, but the fish didn't get hurt. Finally, after hours, he stuck the arrow down in the water, pulled the bow, and waited for a fish to come close and while he was waiting he noticed that the water seemed to make the arrow bend or break in the middle.

Of course—he had forgotten that water refracts, bends light. He had learned that somewhere, in some class, maybe it was biology—he couldn't remember. But it did bend light and that meant the fish were not where they appeared to be. They were lower, just below, which meant he had to aim just under them.

He would not forget his first hit. Not ever. A round-shaped fish, with golden sides, sides as gold as the sun, stopped in front of the arrow and he aimed just beneath it, at the bottom edge of the fish, and released the arrow and there was a bright flurry, a splash of gold in the water. He grabbed the arrow and raised it up and the fish was on the end, wiggling against the blue sky.

He held the fish against the sky until it stopped wiggling, held it and looked to the sky and felt his throat tighten, swell, and fill with pride at what he had done.

He had done food.

With his bow, with an arrow fashioned by his

own hands he had done food, had found a way to live. The bow had given him this way and he exulted in it, in the bow, in the arrow, in the fish, in the hatchet, in the sky. He stood and walked from the water, still holding the fish and arrow and bow against the sky, seeing them as they fit his arms, as they were part of him.

He had food.

He cut a green willow fork and held the fish over the fire until the skin crackled and peeled away and the meat inside was flaky and moist and tender. This he picked off carefully with his fingers, tasting every piece, mashing them in his mouth with his tongue to get the juices out of them, hot steaming pieces of fish . . .

He could not, he thought then, ever get enough. And all that first day, first new day, he spent going to the lake, shooting a fish, taking it back to the fire, cooking it and eating it, then back to the lake, shooting a fish, cooking it and eating it, and on that way until it was dark.

He had taken the scraps back to the water with the thought they might work for bait, and the other fish came by the hundreds to clean them up. He could take his pick of them. Like a store, he thought, just like a store, and he could not remember later how many he ate that day but he thought it must have been over twenty.

It had been a feast day, his first feast day, and a celebration of being alive and the new way he had of getting food. By the end of that day, when it became dark and he lay next to the fire with his stomach full of fish and grease from the meat smeared around his mouth, he could feel new hope building in him. Not hope that he would be rescued—that was gone.

But hope in his knowledge. Hope in the fact that he could learn and survive and take care of himself.

Tough hope, he thought that night. I am full of tough hope.

14

MISTAKES.

Small mistakes could turn into disasters, funny little mistakes could snowball so that while you were still smiling at the humor you could find yourself looking at death. In the city if he made a mistake usually there was a way to rectify it, make it all right. If he fell on his bike and sprained a leg he could wait for it to heal; if he forgot something at the store he could find other food in the refrigerator.

Now it was different, and all so quick, all so incredibly quick. If he sprained a leg here he might starve before he could get around again; if he missed while he was hunting or if the fish moved away he might starve. If he got sick, really sick so he couldn't move he might starve.

Mistakes.

Early in the new time he had learned the most important thing, the truly vital knowledge that drives all creatures in the forest—food is all. Food was simply everything. All things in the woods, from insects to fish to bears, were always, always looking for food—it was the great, single driving influence in nature. To eat. All must eat.

But the way he learned it almost killed him. His second new night, stomach full of fish and the fire smoldering in the shelter, he had been sound asleep when something—he thought later it might be smell—had awakened him.

Near the fire, completely unafraid of the smoking coals, completely unafraid of Brian, a skunk was digging where he had buried the eggs. There was some sliver of a moon and in the faint-pearl light he could see the bushy tail, the white stripes down the back, and he had nearly smiled. He did not know how the skunk had found the eggs, some smell, perhaps some tiny fragment of shell had left a smell, but it looked almost cute, its little head down and its little tail up as it dug and dug, kicking the sand back.

But those were his eggs, not the skunk's, and the half smile had been quickly replaced with fear that he would lose his food and he had grabbed a handful of sand and thrown it at the skunk.

"Get out of here . . ."

He was going to say more, some silly human words, but in less than half a second the skunk had snapped its rear end up, curved the tail over, and sprayed Brian with a direct shot aimed at his head from less than four feet away.

In the tiny confines of the shelter the effect was devastating. The thick sulfurous rotten odor filled the small room, heavy, ugly, and stinking. The corrosive spray that hit his face seared into his lungs and eyes, blinding him.

He screamed and threw himself sideways, taking the entire wall off the shelter; screamed and clawed out of the shelter and fell-ran to the shore of the lake. Stumbling and tripping, he scrambled into the water and slammed his head back and forth trying to wash his eyes, slashing at the water to clear his eyes.

A hundred funny cartoons he had seen about skunks. Cute cartoons about the smell of skunks, cartoons to laugh at and joke about, but when the spray hit there was nothing funny about it—he was completely blind for almost two hours. A lifetime. He thought that he might be permanently blind, or at least impaired—and that would have been the end. As it was the pain in his eyes lasted for days, bothered him after that for two weeks. The smell in the shelter, in his clothes, and in his hair was still there now, almost a month and a half later.

And he had nearly smiled.

Mistakes.

Food had to be protected. While he was in the lake trying to clear his eyes the skunk went ahead and dug up the rest of the turtle eggs and ate every one. Licked all the shells clean and couldn't have cared less that Brian was thrashing around in the water like a dying carp. The skunk had found food and was taking it and Brian was paying for a lesson.

Protect food and have a good shelter. Not just a shelter to keep the wind and rain out, but a shelter to protect, a shelter to make him safe. The day after the skunk he set about making a good place to live.

The basic idea had been good, the place for his shelter was right, but he just hadn't gone far enough. He'd been lazy—but now he knew the second most important thing about nature, what drives nature. Food was first, but the work for the food went on and on. Nothing in nature was lazy. He had tried to take a shortcut and paid for it with his turtle eggs—which he had come to like more than chicken eggs from the store. They had been fuller somehow, had more depth to them.

He set about improving his shelter by tearing it down. From dead pines up the hill he brought down heavier logs and fastened several of them across the opening, wedging them at the top and burying the bottoms in the sand. Then he wove long branches in through them to make a truly tight wall and, still not satisfied, he took even thinner branches and wove those into the first weave. When he was at last finished he could not find a place to put his fist through. It all held together like a very stiff woven basket.

He judged the door opening to be the weakest spot, and here he took special time to weave a door of willows in so tight a mesh that no matter how a skunk tried—or porcupine, he thought, looking at the marks in his leg—it could not possibly get through. He had no hinges but by arranging some cut-off limbs at the top in the right way he had a method to hook the door in place, and when he was in and the door was hung he felt relatively safe. A bear, something big, could still get in by tearing at it, but nothing small could bother him and the weave of the structure still allowed the smoke to filter up through the top and out.

All in all it took him three days to make the shelter, stopping to shoot fish and eat as he went, bathing four times a day to try and get the smell from the skunk to leave. When his house was done, finally done right, he turned to the constant problem—food.

It was all right to hunt and eat, or fish and eat, but what happened if he had to go a long time without food? What happened when the berries were gone and he got sick or hurt or—thinking of the skunk—laid up temporarily? He needed a way to store food, a place to store it, and he needed food to store.

Mistakes.

He tried to learn from the mistakes. He couldn't bury food again, couldn't leave it in the shelter, because something like a bear could get at it right away. It had to be high, somehow, high and safe.

Above the door to the shelter, up the rock face about ten feet, was a small ledge that could make a natural storage place, unreachable to animals—except that it was unreachable to him as well.

A ladder, of course. He needed a ladder. But he had no way to fashion one, nothing to hold the steps on, and that stopped him until he found a dead pine with many small branches still sticking out. Using his hatchet he chopped the branches off so they stuck out four or five inches, all up along the log, then he cut the log off about ten feet long and dragged it down to his shelter. It was a little heavy, but dry and he could manage it, and when he propped it up he found he could climb to the ledge with ease, though the tree did roll from side to side a bit as he climbed.

His food shelf—as he thought of it—had been covered with bird manure and he carefully scraped it clean with sticks. He had never seen birds there, but that was probably because the smoke from his fire went up right across the opening and they didn't like smoke. Still, he had learned and he took time to weave a snug door for the small opening with green willows, cutting it so it jammed in tightly, and when he finished he stood back and looked at the rock face—his shelter below, the food shelf above—and allowed a small bit of pride to come.

Not bad, he had thought, not bad for somebody who used to have trouble greasing the bearings on his bicycle. Not bad at all.

Mistakes.

He had made a good shelter and food shelf, but he had no food except for fish and the last of the berries. And the fish, as good as they still tasted then, were not something he could store. His mother had left some salmon out by mistake one time when they went on an overnight trip to Cape Hesper to visit relatives and when they got back the smell filled the whole house. There was no way to store fish.

At least, he thought, no way to store them dead. But as he looked at the weave of his structure a thought came to him and he moved down to the water.

He had been putting the waste from the fish back in the water and the food had attracted hundreds of new ones.

"I wonder..."

They seemed to come easily to the food, at least the small ones. He had no trouble now shooting them and had even speared one with his old fish spear now that he knew to aim low. He could dangle something in his fingers and they came right up to it. It might be possible, he thought, might just be possible to trap them. Make some kind of pond...

To his right, at the base of the rock bluff, there were piles of smaller rocks that had fallen from the main chunk, splinters and hunks, from double-fist size to some as large as his head. He spent an afternoon carrying rocks to the beach and making what amounted to a large pen for holding live fish—two rock "arms" that stuck out fifteen feet into the lake and curved together at the end. Where the arms came together he left an opening about two feet across, then he sat on the shore and waited.

When he had first started dropping the rocks all the fish had darted away. But his fish-trash pile of bones and skin and guts was in the pond area and the prospect of food brought them back. Soon, under an hour, there were thirty or forty small fish in the enclosure and Brian made a gate by weaving small willows together into a fine mesh and closed them in.

"Fresh fish," he had yelled. "I have fresh fish for sale . . ."

Storing live fish to eat later had been a major breakthrough, he thought. It wasn't just keeping from starving—it was trying to save ahead, think ahead.

Of course he didn't know then how sick he would get of fish.

15

THE DAYS had folded one into another and mixed so that after two or three weeks he only knew time had passed in days because he made a mark for each day in the stone near the door to his shelter. Real time he measured in events. A day was nothing, not a thing to remember—it was just sun coming up, sun going down, some light in the middle.

But events—events were burned into his memory and so he used them to remember time, to know and to remember what had happened, to keep a mental journal.

There had been the day of First Meat. That had been a day that had started like the rest, up after the sun, clean the camp and make sure there is enough wood for another night. But it was a long time, a long time of eating fish and looking for berries, and he craved more, craved more food, heavier food, deeper food.

He craved meat. He thought in the night now of meat, thought of his mother's cooking a roast or dreamed of turkey, and one night he awakened before he had to put wood on the fire with his mouth making saliva and the taste of pork chops in his mouth. So real, so real. And all a dream, but it left him intent on getting meat.

He had been working farther and farther out for wood, sometimes now going nearly a quarter of a mile away from camp for wood, and he saw many small animals. Squirrels were everywhere, small red ones that chattered at him and seemed to swear and jumped from limb to limb. There were also many rabbits—large, gray ones with a mix of reddish fur, smaller fast gray ones that he saw only at dawn. The larger ones sometimes sat until he was quite close, then bounded and jerked two or three steps before freezing again. He thought if he worked at it and practiced he might hit one of the larger rabbits with an arrow or a spear—never the small ones or the squirrels. They were too small and fast.

Then there were the foolbirds.

They exasperated him to the point where they

were close to driving him insane. The birds were everywhere, five and six in a flock, and their camouflage was so perfect that it was possible for Brian to sit and rest, leaning against a tree, with one of them standing right in front of him in a willow clump, two feet away—hidden—only to explode into deafening flight just when Brian least expected it. He just couldn't see them, couldn't figure out how to locate them before they flew, because they stood so perfectly still and blended in so perfectly well.

And what made it worse was that they were so dumb, or seemed to be so dumb, that it was almost insulting the way they kept hidden from him. Nor could he get used to the way they exploded up when they flew. It seemed like every time he went for wood, which was every morning, he spent the whole time jumping and jerking in fright as he walked. On one memorable morning he had actually reached for a piece of wood, what he thought to be a pitchy stump at the base of a dead birch, his fingers close to touching it, only to have it blow up in his face.

But on the day of First Meat he had decided the best thing to try for would be a foolbird and that morning he had set out with his bow and spear to get one; to stay with it until he got one and ate some meat. Not to get wood, not to find berries, but to get a bird and eat some meat.

At first the hunt had not gone well. He saw plenty of birds, working up along the shore of the lake to the end, then down the other side, but he only saw them after they flew. He had to find a way to see them first, see them and get close enough to either shoot them with the bow or use the spear, and he could not find a way to see them.

When he had gone halfway around the lake, and had jumped up twenty or so birds, he finally gave up and sat at the base of a tree. He had to work this out, see what he was doing wrong. There were birds there, and he had eyes—he just had to bring the two things together.

Looking wrong, he thought. I am looking wrong. More, more than that I am being wrong somehow—I am doing it the wrong way. Fine—sarcasm came into his thoughts—I know that, thank you. I know I'm doing it wrong. But what is right? The morning sun had cooked him until it seemed his brain was frying, sitting by the tree, but nothing came until he got up and started to walk again and hadn't gone two steps when a bird got up. It had been there all the time, while he was thinking about how to see them, right next to him—right there.

He almost screamed.

But this time, when the bird flew, something caught his eye and it was the secret key. The bird cut down toward the lake, then, seeing it couldn't land in the water, turned and flew back up the hill into the trees. When it turned, curving through the trees, the sun had caught it, and Brian, for an instant, saw it as a shape; sharp-pointed in front, back from the head in a streamlined bullet shape to the fat body.

Kind of like a pear, he had thought, with a point on one end and a fat little body; a flying pear.

And that had been the secret. He had been looking for feathers, for the color of the bird, for a bird sitting there. He had to look for the outline instead, had to see the shape instead of the feathers or color, had to train his eyes to see the shape . . .

It was like turning on a television. Suddenly he could see things he never saw before. In just moments, it seemed, he saw three birds before they flew, saw them sitting and got close to one of them, moving slowly, got close enough to try a shot with his bow.

He had missed that time, and had missed many more, but he saw them; he saw the little fat shapes with the pointed heads sitting in the brush all over the place. Time and again he drew, held, and let arrows fly but he still had no feathers on the arrows and they were little more than sticks that flopped out of the bow, sometimes going sideways. Even when a bird was seven or eight feet away the arrow would turn without feathers to stabilize it and hit brush or a twig. After a time he gave up with the bow. It had worked all right for the fish, when they came right to the end of the arrow, but it wasn't good for any kind of distance—at least not the way it was now.

But he had carried his fish spear, the original one with the two prongs, and he moved the bow to his left hand and carried the spear in his right.

He tried throwing the spear but he was not good enough and not fast enough—the birds could fly amazingly fast, get up fast. But in the end he found that if he saw the bird sitting and moved sideways toward it—not directly toward it but at an angle, back and forth—he could get close enough to put the spear point out ahead almost to the bird and thrust-lunge with it. He came close twice, and then, down along the lake not far from the beaver house he got his first meat.

The bird had sat and he had lunged and the two points took the bird back down into the ground and killed it almost instantly—it had fluttered a bit—and Brian had grabbed it and held it in both hands until he was sure it was dead.

Then he picked up the spear and the bow and trotted back around the lake to his shelter, where the fire had burned down to glowing coals. He sat looking at the bird wondering what to do. With the fish, he had just cooked them whole, left everything in and picked the meat off. This was different; he would have to clean it.

It had always been so simple at home. He would go to the store and get a chicken and it was all cleaned and neat, no feathers or insides, and his mother would bake it in the oven and he would eat it. His mother from the old time, from the time before, would bake it.

Now he had the bird, but he had never cleaned one, never taken the insides out or gotten rid of the feathers, and he didn't know where to start. But he wanted the meat—had to have the meat—and that drove him.

In the end the feathers came off easily. He tried to pluck them out but the skin was so fragile that it pulled off as well, so he just pulled the skin off the bird. Like peeling an orange, he thought, sort of. Except that when the skin was gone the insides fell out the back end.

He was immediately caught in a cloud of raw odor, a kind of steamy dung odor that came up from the greasy coil of insides that fell from the bird, and he nearly threw up. But there was something else to the smell as well, some kind of richness that went with his hunger and that overcame the sick smell.

He quickly cut the neck with his hatchet, cut the feet off the same way, and in his hand he held something like a small chicken with a dark, fat, thick breast and small legs.

He set it up on some sticks on the shelter wall and took the feathers and insides down to the water, to his fish pond. The fish would eat them, or eat what they could, and the feeding action would bring more fish. On second thought he took out the wing and tail feathers, which were stiff and long and pretty—banded and speckled in browns and grays and light reds. There might be some use for them, he thought, maybe work them onto the arrows somehow.

The rest he threw in the water, saw the small round fish begin tearing at it, and washed his hands. Back at the shelter the flies were on the meat and he brushed them off. It was amazing how fast they came, but when he built up the fire and the smoke increased the flies almost magically disappeared. He pushed a pointed stick through the bird and held it over the fire.

The fire was too hot. The flames hit the fat and the bird almost ignited. He held it higher but the heat was worse and finally he moved it to the side a bit and there it seemed to cook properly. Except that it only cooked on one side and all the juice dripped off. He had to rotate it slowly and that was hard to do with his hands so he found a forked stick and stuck it in the sand to put his cooking stick in. He turned it, and in this way he found a proper method to cook the bird.

In minutes the outside was cooked and the odor that came up was almost the same as the odor when his mother baked chickens in the oven and he didn't think he could stand it but when he tried to pull a piece of the breast meat off the meat was still raw inside.

Patience, he thought. So much of this was patience—waiting and thinking and doing things right. So much of all this, so much of all living was patience and thinking.

He settled back, turning the bird slowly, letting the juices go back into the meat, letting it cook and smell and smell and cook and there came a time when it didn't matter if the meat was done or not; it was black on the outside and hard and hot, and he would eat it.

He tore a piece from the breast, a sliver of meat, and put it in his mouth and chewed carefully, chewed as slowly and carefully as he could to get all the taste and he thought:

Never. Never in all the food, all the hamburgers

and malts, all the fries or meals at home, never in all the candy or pies or cakes, never in all the roasts or steaks or pizzas, never in all the submarine sandwiches, never never never had he tasted anything as fine as that first bite.

First Meat.

16

AND NOW he stood at the end of the long part of the lake and was not the same, would not be the same again.

There had been many First Days.

First Arrow Day—when he had used thread from his tattered old piece of windbreaker and some pitch from a stump to put slivers of feather on a dry willow shaft and make an arrow that would fly correctly. Not accurately—he never got really good with it—but fly correctly so that if a rabbit or a foolbird sat in one place long enough, close enough, and he had enough arrows, he could hit it.

That brought First Rabbit Day—when he killed one of the large rabbits with an arrow and skinned it as he had the first bird, cooked it the same to find the meat as good—not as rich as the bird, but still good—and there were strips of fat on the back of the rabbit that cooked into the meat to make it richer.

Now he went back and forth between rabbits and foolbirds when he could, filling in with fish in the middle.

Always hungry.

I am always hungry but I can do it now, I can get food and I know I can get food and it makes me more. I know what I can do.

He moved closer to the lake to a stand of nut brush. These were thick bushes with little stickler pods that held green nuts—nuts that he thought he might be able to eat but they weren't ripe yet. He was out for a foolbird and they liked to hide in the base of the thick part of the nut brush, back in where the stems were close together and provided cover.

In the second clump he saw a bird, moved close to it, paused when the head feathers came up and it made a sound like a cricket—a sign of alarm just before it flew—then moved closer when the feathers went down and the bird relaxed. He did this four times, never looking at the bird directly, moving toward it at an angle so that it seemed he was moving off to the side—he had perfected this method after many attempts and it worked so well that he had actually caught one with his bare hands—until he was standing less than three feet from the bird, which was frozen in a hiding attitude in the brush.

The bird held for him and he put an arrow to the bow, one of the feathered arrows, not a fish arrow, and drew and released. It was a clean miss and he took another arrow out of the cloth pouch, at his belt, which he'd made from a piece of his windbreaker sleeve, tied at one end to make a bottom. The foolbird sat still for him and he did not look directly at it until he drew the second arrow and aimed and released and missed again.

This time the bird jerked a bit and the arrow stuck next to it so close it almost brushed its breast. Brian only had two more arrows and he debated moving slowly to change the spear over to his right hand and use that to kill the bird. One more shot, he decided, he would try it again. He slowly brought another arrow out, put it on the string, and aimed and released and this time saw the flurry of feathers that meant he had made a hit.

The bird had been struck off-center and was flopping around wildly. Brian jumped on it and grabbed it and slammed it against the ground once, sharply, to kill it. Then he stood and retrieved his arrows and made sure they were all right and went down to the lake to wash the blood off his hands. He kneeled at the water's edge and put the dead bird and his weapons down and dipped his hands into the water.

It was very nearly the last act of his life. Later he would not know why he started to turn—some smell or sound. A tiny brushing sound. But something caught his ear or nose and he began to turn, and had his head half around, when he saw a brown wall of fur detach itself from the forest to his rear and come down on him like a runaway truck. He just had time to see that it was a moose—he knew them from pictures but did not know, could not guess how large they were—when it hit him. It was a cow and she had no horns, but she took him in the left side of the back with her forehead, took him and threw him out into the water and then came after him to finish the job.

He had another half-second to fill his lungs with air and she was on him again, using her head to drive him down into the mud of the bottom. Insane, he thought. Just that, the word, insane. Mud filled his eyes, his ears, the horn boss on the moose drove him deeper and deeper into the bottom muck, and suddenly it was over and he felt alone.

He sputtered to the surface, sucking air and fighting panic, and when he wiped the mud and water out of his eyes and cleared them he saw the cow standing sideways to him, not ten feet away, calmly chewing on a lilypad root. She didn't appear to even see him, or didn't seem to care about him, and Brian turned carefully and began to swim-crawl out of the water.

As soon as he moved, the hair on her back went up and she charged him again, using her head and front hooves this time, slamming him back and down into the water, on his back this time, and he screamed the air out of his lungs and hammered on her head with his fists and filled his throat with water and she left again.

Once more he came to the surface. But he was hurt now, hurt inside, hurt in his ribs and he stayed hunched over, pretended to be dead. She was standing again, eating. Brian studied her out of one eye, looking to the bank with the other, wondering how seriously he was injured, wondering if she would let him go this time.

Insane.

He started to move, ever so slowly; her head turned and her back hair went up—like the hair on an angry dog—and he stopped, took a slow breath, the hair went down and she ate. Move, hair up, stop, hair down, move, hair up—a half-foot at a time until he was at the edge of the water. He stayed on his hands and knees—indeed, was hurt so he wasn't sure he could walk anyway, and she seemed to accept that and let him crawl, slowly, out of the water and up into the trees and brush.

When he was behind a tree he stood carefully and took stock. Legs seemed all right, but his ribs were hurt bad—he could only take short breaths and then he had a jabbing pain—and his right shoulder seemed to be wrenched somehow. Also his bow and spear and foolbird were in the water.

At least he could walk and he had just about decided to leave everything when the cow moved out of the deeper water and left him, as quickly as she'd come, walking down along the shoreline in the shallow water, with her long legs making sucking sounds when she pulled them free of the mud. Hanging on a pine limb, he watched her go, half expecting her to turn and come back to run over him again. But she kept going and when she was well gone from sight he went to the bank and found the bird, then waded out a bit to get his bow and spear. Neither of them were broken and the arrows, incredibly, were still on his belt in the pouch, although messed up with mud and water.

It took him most of an hour to work his way back around the lake. His legs worked well enough, but if he took two or three fast steps he would begin to breath deeply and the pain from his ribs would stop him and he would have to lean against a tree until he could slow back down to shallow breathing. She had done more damage than he had originally thought, the insane cow—no sense at all to it. Just madness. When he got to the shelter he crawled inside and was grateful that the coals were still glowing and that he had thought to get wood first thing in the mornings to be ready for the day, grateful that he had thought to get enough wood for two or three days at a time, grateful that he had fish nearby if he needed to eat, grateful, finally, as he dozed off, that he was alive.

So insane, he thought, letting sleep cover the pain in his chest—such an insane attack for no reason and he fell asleep with his mind trying to make the moose have reason.

The noise awakened him.

It was a low sound, a low roaring sound that came from wind. His eyes snapped open not because it was loud but because it was new. He had felt wind in his shelter, felt the rain that came with wind and had heard thunder many times in the past forty-seven days but not this, not this noise. Low, almost alive, almost from a throat somehow, the sound, the noise was a roar, a far-off roar but coming at him and when he was fully awake he sat up in the darkness, grimacing with pain from his ribs.

The pain was different now, a tightened pain, and it seemed less—but the sound. So strange, he thought. A mystery sound. A spirit sound. A bad sound. He took some small wood and got the fire going again, felt some little comfort and cheer from the flames but also felt that he should get ready. He did not know how, but he should get ready. The sound was coming for him, was coming just for him, and he had to get ready. The sound wanted him.

He found the spear and bow where they were hanging on the pegs of the shelter wall and brought his weapons to the bed he had made of pine boughs. More comfort, but like the comfort of the flames it didn't work with this new threat that he didn't understand yet.

Restless threat, he thought, and stood out of the shelter away from the flames to study the sky but it was too dark. The sound meant something to him, something from his memory, something he had read about. Something he had seen on television. Something... oh, he thought. Oh no.

It was wind, wind like the sound of a train, with the low belly roar of a train. It was a tornado. That was it! The roar of a train meant bad wind and it was coming for him. God, he thought, on top of the moose not this—not this.

But it was too late, too late to do anything. In the strange stillness he looked to the night sky, then turned back into his shelter and was leaning over to go through the door opening when it hit. Later he would think of it and find that it was the same as the moose. Just insanity. He was taken in the back by some mad force and driven into the shelter on his face, slammed down into the pine branches of his bed.

At the same time the wind tore at the fire and sprayed red coals and sparks in a cloud around him. Then it backed out, seemed to hesitate momentarily, and returned with a massive roar; a roar that took his ears and mind and body.

He was whipped against the front wall of the shelter like a rag, felt a ripping pain in his ribs again, then was hammered back down into the sand once more while the wind took the whole wall, his bed, the fire, his tools—all of it—and threw it out into the lake, gone out of sight, gone forever. He felt a burning on his neck and reached up to find red coals there. He brushed those off, found more in his pants, brushed those away, and the wind hit again, heavy gusts, tearing gusts. He heard trees snapping in the forest around the rock, felt his body slipping out and clawed at the rocks to hold himself down. He couldn't think, just held and knew that he was praying but didn't know what the prayer was—knew that he wanted to be, stay and be, and then the wind moved to the lake.

Brian heard the great, roaring sucking sounds of water and opened his eyes to see the lake torn by the wind, the water slamming in great waves that went in all ways, fought each other and then rose in a spout of water going up into the night sky like a wet column of light. It was beautiful and terrible at the same time.

The tornado tore one more time at the shore on the opposite side of the lake—Brian could hear trees being ripped down—and then it was done, gone as rapidly as it had come. It left nothing, nothing but Brian in the pitch dark. He could find nothing of where his fire had been, not a spark, nothing of his shelter, tools, or bed, even the body of the foolbird was gone. I am back to nothing he thought, trying to find things in the dark—back to where I was when I crashed. Hurt, in the dark, just the same.

As if to emphasize his thoughts the mosquitos—with the fire gone and protective smoke no longer saving him—came back in thick, nostril-clogging swarms. All that was left was the hatchet at his belt. Still there. But now it began to rain and in the downpour he would never find anything dry enough to get a fire going, and at last he pulled his battered body back in under the overhang, where his bed had been, and wrapped his arms around his ribs.

Sleep didn't come, couldn't come with the insects ripping at him, so he lay the rest of the night, slapping mosquitos and chewing with his mind on the day. This morning he had been fat—well, almost fat—and happy, sure of everything, with good weapons and food and the sun in his face and things looking good for the future, and inside of one day, just one day, he had been run over by a moose and a tornado, had lost everything and was back to square one. Just like that.

A flip of some giant coin and he was the loser.

But there is a difference now, he thought—there really is a difference. I might be hit but I'm not done. When the light comes I'll start to rebuild. I still have the hatchet and that's all I had in the first place.

Come on, he thought, baring his teeth in the darkness—come on. Is that the best you can do? Is that all you can hit me with—a moose and a tornado? Well, he thought, holding his ribs and smiling, then spitting mosquitos out of his mouth. Well, that won't get the job done. That was the difference now. He had changed, and he was tough. I'm tough where it counts—tough in the head.

In the end, right before dawn a kind of cold snap came down—something else new, this cold snap—and the mosquitos settled back into the damp grass and under the leaves and he could sleep. Or doze. And the last thought he had that morning as he closed his eyes was: I hope the tornado hit the moose.

When he awakened the sun was cooking the inside of his mouth and had dried his tongue to leather. He had fallen into a deeper sleep with his mouth open just at dawn and it tasted as if he had been sucking on his foot all night.

He rolled out and almost bellowed with pain from his ribs. They had tightened in the night and seemed to pull at his chest when he moved. He slowed his movements and stood slowly, without stretching unduly, and went to the lake for a drink. At the shore he kneeled, carefully and with great gentleness, and drank and rinsed his mouth. To his right he saw that the fish pond was still there, although the willow gate was gone and there were no fish. They'll come back, he thought, as soon as I can make a spear or bow and get one or two for bait they'll come back.

He turned to look at his shelter—saw that some of the wood for the wall was scattered around the beach but was still there, then saw his bow jammed into a driftwood log, broken but with the precious string still intact. Not so bad now—not so bad. He looked down the shoreline for other parts of his wall and that's when he saw it.

Out in the lake, in the short part of the L, something curved and yellow was sticking six or eight inches out of the water. It was a bright color, not an earth or natural color, and for a second he could not place it, then he knew it for what it was.

"It's the tail of the plane." He said it aloud, half expecting to hear somebody answer him. There it was, sticking up out of the water. The tornado must have flipped the plane around somehow when it hit the lake, changed the position of the plane and raised the tail. Well, he thought. Well, just look at that. And at the same moment a cutting thought hit him. He thought of the pilot, still in the plane, and that brought a shiver and massive sadness that seemed to settle on him like a weight and he thought that he should say or do something for the pilot; some words but he didn't know any of the right words, the religious words.

So he went down to the side of the water and looked at the plane and focused his mind, the way he did when he was hunting the foolbirds and wanted to concentrate, focused it on the pilot and thought: Have rest. Have rest forever.

17

He Turned Back to his campsite and looked to the wreckage. He had a lot to do, rebuild his shelter, get a new fire going, find some food or get ready to find some food, make weapons—and he had to work slowly because his ribs hurt.

First things first. He tried to find some dry grass and twigs, then peeled bark from a nearby birch to shred into a fire nest. He worked slowly but even so, with his new skill he had a fire going in less than an hour. The flames cut the cool damp morning, crackled and did much to bring his spirits up, not to mention chasing away the incessant mosquitos. With the fire going he searched for dry wood—the rain had driven water into virtually all the wood he could find—and at last located some in a thick evergreen where the top branches had covered the lower dead ones, keeping them dry.

He had great difficulty breaking them, not being able to pull much with his arm or chest muscles, but finally got enough to keep the fire going all day and into the night. With that he rested a bit, eased his chest, and then set about getting a shelter squared away.

Much of the wood from his original wall was still nearby and up in back of the ridge he actually found a major section of the weave still intact. The wind had torn it out, lifted it, and thrown it to the top of the ridge and Brian felt lucky once more that he had not been killed or more seriously injured—which would have been the same, he thought. If he couldn't hunt he would die and if he were injured badly he would not be able to hunt.

He jerked and dragged wood around until the wall was once more in place—crudely, but he could improve it later. He had no trouble finding enough pine boughs to make a new bed. The storm had torn the forest to pieces—up in back of the ridge it looked like a giant had become angry and used some kind of a massive meatgrinder on the trees. Huge pines were twisted and snapped off, blown sideways. The ground was so littered, with limbs and tree-tops sticking every which way, that it was hard to get through. He pulled enough thick limbs in for a bed, green and spicy with the new broken sap smell, and by evening he was exhausted, hungry, and hurting, but he had something close to a place to live again, a place to be.

Tomorrow, he thought, as he lay back in the darkness. Tomorrow maybe the fish would be back and he would make a spear and new bow and get some food. Tomorrow he would find food and refine the camp and bring things back to sanity from the one completely insane day.

He faced the fire. Curving his body, he rested his head on his arm, and began to sleep when a picture came into his head. The tail of the plane sticking out of the water. There it was, the tail sticking up. And inside the plane, near the tail somewhere, was the survival pack. It must have survived the crash because the plane's main body was still intact. That was the picture—the tail sticking up and the survival pack inside—right there in his mind as he dozed. His eyes snapped opened. If I could get at the pack, he thought. Oh, if I could get at the pack. It probably had food and knives and matches. It might have a sleeping bag. It might have fishing gear. Oh, it must have so many wonderful things—if I could get at the pack and just get some of those things. I would be rich. So rich if I could get at the pack.

Tomorrow. He watched the flames and smiled. Tomorrow I'll see. All things come tomorrow.

He slept, deep and down with only the picture of the plane tail sticking up in his mind. A healing sleep.

In the morning he rolled out before true light. In the gray dawn he built up the fire and found more wood for the day, feeling almost chipper because his ribs were much better now. With camp ready for the day he looked to the lake. Part of him half-expected the plane tail to be gone, sunk back into the depths, but he saw that it was still there, didn't seem to have moved at all.

He looked down at his feet and saw that there were some fish in his fish pen looking for the tiny bits of bait still left from before the wind came. He fought impatience to get on the plane project and remembered sense, remembered what he had learned. First food, because food made strength; first food, then thought, then action. There were fish at hand here, and he might not be able to get anything from the plane. That was all a dream.

The fish were real and his stomach, even his new

shrunken stomach, was sending signals that it was savagely empty.

He made a fish spear with two points, not peeling the bark all the way back but just working on the pointed end. It took him an hour or so and all the time he worked he sat looking at the tail of the plane sticking up in the air, his hands working on the spear, his mind working on the problem of the plane.

When the spear was done, although still crude, he jammed a wedge between the points to spread them apart and went to the fish pond. There were not clouds of fish, but at least ten, and he picked one of the larger ones, a round fish almost six inches long, and put the spear point in the water, held it, then thrust with a flicking motion of his wrist when the fish was just above the point.

The fish was pinned neatly and he took two more with the same ease, then carried all three back up to the fire. He had a fish board now, a piece of wood he had flattened with the hatchet, that leaned up by the fire for cooking fish so he didn't have to hold a stick all the time. He put the three fish on the board, pushed sharpened pegs through their tails into cracks on the cooking board, and propped it next to the reddest part of the coals. In moments the fish were hissing and cooking with the heat and as soon as they were done, or when he could stand the smell no longer, he picked the steaming meat from under the loosened skin and ate it.

The fish did not fill him, did not even come close—fish meat was too light for that. But they gave him strength—he could feel it moving into his arms and legs—and he began to work on the plane project.

While making the spear he had decided that what he would have to do was make a raft and push-paddle the raft to the plane and tie it there for a working base. Somehow he would have to get into the tail, inside the plane—rip or cut his way in—and however he did it he would need an operating base of some kind. A raft.

Which, he found ruefully, was much easier said than done. There were plenty of logs around. The shore was littered with driftwood, new and old, tossed up and scattered by the tornado. And it was a simple matter to find four of them about the same length and pull them together.

Keeping them together was the problem. Without rope or crosspieces and nails the logs just rolled and separated. He tried wedging them together, crossing them over each other—nothing seemed to work. And he needed a stable platform to get the job done. It was becoming frustrating and he had a momentary loss of temper—as he would have done in the past, when he was the other person.

At that point he sat back on the beach and studied the problem again. Sense, he had to use his sense. That's all it took to solve problems—just sense.

It came then. The logs he had selected were smooth and round and had no limbs. What he needed were logs with limbs sticking out, then he could cross the limbs of one log over the limbs of another and "weave" them together as he had done his wall, the food shelf cover, and the fish gate. He scanned the area above the beach and found four dry treetops that had been broken off by the storm. These had limbs and he dragged them down to his work area at the water's edge and fitted them together.

It took most of the day. The limbs were cluttered and stuck any which way and he would have to cut one to make another fit, then cut one from another log to come back to the first one, then still another from a third log would have to be pulled in.

But at last, in the late afternoon he was done and the raft—which he called Brushpile One for its looks—hung together even as he pulled it into the water off the beach. It floated well, if low in the water, and in the excitement he started for the plane. He could not stand on it, but would have to swim alongside.

He was out to chest depth when he realized he had no way to keep the raft at the plane. He needed some way to tie it in place so he could work from it.

And for a moment he was stymied. He had no rope, only the bowstring and the other cut shoestring in his tennis shoes—which were by now looking close to dead, his toes showing at the tops. Then he remembered his windbreaker and he found the tattered part he used for an arrow pouch. He tore it into narrow strips and tied them together to make a rope or tie-down about four feet long. It wasn't strong, he couldn't use it to pull a Tarzan and swing from a tree, but it should hold the raft to the plane.

Once more he slid the raft off the beach and out into the water until he was chest deep. He had left his tennis shoes in the shelter and when he felt the sand turn to mud between his toes he kicked off the bottom and began to swim.

Pushing the raft, he figured, was about like trying to push an aircraft carrier. All the branches that stuck down into the water dragged and pulled and the logs themselves fought any forward motion and he hadn't gone twenty feet when he realized that it was going to be much harder than he thought to get the raft to the plane. It barely moved and if he kept going this way he would just about reach the plane at dark. He decided to turn back again, spend the night and start early in the morning, and he pulled the raft once more onto the sand and wipe-scraped it dry with his hand.

Patience. He was better now but impatience still ground at him a bit so he sat at the edge of the fish pond with the new spear and took three more fish, cooked them up and ate them, which helped to pass the time until dark. He also dragged in more wood—endless wood—and then relaxed and watched the sun set over the trees in back of the ridge. West, he thought. I'm watching the sun set in the west. And that way was north where his father was, and that way east and that way south—and somewhere to the south and east his mother would be. The news would be on the television. He could visualize more easily his mother doing things than his father because he had never been to where his father lived now. He knew everything about how his mother lived. She would have the small television on the kitchen counter on and be watching the news and talking about how awful it was in South Africa or how cute the baby in the commercial looked. Talking and making sounds, cooking sounds.

He jerked his mind back to the lake. There was

great beauty here—almost unbelievable beauty. The sun exploded the sky, just blew it up with the setting color, and that color came down into the water of the lake, lit the trees. Amazing beauty and he wished he could share it with somebody and say, "Look there, and over there, and see that . . ."

But even alone it was beautiful and he fed the fire to cut the night chill. There it is again, he thought, that late summer chill to the air, the smell of fall. He went to sleep thinking a kind of reverse question. He did not know if he would ever get out of this, could not see how it might be, but if he did somehow get home and go back to living the way he had lived, would it be just the opposite? Would he be sitting watching television and suddenly think about the sunset up in back of the ridge and wonder how the color looked in the lake?

Sleep.

In the morning the chill was more pronounced and he could see tiny wisps of vapor from his breath. He threw wood on the fire and blew until it flamed, then banked the flames to last and went down to the lake. Perhaps because the air was so cool the water felt warm as he waded in. He made sure the hatchet was still at his belt and the raft still held together, then set out pushing the raft and kick-swimming toward the tail of the plane.

As before, it was very hard going. Once an eddy of breeze came up against him and he seemed to be standing still and by the time he was close enough to the tail to see the rivets in the aluminum he had pushed and kicked for over two hours, was nearly exhausted and wished he had taken some time to get a fish or two and have breakfast. He was also wrinkled as a prune and ready for a break.

The tail looked much larger when he got next to it, with a major part of the vertical stabilizer showing and perhaps half of the elevators. Only a short piece of the top of the fuselage, the plane's body toward the tail, was out of the water, just a curve of aluminum, and at first he could see no place to tie the raft. But he pulled himself along the elevators to the end and there he found a gap that went in up by the hinges where he could feed his rope through.

With the raft secure he climbed on top of it and lay on his back for fifteen minutes, resting and letting the sun warm him. The job, he thought, looked impossible. To have any chance of success he would have to be strong when he started.

Somehow he had to get inside the plane. All openings, even the small rear cargo hatch, were underwater so he couldn't get at them without diving and coming up inside the plane.

Where he would be trapped.

He shuddered at that thought and then remembered what was in the front of the plane, down in the bottom of the lake, still strapped in the seat, the body of the pilot. Sitting there in the water—Brian could see him, the big man with his hair waving in the current, his eyes open...

Stop, he thought. Stop now. Stop that thinking. He was nearly at the point of swimming back to shore and forgetting the whole thing. But the image of the survival pack kept him. If he could get it out of the plane, or if he could just get into it and pull something out. A candy bar.

Even that—just a candy bar. It would be worth it.

But how to get at the inside of the plane?

He rolled off the raft and pulled himself around the plane. No openings. Three times he put his face in the water and opened his eyes and looked down. The water was murky, but he could see perhaps six feet and there was no obvious way to get into the plane. He was blocked.

18

BRIAN WORKED around the tail of the plane two more times, pulling himself along on the stabilizer and the elevator, but there simply wasn't a way in.

Stupid, he thought. I was stupid to think I could just come out here and get inside the plane. Nothing is that easy. Not out here, not in this place. Nothing is easy.

He slammed his fist against the body of the plane and to his complete surprise the aluminum covering gave easily under his blow. He hit it again, and once more it bent and gave and he found that even when he didn't strike it but just pushed, it still moved. It was really, he thought, very thin aluminum skin over a kind of skeleton and if it gave that easily he might be able to force his way through . . .

The hatchet. He might be able to cut or hack with the hatchet. He reached to his belt and pulled the hatchet out, picked a place where the aluminum gave to his push and took an experimental swing at it.

The hatchet cut through the aluminum as if it were soft cheese. He couldn't believe it. Three more hacks and he had a triangular hole the size of his hand and he could see four cables that he guessed were the control cables going back to the tail and he hit the skin of the plane with a frenzied series of hacks to make a still larger opening and he was bending a piece of aluminum away from two aluminum braces of some kind when he dropped the hatchet.

It went straight down past his legs. He felt it bump his foot and then go on down, down into the water and for a second he couldn't understand that he had done it. For all this time, all the living and fighting, the hatchet had been everything—he had always worn it. Without the hatchet he had nothing—no fire, no tools, no weapons—he was nothing. The hatchet was, had been him.

And he had dropped it.

"Arrrgghhh!" He yelled it, choked on it, a snarl-cry of rage at his own carelessness. The hole in the plane was still too small to use for anything and now he didn't have a tool.

"That was the kind of thing I would have done before," he said to the lake, to the sky, to the trees. "When I came here—I would have done that. Not now. Not now . . ."

Yet he had and he hung on the raft for a moment and felt sorry for himself. For his own stupidity. But as before, the self-pity didn't help and he knew that he had only one course of action.

He had to get the hatchet back. He had to dive and get it back.

But how deep was it? In the deep end of the gym pool at school he had no trouble getting to the bottom and that was, he was pretty sure, about eleven feet.

Here it was impossible to know the exact depth. The front end of the plane, anchored by the weight of the engine, was obviously on the bottom but it came back up at an angle so the water wasn't as deep as the plane was long.

He pulled himself out of the water so his chest could expand, took two deep breaths and swiveled and dove, pulling his arms and kicking off the raft bottom with his feet.

His first thrust took him down a good eight feet but the visibility was only five feet beyond that and he could not see bottom yet. He clawed down six or seven more feet, the pressure pushing in his ears until he held his nose and popped them and just as he ran out of breath and headed back up he thought he saw the bottom—still four feet below his dive.

He exploded out of the surface, bumping his head on the side of the elevator when he came up and took air like a whale, pushing the stale air out until he wheezed, taking new in. He would have to get deeper yet and still have time to search while he was down there.

Stupid, he thought once more, cursing himself—just dumb. He pulled air again and again, pushing his chest out until he could not possibly get any more capacity, then took one more deep lungful, wheeled and dove again.

This time he made an arrow out of his arms and used his legs to push off the bottom of the raft, all he had in his legs, to spring-snap and propel him down. As soon as he felt himself slowing a bit he started raking back with his arms at his sides, like paddles, and thrusting with his legs like a frog and this time he was so successful that he ran his face into the bottom mud.

He shook his head to clear his eyes and looked around. The plane disappeared out and down in front of him. He thought he could see the windows and that made him think again of the pilot sitting inside and he forced his thoughts from it—but he could see no hatchet. Bad air triggers were starting to go off in his brain and he knew he was limited to seconds now but he held for a moment and tried moving out a bit and just as he ran out of air, knew that he was going to have to blow soon, he saw the handle sticking out of the mud. He made one grab, missed, reached again and felt his fingers close on the rubber. He clutched it and in one motion slammed his feet down into the mud and powered himself up. But now his lungs were ready to explode and he had flashes of color in his brain, explosions of color, and he would have to take a pull of water, take it into his lungs and just as he opened his mouth to take it in, to pull in all the water in the lake his head blew out of the surface and into the light.

"*Tchaaak!*" It was as if a balloon had exploded. Old air blew out of his nose and mouth and he pulled new in again and again. He reached for the side of the raft and hung there, just breathing, until he could think once more—the hatchet clutched and shining in his right hand.

"All right . . . the plane. Still the plane . . ."

He went back to the hole in the fuselage and began to chop and cut again, peeling the aluminum skin off in pieces. It was slow going because he was careful, very careful with the hatchet, but he hacked and pulled until he had opened a hole large enough to pull his head and shoulders in and look down into the water. It was very dark inside the fuselage and he could see nothing—certainly no sign of the survival pack. There were some small pieces and bits of paper floating on the surface inside the plane—dirt from the floor of the plane that had floated up—but nothing substantial.

Well, he thought. Did you expect it to be easy? So easy that way? Just open her up and get the pack—right?

He would have to open it more, much more so he could poke down inside and see what he could find. The survival pack had been a zippered nylon bag, or perhaps canvas of some kind, and he thought it had been red, or was it gray? Well, that didn't matter. It must have been moved when the plane crashed and it might be jammed down under something else.

He started chopping again, cutting the aluminum away in small triangles, putting each one on the raft as he chopped—he could never throw anything away again, he thought—because they might be useful later. Bits of metal, fish arrowheads or lures, maybe. And when he finally finished again he had cleaned away the whole side and top of the fuselage that stuck out of the water, had cut down into the water as far as he could reach and had a hole almost as big as he was, except that it was crossed and crisscrossed with aluminum—or it might be steel, he couldn't tell—braces and formers and cables. It was an awful tangled mess, but after chopping some braces away there was room for him to wiggle through and get inside.

He held back for a moment, uncomfortable with the thought of getting inside the plane. What if the tail settled back to the bottom and he got caught and couldn't get out? It was a horrible thought. But then he reconsidered. The thing had been up now for two days, plus a bit, and he had been hammering and climbing on it and it hadn't gone back down. It seemed pretty solid.

He eeled in through the cables and formers, wiggling and pulling until he was inside the tail with his head clear of the surface of the water and his legs down on the angled floor. When he was ready, he took a deep breath and pushed down along the floor with his legs, feeling for some kind of fabric or cloth—anything—with his bare feet. He touched nothing but the floor plates.

Up, a new breath, then he reached down to formers underwater and pulled himself beneath the water, his legs pushing down and down almost to the backs of the front seats and finally, on the left side of the plane, he thought he felt his foot hit cloth or canvas.

Up for more air, deep breathing, then one more grab at the formers and pushing as hard as he could he jammed his feet down and he hit it again, definitely canvas or heavy nylon, and this time when he pushed his foot he thought he felt something inside it; something hard.

It had to be the bag. Driven forward by the crash, it was jammed into the backs of the seats and caught on something. He tried to reach for it and pull but didn't have the air left and went up for more.

Lungs filled in great gulps, he shot down again, pulling on the formers until he was almost there, then wheeling down head first he grabbed at the cloth. It was the survival bag. He pulled and tore at it to loosen it and just as it broke free and his heart leaped to feel it rise he looked up, above the bag. In the light coming through the side window, the pale green light from the water, he saw the pilot's head only it wasn't the pilot's head any longer.

The fish. He'd never really thought of it, but the fish—the fish he had been eating all this time had to eat, too. They had been at the pilot all this time, almost two months, nibbling and chewing and all that remained was the not quite cleaned skull and when he looked up it wobbled loosely.

Too much. Too much. His mind screamed in horror and he slammed back and was sick in the water, sick so that he choked on it and tried to breathe water and could have ended there, ended with the pilot where it almost ended when they first arrived except that his legs jerked. It was instinctive, fear more than anything else, fear of what he had seen. But they jerked and pushed and he was headed up when they jerked and he shot to the surface, still inside the birdcage of formers and cables.

His head slammed into a bracket as he cleared and he reached up to grab it and was free, in the air, hanging up in the tail.

He hung that way for several minutes, choking and heaving and gasping for air, fighting to clear the picture of the pilot from his mind. It went slowly—he knew it would never completely leave—but he looked to the shore and there were trees and birds, the sun was getting low and golden over his shelter and when he stopped coughing he could hear the gentle sounds of evening, the peace sounds, the bird sounds and the breeze in the trees.

The peace finally came to him and he settled his breathing. He was still a long way from being finished—had a lot of work to do. The bag was floating next to him but he had to get it out of the plane and onto the raft, then back to shore.

He wiggled out through the formers—it seemed harder than when he came in—and pulled the raft around. The bag fought him. It was almost as if it didn't want to leave the plane. He pulled and jerked and still it wouldn't fit and at last he had to change the shape of it, rearranging what was inside by pushing and pulling at the sides until he had narrowed it and made it longer. Even when it finally came it was difficult and he had to pull first at one side, then another, an inch at a time, squeezing it through.

All of this took some time and when he finally got the bag out and tied on top of the raft it was nearly dark, he was bone tired from working in the water all day, chilled deep, and he still had to push the raft to shore.

Many times he thought he would not make it. With the added weight of the bag—which seemed to get heavier by the foot—coupled with the fact that he was getting weaker all the time, the raft seemed barely to move. He kicked and pulled and pushed, taking the shortest way straight back to shore, hanging to rest many times, then surging again and again.

It seemed to take forever and when at last his feet hit bottom and he could push against the mud and slide the raft into the shore weeds to bump against the bank he was so weak he couldn't stand, had to crawl; so tired he didn't even notice the mosquitos that tore into him like a gray, angry cloud.

He had done it.

That's all he could think now. He had done it.

He turned and sat on the bank with his legs in the water and pulled the bag ashore and began the long drag—he couldn't lift it—back down the shore-line to his shelter. Two hours, almost three he dragged and stumbled in the dark, brushing the mosquitos away, sometimes on his feet, more often on his knees, finally to drop across the bag and to sleep when he made the sand in front of the doorway.

He had done it.

19

TREASURE.

Unbelievable riches. He could not believe the contents of the survival pack.

The night before he was so numb with exhaustion he couldn't do anything but sleep. All day in the water had tired him so much that, in the end, he had fallen asleep sitting against his shelter wall, oblivious even to the mosquitos, to the night, to anything. But with false gray dawn he had awakened, instantly, and began to dig in the pack—to find amazing, wonderful things.

There was a sleeping bag—which he hung to dry over his shelter roof on the outside—and foam sleeping pad. An aluminum cookset with four little pots and two frying pans; it actually even had a fork and knife and spoon. A waterproof container with matches and two small butane lighters. A sheath knife with a compass in the handle. As if a compass would help him, he thought, smiling. A first-aid kit with bandages and tubes of antiseptic paste and small scissors. A cap that said CESSNA across the front in large letters. Why a cap? he wondered. It was adjustable and he put it on immediately. A fishing kit with four coils of line, a dozen small lures, and hooks and sinkers.

Incredible wealth. It was like all the holidays in the world, all the birthdays there were. He sat in the sun by the doorway where he had dropped the night before and pulled the presents—as he thought of them—out one at a time to examine them, turn them in the light, touch them and feel them with his hands and eyes.

Something that at first puzzled him. He pulled out what seemed to be the broken-off, bulky stock of a rifle and he was going to put it aside, thinking it might be for something else in the pack, when he shook it and it rattled. After working at it a moment he found the butt of the stock came off and inside there was a barrel and magazine and action assembly, with a clip and a full box of fifty shells. It was a .22 survival rifle—he had seen one once in the sporting goods store where he went for bike parts—and the barrel screwed onto the stock. He had never owned a rifle, never fired one, but had seen them on television, of course, and after a few moments figured out how to put it together by screwing the action onto the stock, how to load it and put the clip full of bullets into the action.

It was a strange feeling, holding the rifle. It somehow removed him from everything around him. Without the rifle he had to fit in, to be part of it all, to understand it and use it—the woods, all of it. With the rifle, suddenly, he didn't have to know; did not have to be afraid or understand. He didn't have to get close to a foolbird to kill it—didn't have to know how it would stand if he didn't look at it and moved off to the side.

The rifle changed him, the minute he picked it up, and he wasn't sure he liked the change very much. He set it aside, leaning it carefully against the wall. He could deal with that feeling later. The fire was out and he used a butane lighter and a piece of birchbark with small twigs to get another one started—marveling at how easy it was but feeling again that the lighter somehow removed him from where he was, what he had to know. With a ready flame he didn't have to know how to make a spark nest, or how to feed the new flames to make them grow. As with the rifle, he wasn't sure he liked the change.

Up and down, he thought. The pack was wonderful but it gave him up and down feelings.

With the fire going and sending up black smoke and a steady roar from a pitch-smelling chunk he put on, he turned once more to the pack. Rummaging through the food packets—he hadn't brought them out yet because he wanted to save them until last, glory in them—he came up with a small electronic device completely encased in a plastic bag. At first he thought it was a radio or cassette player and he had a surge of hope because he missed music, missed sound, missed hearing another voice. But when he opened the plastic and took the thing out and turned it over he could see that it wasn't a receiver at all. There was a coil of wire held together on the side by tape and it sprung into a three foot long antenna when he took the tape off. No speaker, no lights, just a small switch at the top and on the bottom he finally found, in small print:

Emergency Transmitter.

That was it. He turned the switch back and forth a few times but nothing happened—he couldn't even hear static—so, as with the rifle, he set it against the wall and went back to the bag. It was probably ruined in the crash, he thought.

Two bars of soap.

He had bathed regularly in the lake, but not with soap and he thought how wonderful it would be to wash his hair. Thick with grime and smoke dirt, frizzed by wind and sun, matted with fish and foolbird grease, his hair had grown and stuck and tangled and grown until it was a clumped mess on his head. He could use the scissors from the first-aid kit to cut it off, then wash it with soap.

And then, finally—the food.

It was all freeze-dried and in such quantity that he thought, With this I could live forever. Package after package he took out, beef dinner with potatoes, cheese and noodle dinners, chicken dinners, egg and potato breakfasts, fruit mixes, drink mixes, dessert mixes, more dinners and breakfasts than he could count easily, dozens and dozens of them all packed in waterproof bags, all in perfect shape and when he had them all out and laid against the wall in stacks he couldn't stand it and he went through them again.

If I'm careful, he thought, they'll last as long as... as long as I need them to last. If I'm careful.... No. Not yet. I won't be careful just yet. First I am going to have a feast. Right here and now I am going to cook up a feast and eat until I drop and then I'll be careful.

He went into the food packs once more and selected what he wanted for his feast: a four-person beef and potato dinner, with orange drink for an appetizer and something called a peach whip for dessert. Just add water, it said on the packages, and cook for half an hour or so until everything was normal-size and done.

Brian went to the lake and got water in one of the aluminum pots and came back to the fire. Just that amazed him—to be able to carry water to the fire in a pot. Such a simple act and he hadn't been able to do it for almost two months. He guessed at the amounts and put the beef dinner and peach dessert on to boil, then went back to the lake and brought water to mix with the orange drink.

It was sweet and tangy—almost too sweet—but so good that he didn't drink it fast, held it in his mouth and let the taste go over his tongue. Tickling on the sides, sloshing it back and forth and then down, swallow, then another.

That, he thought, that is just fine. Just fine. He got more lake water and mixed another one and drank it fast, then a third one, and he sat with that near the fire but looking out across the lake, thinking how rich the smell was from the cooking beef dinner. There was garlic in it and some other spices and the smells came up to him and made him think of home, his mother cooking, the rich smells of the kitchen, and at that precise instant, with his mind full of home and the smell from the food filling him, the plane appeared.

He had only a moment of warning. There was a tiny drone but as before it didn't register, then suddenly, roaring over his head low and in back of the ridge a bushplane with floats fairly exploded into his life.

It passed directly over him, very low, tipped a wing sharply over the tail of the crashed plane in the lake, cut power, glided down the long part of the L of the lake, then turned and glided back, touching the water gently once, twice, and settling with a spray to taxi and stop with its floats gently bumping the beach in front of Brian's shelter.

He had not moved. It had all happened so fast that he hadn't moved. He sat with the pot of orange drink still in his hand, staring at the plane, not quite understanding it yet; not quite knowing yet that it was over.

The pilot cut the engine, opened the door, and got out, balanced, and stepped forward on the float to hop onto the sand without getting his feet wet. He was wearing sunglasses and he took them off to stare at Brian.

"I heard your emergency transmitter—then I saw the plane when I came over..." He trailed off, cocked his head, studying Brian. "Damn. You're him, aren't you? You're that kid. They quit looking, a month, no, almost two months ago. You're him, aren't you? You're that kid . . . "

Brian was standing now, but still silent, still holding the drink. His tongue seemed to be stuck to the roof of his mouth and his throat didn't work right. He looked at the pilot, and the plane, and down at himself—dirty and ragged, burned and lean and tough—and he coughed to clear his throat.

"My name is Brian Robeson," he said. Then he saw that his stew was done, the peach whip almost done, and he waved to it with his hand. "Would you like something to eat?"

Epilogue

THE PILOT who landed so suddenly in the lake was a fur buyer mapping Cree trapping camps for future buying runs—drawn by Brian when he unwittingly turned on the emergency transmitter and left it going. The Cree move into the camps for fall and winter to trap and the buyers fly from camp to camp on a regular route.

When the pilot rescued Brian he had been alone on the L-shaped lake for fifty-four days. During that time he had lost seventeen percent of his body weight. He later gained back six percent, but had virtually no body fat—his body had consumed all extra weight and he would remain lean and wiry for several years.

Many of the changes would prove to be permanent. Brian had gained immensely in his ability to observe what was happening and react to it; that would last him all his life. He had become more thoughtful as well, and from that time on he would think slowly about something before speaking.

Food, all food, even food he did not like, never lost its wonder for him. For years after his rescue he would find himself stopping in grocery stores to just stare at the aisles of food, marveling at the quantity and the variety.

There were many questions in his mind about what he had seen and known, and he worked at research when he got back, identifying the game and berries. Gut cherries were termed choke cherries, and made good jelly. The nut bushes where the foolbirds hid were hazelnut bushes. The two kinds of rabbits were snowshoes and cottontails; the foolbirds were ruffed grouse (also called fool hens by trappers, for their stupidity); the small food fish were bluegills, sunfish, and perch; the turtle eggs were laid by a snapping turtle, as he had thought; the wolves were timber wolves, which are not known to attack or bother people; the moose was a moose.

There were also the dreams—he had many dreams about the lake after he was rescued. The

Canadian government sent a team in to recover the body of the pilot and they took reporters, who naturally took pictures and film of the whole campsite, the shelter—all of it. For a brief time the press made much of Brian and he was interviewed for several networks but the furor died within a few months. A writer showed up who wanted to do a book on the "complete adventure" (as he called it) but he turned out to be a dreamer and it all came to nothing but talk. Still Brian was given copies of the pictures and tape, and looking at them seemed to trigger the dreams. They were not nightmares, none of them were frightening, but he would awaken at times with them; just awaken and sit up and think of the lake, the forest, the fire at night, the night birds singing, the fish jumping—sit in the dark alone and think of them and it was not bad and would never be bad for him.

Predictions are, for the most part, ineffective; but it might be interesting to note that had Brian not been rescued when he was, had he been forced to go into hard fall, perhaps winter, it would have been very rough on him. When the lake froze he would have lost the fish, and when the snow got deep he would have had trouble moving at all. Game becomes seemingly plentiful in the fall (it's easier to see with the leaves off the brush) but in winter it gets scarce and sometimes simply nonexistent as predators (fox, lynx, wolf, owls, weasels, fisher, martin, northern coyote) sweep through areas and wipe things out. It is amazing what a single owl can do to a local population of ruffed grouse and rabbits in just a few months.

After the initial surprise and happiness from his parents at his being alive—for a week it looked as if they might actually get back together—things rapidly went back to normal. His father returned to the northern oil fields, where Brian eventually visited him, and his mother stayed in the city, worked at her career in real estate, and continued to see the man in the station wagon.

Brian tried several times to tell his father, came really close once to doing it, but in the end never said a word about the man or what he knew, the Secret.